Praise for th

"A thoroughly entertaining series debut, with enjoyable yet realistic characters and enough plot twists—and dead ends—to appeal from beginning to end."
—*Booklist*, starred review, on *Booked 4 Murder*

"Filled with clues that make you go 'Huh?' and a list of potential subjects that range from the charming to the witty to the intense. Readers root for Phee as she goes up against a killer who may not stop until Phee is taken out well before her time. Enjoy this laugh-out-loud funny mystery that will make you scream for the authors to get busy on the next one."
—*Suspense Magazine* on *Molded 4 Murder*

"Engaging characters and a stirring mystery kept me captivated from the first page to the last."
—Dollycas, Amazon Vine Voice, on *Divide and Concord*

"Well-crafted sleuth, enjoyable supporting characters. This is a series not to be missed."
—*Cozy Cat Reviews* on *Death, Dismay and Rosé*

"A sparkling addition to the Wine Trail Mystery series. A toast to protagonist Norrie and Two Witches Winery, where the characters shine and the mystery flows. This novel is a perfect blend of suspense and fun!"
—Carlene O'Neil, author of the Cypress Cove Mysteries, on *Chardonnayed to Rest*

Books by J. C. Eaton

The Wine Trail Mysteries

A Riesling to Die
Chardonnayed to Rest
Pinot Red or Dead?
Sauvigone for Good
Divide and Concord
Death, Dismay and Rosé
From Port to Rigor Morte
Mischief, Murder and Merlot
Caught in the Traminette

The Sophie Kimball Mysteries

Booked 4 Murder
Ditched 4 Murder
Staged 4 Murder
Botched 4 Murder
Molded 4 Murder
Dressed Up 4 Murder
Broadcast 4 Murder
Railroaded 4 Murder
Saddled Up 4 Murder
Grilled 4 Murder
Strike Out 4 Murder
Revved Up 4 Murder
Pinned 4 Murder
Planted 4 Murder

The Marcie Rayner Mysteries

Murder in the Crooked Eye Brewery
Murder at the Mystery Castle
Murder at Classy Kitchens

The Charcuterie Shop Mysteries

Laid Out to Rest
Sliced, Diced and Dead
Death on a Serving Board
A Plattering of Murder

Planted
4
Murder

J. C. Eaton

Planted 4 Murder
J. C. Eaton
Copyright © 2025 J. C. Eaton
Cover design and illustration by Dar Albert, Wicked Smart Designs

Beyond the Page Books
are published by
Beyond the Page Publishing
www.beyondthepagepub.com

ISBN: 978-1-966322-30-6

All rights reserved under International and Pan-American Copyright Conventions. By payment of required fees, you have been granted the non-exclusive, non-transferable right to access and read the text of this book. No part of this text may be reproduced, transmitted, downloaded, decompiled, reverse engineered, or stored in or introduced into any information storage and retrieval system, in any form or by any means, whether electronic or mechanical, now known or hereinafter invented without the express written permission of both the copyright holder and the publisher.

This is a work of fiction. Names, characters, places, and incidents either are the product of the author's imagination or are used fictitiously, and any resemblance to actual persons, living or dead, business establishments, events or locales is entirely coincidental. The publisher does not have any control over and does not assume any responsibility for author or third-party websites or their content.

The scanning, uploading, and distribution of this book via the Internet or via any other means without the permission of the publisher is illegal and punishable by law. Your support of the author's rights is appreciated.

No AI Training: Without in any way limiting the author's and Beyond the Page's exclusive rights under copyright, any use of this publication to "train" generative artificial intelligence (AI) technologies to generate text is expressly prohibited. The author reserves all rights to license uses of this work for generative AI training and development of machine learning language models.

To our dear friends at New Hope Fellowship, Sun City West, Arizona, whose kindness, care, and love of God make this a better world for all of us

Acknowledgments

So many accolades for the amazing scrutiny and attention given to our manuscript by Regina Kotkowski from the U.S. and Susan Schwartz from Australia! How we ever managed to find these incredibly savvy and discerning "first round" editors is beyond anyone's imagination!

And talk about editors—Thank you, Bill Harris at Beyond the Page, for your insight, humor, and guidance. It is a joy to work with you!

Thank you so much, Renee Gauthier and Sandy Miller from the Sun City West Agriculture Club. From on-site tours to in-depth information, you gave us so much "fodder" for our book. We are indeed in your debt.

Dar Albert, from Wicked Smart Designs, you dazzle us no end and we are so fortunate to have found you!

Cast of Characters

Protagonist:

Sophie (Phee) Kimball, forty-something bookkeeper/accountant from Mankato, Minnesota, turned amateur sleuth

The Sun City West, Arizona, Book Club Ladies:

Harriet Plunkett, seventy-something, Phee's mother and book club organizer; owner of a neurotic chiweenie named Streetman and a cat named Essie

Shirley Johnson, seventy-something, retired milliner and teddy bear maker

Cecilia Flanagan, seventy-something, devout churchgoer and more modest than most nuns; sneaks off holy water when needed

Lucinda Espinoza, seventy-something, attends Cecilia's church and translates Telemundo soap operas for the club

Myrna Mittleson, former seventy-something New Yorker and aspiring bocce player with a penchant for self-defense weapons

Louise Munson, seventy-something avid bird lover and owner of precocious African gray parrot

Ina Melinsky, Harriet's sister and Phee's aunt, married to saxophone player and gambler *Louis Melinsky*; more eccentric than Lady Gaga and Andy Warhol combined; seventy-something but don't tell her that

The Sun City West, Arizona, Pinochle Crew:

Herb Garrett, Harriet's neighbor and pinochle crew organizer, seventy-something

Bill Sanders, seventy-something bocce player

Wayne, seventy-something carpenter, jack-of-all-trades

Cast of Characters

Kevin, seventy-something

Kenny, seventy something, married

Williams Investigations in Glendale, Arizona:

Nate Williams, sixties, owner, retired detective from the Mankato, Minnesota, Police Department

Marshall Gregory, forties, partner and retired detective from the Mankato, Minnesota, Police Department, Phee's husband

Augusta Hatch, secretary and Wisconsin transplant from a tool and die company, sixty-something; as quick with a canasta hand as she is with her Smith & Wesson

Rolo Barnes, cyber-sleuth extraordinaire, puts the CIA, FBI and Homeland Security to shame

Maricopa County Sheriff's Office:

Deputy Bowman, fiftyish, grizzly in looks and personality

Deputy Ranston, fiftyish, somewhat toadish in looks and personality

Sun City West Residents:

Cindy Dolton, sixty- or seventy-something, local community gossip and dog park aficionado

Gloria Wong, sixties or seventies, Harriet's former neighbor and unofficial book club member

Paul Schmidt, seventies, avid fisherman and radio show host

Lyndy Ellsworth, forties, widowed, Phee's neighbor and best friend; works for a medical billing company

Chapter 1

I was less than two miles to my office at Williams Investigations when my mother's phone call came through like a public service announcement.

"Phee! Can you hear me? I figured you're probably on the way to work so I'll speak nice and loud so you can hear me from the car's blue thing and not your phone."

"Bluetooth."

"I just said that."

"Okay. And you don't have to scream. I can hear you."

"Good. I meant to call you last night but I got home late from mahjongg. Anyway, all of us are going to Bagels 'n More tomorrow morning for our usual Saturday brunch and you really should join us. Late September is the perfect time of year. The humidity is gone and the sweltering heat is slowly dissipating. Besides, it's the grand opening of their new patio. It's a double-tiered pergola with lattice and beam coverings so we won't get wet if it rains. It's even handicapped accessible with ramps and lots of comfortable seating. Not at all like those three small tables they used to have out front with the umbrellas that kept falling over. Besides, Herb has information he wants to share."

"The last time your neighbor shared information, we were all suckered into watching the Sun City West men's slow pitch."

"Aren't you the least bit curious about the pergola?"

"Nope. I've seen them before. And as for Herb's earth-shattering information, I might be better off not knowing."

"Come on, Phee. The book club ladies haven't seen you in a few weeks and the same goes for your aunt Ina. She'll be there as well. I know Marshall has to work, but it's one of your Saturdays off. And here's the best news—it's an outdoor patio so I can bring Streetman."

"Streetman? That's a reason for me *not* to go. That neurotic little chiweenie of yours is way too unpredictable."

"Well, I suppose you can always take him to the dog park instead. You're far more agile chasing him around than I am."

Terrific. She set a trap and I'm about to fall in.

"Okay, fine. What time?"

"Ten thirty. But Herb's pinochle crew is likely to straggle in. So, figure ten thirtyish."

"Ten thirtyish it is. See you Saturday."

I ended the call just as I pulled up to our office in search of a parking spot.

I'm Sophie Kimball Gregory, better known as Phee, and I never thought I'd leave my bookkeeping/accounting job at the police department in Mankato, Minnesota, and settle in Peoria, Arizona, a stone's throw from my mother's Sun City West retirement community. What can I say? Everyone has a moment of weakness.

Mine came when Detective Nate Williams retired and started his own agency not far from where I live. He managed to twist my arm and convince me to work in the same capacity as I did in Mankato, only with a higher salary and the perk of not having to shovel snow.

But the biggest perk of all was when he hired Detective Marshall Gregory, also from the Mankato police department, to join him. Sparks flew and ignited. Need I say more? Marshall and I have been married for a few years now and neither of us have any intention of ever moving back to snowy winters, blinding snow, and murky gray skies.

Unfortunately, our newfound careers and location came at a price—my mother's quirky book club ladies and her neighbor Herb's wacky pinochle buddies. Well, no one's perfect. Throw in my aunt Ina, and you are looking at the cast from a Marx Brothers movie.

"Guess where I'm headed tomorrow morning?" I asked our secretary, Augusta, the second I opened the office door.

She pushed her tortoiseshell glasses further up her nose and raised her head above the computer screen. "Let me guess. Tomorrow's Saturday and the earth will cease from spinning if your mother's friends don't have brunch at Bagels 'n More. Next time, hit me with a tougher question."

I walked to the Keurig, plopped in a dark roast K-Cup and smiled. "They're celebrating the new pergola out back. Spacious, double-tiered and handicapped accessible. From the way my mother described it, it might as well be the eighth wonder of the world."

"Uh-oh. A new patio, oops, I mean *pergola*, for outdoor dining. You know who else will be enjoying the ambience."

"Don't remind me. At least she's not bringing the cat."

"Funny you should mention cats. Mr. Williams is on his way to Estrella Mountain Ranch in Goodyear to investigate a cat theft."

"Seriously? A cat?"

"Not just any cat. Do you follow Princess and Queen Empress Trudalia on Facebook? She's a specially bred sphynx worth a fortune."

I retrieved my coffee and took a sip. "Uh, no."

"The cat has more followers than most Hollywood moguls."

"Keep that information away from my mother or next thing we know, she'll be hiring a professional photographer for Essie. At least Marshall's day will be a tad more normal. He said he's trying to locate a possible triplet. Twin sisters, who recently connected, having been adopted by

Planted 4 Murder

different families, learned that they might have another sibling, making them triplets."

"I'd say the men deserve a breather for a while. It's been one murder after another, topped with blackmail, extortion and bribery. Might as well tune into an old noir movie."

"You forgot the femme fatale."

"Give it time."

I laughed as I grabbed a sugar cookie from our not-so-secret stash and headed to my office.

• • •

"Don't get up on my behalf," Marshall called out from the shower the following morning. He toweled himself dry in the small space that separated our bedroom from the en suite before planting a kiss on my forehead. "Enjoy your day off. I'll pick up a coffee on my way to the office." Then he burst out laughing. "Should be a humdinger in the pergola. I can picture it now. Your mother will bring both pets in that combo stroller of hers and Gloria will arrive with Thor. All ninety pounds of him."

"Let's pray no one invents a parrot stroller or Lucifer would fill out the menagerie. You know how Louise is with that parrot."

"I thought his name was Leviticus."

"It is. But Lucifer is much more fitting."

Marshall laughed. "I'll text you later. And have an extra bagel for me."

I pulled the covers up to my neck and reset my phone alarm to give me an additional thirty minutes of shut-eye. When I got to Bagels 'n More a few hours later, I had already cleaned the house and changed the linens on the bed. A few more months of cotton percale and then flannel. My Minnesota friends would laugh their heads off if they knew I froze to death at sixty degrees. But today promised to be in the low nineties with nothing but bright sunshine.

"Phee! We're so glad you could make it," Cecilia called out when I made my way across the large rectangular deck that was the bottom level of the pergola. When my mother said *tiered*, I pictured an upper level, but what Bagels 'n More designed was truly spectacular. I only hoped it wouldn't be reflected in their prices.

There were three levels in all, staggered so that ramps could accommodate walkers and wheelchairs. Greenery that consisted of Ficus trees and small palms invited patrons to enjoy dining al fresco. I imagined it also invited pampered dogs to enjoy it in their own way.

I spied my mother and my aunt as well as some of the book club ladies at a long oval table. Then I also saw Paul Schmidt with Herb and the pinochle men. *Please don't tell me he came back from fishing somewhere.* Without wasting a second, I nabbed the seat next to Shirley just as Myrna plopped down on the other side of me. "Lucinda should be here any second," she said. "She was parking her car but I didn't want to wait. It takes her at least three tries to line it up. Then, when she gets out, she goes back and straightens it again."

"I hope she hurries up." Herb stood and looked around. "Who else are we missing?"

"I didn't know you were taking attendance," Myrna said. "Look to your left. Bill's coming in and so are Gloria and Wayne. I'm glad she had the good sense to leave the dog home. He'd knock over everything."

My mother adjusted the double stroller next to her on the aisle. "I'm glad my fur-babies are small. They need to enjoy the outdoor air. Too bad I can't let Streetman loose to practice his scent identification training."

"His what?" I asked.

"Scent identification. I've decided to train him to detect certain scents. That way I could get him registered as a service dog."

I was positive the color left my face but I had no way to be sure. "Um, how exactly are you doing that?"

"With a special training program on YouTube. We use the large TV in the living room and practice the exercises around the house. He has different scented toys that I bought and he learns to find the source. When it gets cooler, we'll practice outside. And who knows? He may be needed by the sheriff's office sometime."

Herb burst out laughing. "Not in my lifetime, Harriet."

A few chuckles followed just as Wayne and Gloria sat down. "Where's Louis?" Wayne asked my aunt. "Thought he'd be here."

"Sound asleep. He got in at three a.m. from an anniversary celebration at the Omni Resort. I nearly tripped over his saxophone on the way out the door. He left the case leaning over a table in our entryway."

"Good! Everyone is here." Herb leaned back, sucked in his stomach and puffed out his chest. In that instant, I feared for the worst. *Please don't tell me he joined another sport. Or worse yet, signed up for a baking class and all of us would be compelled to taste test his projects.*

I held my breath and waited for the announcement, but no one on God's green earth would have ever expected what came out of his mouth.

Chapter 2

Herb's voice exploded and I was thankful we were outside. "Solar flares are intensifying and we need to take action now!"

Myrna looked up and turned to Cecilia. "Pass me one of those complimentary mini-bagels, please."

"This is serious, Myrna," he said. "If they continue to fire up, they could cause the worst geomagnetic storm in over 165 years! But don't take my word for it—check NASA, check NOAA. Good grief, check Google."

"In that case," my aunt said, "we'd better order right now."

"Don't you people have anything better to think about than food at a time like this?" Herb's face turned crimson and he crossed his arms. Bill patted his shoulder and chuckled. "Hey, lighten up. We're eating out. What are we supposed to think of?"

"Fine. But don't say I didn't warn you."

My mother adjusted the stroller so that Streetman could have a better view of the table. "All right, Herb. Tell us exactly what we're supposed to do. Fire off a giant ice-ball? It's not like an asteroid that someone can detonate."

"Don't be ridiculous. We can't stop the solar flares but we can save ourselves from starvation."

"If that waitress doesn't show up soon," my aunt said, "it won't matter. We'll all die of starvation."

Lucinda leaned across the table and eyeballed Herb. "What are you saying, Herb?"

"Simply put, if a solar flare disrupts the earth's power grids, and believe me, it's possible, then the entire food chain goes down the tubes. Remember the great toilet paper disaster? That will be nothing compared to this."

"Are you suggesting hoarding food?" Gloria furrowed her brow and reached for the carafe of coffee.

"Not hoarding it, *growing* it."

Suddenly, the entire table went silent. I couldn't tell if the stricken looks on everyone's faces were out of fear, or a result of holding back laughter. Finally, Lucinda spoke.

"Let me get this straight, Herb. You want us to grow our own food?"

"Vegetables to be precise. We need to start growing our own vegetables."

"Why on earth would I do that when I can go to Sprouts or any of the farmer's markets?" My aunt spied a waitress off to the left and waved her over.

"Because Sprouts wouldn't be able to acquire food if the power grid went down and transportation went along with it. All of us need to chew on that one."

"I need to chew on something," Bill muttered.

"You can say that," Kenny chimed in. "But after listening to Herb, I'm ordering the garden vegetable shmear for my bagels."

At that moment the waitress arrived and all thoughts turned to what was on the menu, not what awaited planting. But once all of us were satiated, the topic of growing our own vegetables returned like the seven-year-itch.

"All of you will thank me for this," Herb said. "I signed up for the Sun City West Agriculture Club. Membership is only ten dollars a year. Not only that, but I rented four of the large plots of land for our farming."

"Farming? Did you rent us a plow and an ox, too?" Myrna couldn't stop laughing.

"I'm serious." Herb furrowed his brow and continued to speak. "The club provides rototillers and all sorts of equipment."

"Lordy, I don't even know where these plots are, and I've lived here for over twenty-seven years," Shirley said.

"Off of 137th Drive, which is off of Gemstone Drive."

"Heavens, Herb, none of us knows where Gemstone Drive is." Shirley took a sip of her coffee and shook her head.

Cecilia literally waved her hands in the air. "I do! I do! Take West Aleppo Drive east and you'll find it. I had to deliver a condolence basket to a family in our church not too long ago. Poor Ernest Kinsley passed away a few days before his hundredth birthday. Very unexpected."

"At a hundred years old?" Kenny widened his eyes and then rolled them.

"Forget Kinsley, or whatever his name is. I'm serious. We need to prepare for the unexpected." Herb devoured a mini-bagel in a nanosecond. Then Cecilia sighed.

"Too bad poor Ernest didn't prepare."

"Now then, this is what I suggest." Herb leaned his elbows on the table as if he was about to read a proclamation. "The plots are large enough so that all of us will be able to cultivate them and plant an assortment of leafy greens, tomatoes, squash, peppers, radishes, and melons."

"Not in this lifetime!" Shirley held up her hands for everyone to see. "The days of two-dollars-a-nail for a manicure are long gone. It's a least fifty dollars and that doesn't include the tip. Then, if you want to add bling to it, you'll cough up at least twenty more. There is no way I'm getting soil under my nails. Count me out."

"You could always buy garden gloves," Kevin said before Louise nudged his elbow.

Then Paul, who finished off two plates of smoked salmon, wiped his lips and bellowed, "I have a better idea. A much better idea."

If I could have held a mirror to my face, I would have been sure it had turned ashen. I clenched my teeth and waited for the worst. Sure enough, it came.

"Why plant and get dirt on your hands when you can fish? That's right—fish! I can teach all of you how to select the best bait, cast that first line into the water, reel that baby in, remove it, and gut it." Then he turned to my mother and Myrna. "By the way, I was thinking about devoting some radio time to gutting and fileting fish."

At the mention of the words *radio time*, I shuddered. My mother, along with Myrna and Paul, shared a dreadful radio show on KSCW, the voice of Sun City West. "The Cozy Mystery Fishing Hour," or something like that. I try not to think about it for fear of getting hives. Initially, my mother and Myrna had, and still do, their own murder mystery show where they talk about cozy mysteries and any other rambling thoughts that get into their heads. Gossip included. It still amazes me that they haven't been taken off the air, jailed, or sued.

Paul also has his own show, "Lake Fishing with Paul." One unfortunate day a while back, all three of them got scheduled for the same time and all of them refused to leave. As a result, the airtime consisted of a hodgepodge of cozy mystery discussion interspersed with fishing and bait tips. Horrific doesn't come close to describing it. Oddly enough, the audience loved it, and when the station manager found out, the three of them wound up with a shared show. Go figure.

"As I was saying," Paul continued, "gutting fish is an art. I'll add it to the program."

Herb was undaunted regarding the solar flare threat. "Fish have to be cooked, Paul. Can't very well do that if there's no power."

"We can build a campfire."

"No one is building a campfire, reeling in and gutting fish, or getting their hands dirty by planting things," my mother said. "I'm willing to take my chances with the solar flares."

Just then, our waitress reappeared. "I didn't mean to eavesdrop, but did you mention solar flares? It was on the news a few minutes ago. Scientists are predicting one heck of a stormy year ahead with unforeseeable consequences. They suggested people consider home gardens and stockpiling nonperishable items."

"That cinches it for me," my aunt announced. "I'm sending Louis to Costco to buy out the place."

"Got a deal on angleworms. Sure none of you want to take a stab at putting them on a hook?" Paul narrowed his eyes and looked at my mother. She immediately turned to face Herb. "Maybe I spoke too soon. Gardening may not be all that bad. After all, Martha Stewart does it."

Martha Stewart does it, all right. With a crew of twenty or more people. And this isn't gardening per se, it's growing vegetables!

"That's wonderful, Harriet!" Herb lifted his coffee mug in the air. "Who else is on board?"

Lucinda scratched her head and wisps of blond-gray hair flew across her forehead. "I had a nice geranium once. As I recall, it wasn't too much trouble."

"Is that a yes?" Herb asked.

"Oh, I suppose." Then she looked at Louise. "You had those adorable green plants on your windowsill. Whatever happened to them?"

Louise shrugged. "They died. From overwatering. I was so used to filling up Leviticus's water feeder that I kept giving the plants water at the same time."

"Sounds like another yes to me," Herb announced.

"Sure I can't twist anyone's arm into fishing instead?" Paul reached for the last mini-bagel and popped it in his mouth.

"No!" everyone bellowed at once.

"I snagged this neat mini rod-reel combo on Amazon and want to try it out. It's pocket-sized so I can carry it on me all the time. Sure you won't change your minds?"

Again, another *"No!"* resounded from the crowd.

Paul shrugged and chomped on the mini-bagel that was in his mouth. "Got to have the waitress bring us more of these."

When we finally paid the bill and got up to leave, Herb walked toward my mother and me. "You'll thank me for this opportunity, Harriet. Imagine—the open air, the close encounter with nature, and the knowledge that we won't go hungry when those solar flares attack the earth."

Yep, we can all munch on our lettuce leaves in the hot, humid air, filled with lots of little bugs, compliments of nature.

"Oh, I'm not concerned about going hungry, I've got a full freezer and dry ice will work just fine if we lose power. I just thought planting and sowing would be a wonderful pastime for Streetman. He can romp around the garden area to his heart's delight."

"And to the horror of everyone else, Mom! Are you sure they allow dogs?"

"They do," Kevin said. "My neighbor has a boxer and they bring

Archie all the time when they work in their garden."

"You see? There's nothing to worry about, Phee. What possible harm will come from a little chiweenie running about in a community garden?"

"As long as that's all he'll do." *Which I doubt.*

"Honestly, from the way you're acting, you'd think my little man was a magnet for mayhem."

"You said it, not me."

We walked down the path that led to our cars, and as I was about to tap the fob to open my car door, she called out, "I'll let you know when we check it out so you can join us!"

I pretended not to hear but it wouldn't have mattered. Somehow, I knew I'd get coerced into the bird's-eye tour of the Sun City West Agriculture Club's plots. What I didn't know was that the tour would turn into a full-blown excursion. And soil under everyone's fingernails would be the least of their concerns.

Chapter 3

Augusta nearly spit out her coffee when I got to work on Monday and told her about my mother's latest venture.

"That takes the cake, Phee! Of all the wacky things those book club ladies have done, this one outdoes it. Planting? Gardening? Farming? You have *got* to be kidding me."

"I wish I was. Right now it's only my mom, Lucinda and Louise. That doesn't include the men. I think Herb managed to convince Bill, Kevin, and Kenny to join him."

"Have any of them had any actual experience growing anything?"

"Yep—food mold."

Augusta laughed and took another sip of her coffee. "One thing for sure, it'll keep them occupied. They'll have to decide what they want to grow and if they're going to purchase seeds, transplants or a combination. They should also read up on pest-resilient plant varieties."

"I doubt that will happen. They'll pick what they're familiar eating—tomatoes, carrots, zucchini . . . you know, vegetables that are recognizable."

"I grow what I can eat, freeze or can. Tell them they can go online for the vegetable planting calendar for Maricopa County. September and October are really good months. Not like back East when we had to wait for the great spring thaw before we could plant anything. Say, have they given any thought to pest management?"

"No, but I have and it's my mother's four-legged pest."

"Yikes, forgot about Streetman for a minute. Anyway, those women should really become somewhat knowledgeable about plant diseases. The seeds and transplants have letters that indicate what they're resistant to. It's not the same with all plants. Take tomatoes, for example. They'll have the letter V for resistance to Verticillium disease."

"Uh-oh. This is sounding more complicated by the minute."

"Oh, it gets better. Did you know there were pest seasons?"

"Nope. Only tourist and snowbird ones."

"Okay. Just tell her to wait until it cools down a bit and the whitefly population dwindles."

"Trust me. If she or any of the women are bothered by flies of any variety or color, they'll hightail it out of there and over to Bagels 'n More to complain."

"Mr. Gregory said you ate out on their new deck this past Saturday. Fancy-dancy or what?"

"Three-tiered. The perfect venue for people watching, and believe me, those women will do lots of that. Anyway, I should get behind my desk and start on those invoices. I take it the men are out on cases. It's pretty quiet in here, other than us."

"Yep. First appointment isn't until ten. Mr. Gregory should be back by then. And Mr. Williams will be tied up all morning with the cat case. He's picked up a few good leads and is running with them."

I headed to my office and didn't emerge for over two hours. And just as I plunked a K-Cup of McCafé into the Keurig, Augusta took a call and handed the phone to me. "Your mother." She put her palm over the receiver. "She's not frantic. You can enjoy your coffee."

"Hey, Mom, what's up?" I watched the machine, ready to snatch my coffee in a nanosecond.

"Someone named Gussie, who also goes by Big Gus, is giving Herb a tour of the facility Wednesday morning at six thirty before the heat rises. Lucinda, Louise and I are going."

"Have fun."

"Wait! You didn't let me finish. Since you don't have to be at the office until nine, you really should join us."

"Why? I know what community gardens look like. There was a big one in Mankato."

"What if you try to reach me one day and I don't answer? I could be face down in a radish patch or worse. You need to know where it is."

"Oh, brother. Talk about overexaggerating. If you wind up face down in a radish patch, someone is bound to notice."

"Exactly. And that someone should be my daughter."

I shut my eyes, inhaled and silently counted to ten. When I opened my eyes, Augusta mouthed, "Just go! Get it over with."

I gave Augusta "the eye" and sighed. Loudly. "I will give you one hour and one hour only. And if I don't see a radish patch, I'm out of there."

"Very funny. I'll email you the directions. Oh, and don't wear good shoes. It may be dusty, or muddy, or both. You never know what you'll find."

"As long as it's not the dog. Got to get to work. Have a good day, Mom."

I handed the receiver back to Augusta and took my first taste of the McCafé. "I can't believe I caved in."

"Think of it this way. You'll get your good deed over with early in the day."

"So can you. Bring donuts to the office."

. . .

That Wednesday, when I pulled up to the garden gate with its five-mile-an-hour sign, I didn't know which one to read next—"Please close gate and sign in after entering the garden," "No Trespassing, No Trash," "Last Person Leaving the Garden, Please Lock the Gate," and "No Firearms."

Given the narrow gravel road that was intended for golf carts and walkers, I parked my car on the adjacent street and walked to the entrance. With the exception of its desert landscaping, the area looked like every other community garden I'd seen. However, there was one exception—the people cultivating it.

At first I thought I had been transported back to 1969, but once I got over the initial shock of seeing an eighty-something man in a bright tie-dyed Grateful Dead shirt, and two senior women with long gauze sundresses and ribbons in their hair, I realized that conformity didn't come with retirement.

Apparently, I was the only one to arrive on time and must have looked like a deer in the headlights, because the next thing I knew, a red-haired rotund man, barefooted and sporting a beard, approached me.

"Good morning. I'm Gussie, the president of the agriculture club. How can I help you?"

"Hi! Phee Kimball, visitor. I'm supposed to meet my mother and her friends, along with her neighbor, Herb Garrett, for a tour. You said your name was Gussie? I think you're our tour guide."

"I sure am. Look off to your left. Herb's over there admiring Thira Tillwell's purple artichoke flowers."

And Thira Tillwell, from the look of things.

"Yep. That's Herb all right. I didn't recognize him with that large straw hat."

Gussie laughed. "You can always spot a newbie. They're the ones with the big straw hats. I'll stick to my baseball caps."

Just then, I heard an oh-so-familiar voice.

"Phee! I knew that was your car. Have you seen Herb?"

I turned and saw my mother and Shirley making their way toward us.

"He's over there." I pointed to the left.

"Good heavens! He looks like Farmer Brown."

"Mom, Shirley, this is Gussie. He's the gentleman who'll be giving us the tour." Then I smiled at Shirley. "I didn't know you decided to grow vegetables here as well."

Even with her dark skin, Shirley turned ashen. "Lordy, no. I'm just here to keep your mother company since we're going out to Betty's Rooste for breakfast. It's cannoli pancake day. Lucinda and Louise are coming as well."

Before Shirley could continue, Louise shouted from the gate, "We're here! We had to drive back to Lucinda's for her everyday sneakers."

Thankfully I had thought ahead and left my office shoes in the car, opting for my old sneaks as well. A second or two later, Herb huffed and puffed his way over to us with Bill a few feet behind him.

"Kevin and Kenny had to make a coffee stop. They'll catch up with us. I see all of you have met Gussie."

A few nods and handshakes followed as Gussie cleared his throat. "Don't worry yourselves with all the little details. Just try to get the lay of the land, so to speak. With few exceptions, everyone here is friendly and willing to help. Some folks retired from operating farms. Others are from the big cities and wanted a taste of Mother Nature, southwest style. Come on, let's get moving and I'll point out a few key areas. Feel free to ask any questions."

"Um, this is not so much of a question as it is a statement," I said. "I can only stay for a little while. I need to be at work in Glendale and didn't want you to think I was being rude if I left early."

Gussie chuckled. "Don't worry, I won't."

Then Louise asked, "Can you tell me why you're barefooted?"

Gussie looked down as if it was the first time he realized he didn't have shoes on. Surprising how he wasn't bothered by the gravel and small rocks. "My body needs to feel the energy of the ground. It gives me life. Can't very well do that with shoes and socks on."

My mother looked at Gussie's feet and then at me. "Oh my goodness, that's exactly what your aunt Ina says when she traipses around barefoot and braless in the house."

I looked around for a sinkhole but couldn't find one. It didn't matter because in that second, we all heard a woman shout, "So help me, Barry, if as much as a particle of that pesticide gets on my zucchinis and cukes, you'll wish you stayed in Yakima."

"Get over it, Maybelle. Don't know about you, but I'm growing my veggies in the twenty-first century, not the first."

Gussie shook his head and motioned us on. "Too bad Barry and Maybelle's plots are next to each other's. This has been going on forever, but lately, he's ornerier than usual and she's become super hypersensitive when it comes to her garden. You don't have to worry though; your plots are a way down the road. And it's up to you if you want to use pesticides or rely on the old-fashioned natural methods."

Shirley poked my mother's elbow. "Are you sure you want to do this, Harriet? You don't know anything about pesticides, or natural methods, come to think of it."

"What's to know? I plop the seed or the little plant in the ground, give it water and wait until it's edible."

The look of terror on Gussie's face was unmistakable. "I wish it was that easy, but there's all sorts of insects, critters, and pests waiting to devour your next meal. Nematodes, aphids, slugs, spider mites, ants, earwigs, cutworms, mealybugs, and don't get me started on blister beetles. Did you know they carry cantharidin?"

"Can what?" Shirley asked.

"Cantharidin. It's a defense chemical for those little stinkers and it's harmful to humans."

"Pesticides it is!" my mother shouted. "And I'll use some of Myrna's defense sprays, too."

"Those are for attackers," Lucinda said.

My mother widened her eyes. "What do you think those things are?"

And with that, I made my excuses and headed back to the car and the office. I'd had enough insanity for the day. Unfortunately, had I known at the time what awaited the crew, I would have talked my mother out of veggie farming with the agriculture club and purchased her a gift certificate for Sprouts.

Chapter 4

"I see you're still in one piece," Augusta laughed when I walked into the office. I had changed my shoes in the car and dusted off my slacks and top. The agricultural area was a magnet for anything the wind could blow.

"Let's put it this way, I don't expect to be going back any time soon."

"Let me guess. A cadre of veggie-growing personalities?"

"I only met one but observed two others bickering over pesticides. And as for the characters, those book club ladies and whoever Herb musters up in addition to Kevin and Kenny should be a real sideshow. At least it'll be a different kind of diversion for my mother."

"Speaking of diversions, Mr. Williams will be attending the International Cat Fanciers' Show at the Phoenix Convention Center this weekend. He's following up on that lead."

"Uh-huh."

"That's not all. Your husband will be joining him. They just decided a few minutes ago before they took off."

"As long as Marshall doesn't bring home any four-legged felines, it'll be fine."

"I doubt he will. These are champion cats with exorbitant price tags. Show cats. Breeder cats. You'd have to take out a second mortgage."

I cringed. "And Nate thinks Princess-Queen-Empress-Whatever may be there?"

"Not in person, no. But someone is bound to know something."

"Guess I'll have a nice, quiet weekend at home."

"Sounds good to me."

I moseyed into my office and tackled the usual invoices and spreadsheets for three hours until the inevitable interruption from my mother arrived.

"At least she waited until the midmorning break," Augusta called out as she transferred the call to my office. "Incoming!"

Yep. My mother's voice, right in my ear.

"I hope you have a few minutes to talk, Phee. I need to go over my planting list with you. Lucinda, Louise, and Herb were no help whatsoever. And forget Kevin and Kenny. They're even worse."

"I don't know anything about planting vegetables. I go to the frozen foods section and look to see what's on sale. Unless I'm making a fresh salad. And that's a no-brainer. Lettuce, tomato, the usual."

"Planting them is different. It's a regular science. What can withstand certain insects. What can survive a blight. What won't catch a virus. Did you know plants can get a virus?"

"No, but I'll keep that in mind. Look, I have lots of work to do. I'll touch base later, okay?"

"I suppose. The women were thinking it might be a good idea to divvy up the selections so we'll have a wide variety."

"That makes sense."

"Are you sure you can't spare an hour to glance at my planting list?"

"Why don't you drive back and ask Gussie. He seemed helpful. Or maybe that hippie lady. The one who argued with Barry."

"Goodness, speaking of Barry, Gussie gave us the lowdown on him. Including a ten-year smoking habit that he's trying to quit. Blames his irritability on it. Bad news. Steer clear."

"Not a problem. Catch you later."

I didn't have to be told to steer clear of Barry. I planned to steer clear of everyone. This was one looney project that didn't need my intervention. Or so I thought. I returned to my work and remained in bookkeeping bliss for the remainder of the afternoon. That's when my mother's second nuisance call came.

"I took your advice."

"Uh, what advice was that?"

"You said we should talk with Gussie, only he wasn't there, but Ona and Aneta were. They're from Macedonia and they gave Lucinda, Louise and me lots of advice about planting. Did you ever hear of companion plants? It's just like Streetman and Essie, only with plants. But instead of playing with each other, it's all about pest control and flavor improvement."

"Uh-huh."

"That means I have to plant basil to help the tomatoes."

"Is that what you decided to plant?"

"That, and a few other things—carrots, beets and peppers. Lucinda is going to plant potatoes and squash, but not near my plot because those vegetables don't play nice with mine. Oh, and Louise wants to plant onions."

"Onions? That's it?"

"She said something about garden peas and lettuce. Before I forget, we have to plant nasturtiums too."

"I don't believe they're edible, but I'm not really sure."

"They keep the aphids away from the vegetables."

"See? You've learned so much already. No need for my help."

"Actually, we will need your help and Marshall's if he ever has time. Our plots have wire cages around them to keep out the rabbits but the wire has to be replaced."

"Isn't that something Herb and his crew can do?"

"Oh, they'll do it all right, but they're starting with Herb's plot, and then Kevin's and Kenny's. By the time those slowpokes finish, it'll be Christmas. It's more grunt work than anything else but the good news is that Herb will purchase and deliver the new rabbit mesh. So all you and Marshall would need to do is replace the wire that's got holes in it. Easy-peasy."

"Does Herb have wire cutters?"

"Those men have everything. And it shouldn't take you and Marshall that long."

"Not Marshall. Me. Marshall has to be in Phoenix at a cat convention."

"A what?"

"Don't get any ideas. It's a purebred cat convention. Essie doesn't qualify. And Marshall and Nate are tracking down a stolen cat. A very valuable, exceedingly rare, stolen cat."

"So this means you'll do it?"

"Oh, I suppose so. But I can't make it an all-day thing. I want to take in some swimming and run errands."

"No problem. I really appreciate it. We all do."

"We?"

"Lucinda and Louise."

And with those words, I pictured my weekend evaporating into thin air. Still, my mother was so enthusiastic about this project that I didn't have the heart to say no.

"I take it we'll be meeting on Saturday. I'll be there at noon. It's one of my half-day work Saturdays."

"That's fine. Besides, we always start Saturday mornings at Bagels 'n More, so the timing should be perfect. I'll bring you a bagel and whatever you want to drink."

"Coffee, but I'll bring my own. Just a pretzel bagel. And thanks."

"You too."

No sooner did I place the receiver back in the cradle when I heard Marshall's voice. "I'll take a round of applause, please!"

I got up from my chair and walked to the outer office. "What are we applauding?"

He grinned from ear to ear. "I located the missing sibling! Identical triplets for sure. Wish all our cases were this satisfying."

"Get that invoice out now, Phee," Augusta said. "Before they all get on each other's nerves."

Marshall grabbed a Coke from the fridge. "Nah, that's only in Phee's family." Then he crinkled his nose and looked at me. "Only kidding, hon."

I rolled my eyes. "I'm not. Between my mother and my aunt Ina, the banter is nonstop. But the good news is that Aunt Ina lives in the Grand and will not be taking part in the great gardening endeavor."

"Uh. So it's really a go?"

I nodded. "Uh-huh. And I'm going over there Saturday afternoon to rewire the plot cages or whatever they call them."

"I'd love to help you, but I'll be—"

"I know. Up to your neck with cat fur."

He looked at Augusta. "You beat me to it. I was going to tell her that Nate and I were going to spend the weekend in a cat house."

Augusta pursed her lips. "She'd probably tell you not to bring any of them home."

With that, we all broke into laughter.

"You've got that right, folks," I said. "Frankly, the cage wiring is beginning to sound better and better."

And while redoing the cage mesh sounded doable, it was everything else that put my nerves on high alert.

Chapter 5

When Saturday finally rolled around, Marshall and Nate headed to the convention center at dawn so that they could "eat a substantial breakfast" on the way. A euphemism for finding a fast-food place that specialized in bacon and egg sandwiches with home fries.

The past few days were uneventful as far as the office was concerned, and even my mother's phone calls dwindled. Augusta began to worry that it was the proverbial calm before the storm, but I knew my mother was saving up all of the gossip and latest rumors for our work weekend in the garden.

At a little after one, I arrived at the agricultural plots and was greeted by Gussie, who happened to be working on some PVC pipes. "Gotta replace some of these pipes that cracked," he said. "By the way, your mother and her two lady friends should be all set. The former plot tenant left a decent grid and a timer."

I nodded, trying not to appear as if I had no idea what he was taking about. "Good to know. Thanks."

"Yeah. Sure beats hand watering with a hose. That would eat up more time than I want to put in, and believe me, I put in a lot. Still, we got some folks who prefer the hand watering. More power to 'em."

"Uh, is there a charge for the water?"

Gussie shook his head. "Not to us. The rec center pays."

"Thanks. I'm here to help my mom redo the cage mesh."

"I know. The whole crew is over there working."

"You wouldn't happen to know if she brought a small dog with her?"

"A little yappy brown one was running all over the place. Could be hers. He growled at some of the sack cloth around the plots."

"Yeah, that's hers all right. Streetman. Very unpredictable. Very spoiled. The two of them are joined at the hip."

"Yep. Kinda got that impression. Have fun re-meshing."

"Thanks."

I ambled down the road, taking in the strange dynamics of the garden. My first impression was that the Doomsday Preppers and the Sixties Love Children joined forces to prevent their mutual starvation. One woman's area was nothing but a small lavender field and the plot next to it was herbs. Nothing but herbs.

Then, plots that resembled small farms with potatoes, squash, beans, corn, and anything dense and caloric.

"I've got scores of extra potatoes if you want some," a robust woman with reddish hair shouted. "What are you growing?"

"I'm not, but thanks. I'm here to help my mother out. She's the lady on the left and her cage meshing needs repair or replacement."

The woman scanned the area. "That's Harriet Plunkett. I know her. I must have been so busy planting and weeding that I didn't notice her come in." She squinted for a second and added, "And she's with Lucinda Espinosa and Louise Munson. I attended a rec center workshop on personal safety for seniors with them. Hmm, seems there was another lady there who had an arsenal of self-defense products with her."

"Myrna Mittleson."

"That's right. Myrna. From New York. I suppose you'd need an arsenal to live there, but frankly, Phoenix is catching up. By the way, I'm Claudia Galen. Lived in Sun City West since the late nineties." She motioned for me to move a bit closer and whispered, "My potato patch is really a front for what I really do."

Wonderful. She's probably on the ten most-wanted list.

"What's that?"

"I sit here and read all day. Occasionally I make it look as if I'm doing something, but once I got these spuds in the ground, I lay back and wait. Everyone minds their own business and I don't have to deal with any of the library fussbudgets."

"I see. Well, it's nice meeting you, Claudia. I'd better get over there and pitch in."

"Before you go, let me give you a piece of advice—stay away from Barry. If you don't know who he is, you will soon enough. Big brawny guy who hasn't seen a razor since the Great Depression. He's terrorized more people here than I can count with both hands. And—" Then she looked around and bent her head down. Still, her whisper was more than audible. "I think he poisoned Maybelle's cucumbers last year. One minute they were shiny and green, the next minute they were shriveled up and brown."

"What makes you think Barry was responsible?"

"He was seen milling around her garden plot more than once or twice."

"Thanks for the heads-up."

"Anytime. And say hi to the ladies for me. Got to get back to the psychological thriller I'm reading."

I smiled. "Enjoy."

• • •

"Phee! What on earth took you so long?" my mother shouted as I approached. "I saw you over there chatting with one of the gardeners. And you complain that I talk too much."

"Her name is Claudia and she attended a self-defense program with all of you and Myrna."

My mother peered across the road and squinted. "Claudia. I remember her. Nice lady. Avid reader, but thrillers mainly. Not cozies. What was she talking about for so long?"

"Actually, she told me what we already heard—to stay away from Barry."

"That may be easier said than done."

"Why?"

"Because he's headed this way."

Lucinda, Louise, and my mom turned and watched as Barry strode toward us. His bellow got to us before he did. "Which of you ladies owns that little brown dog? He peed all over Maybelle's tomatoes!"

I glared at my mother. Before she could take ownership, Barry continued. "Not that I give a hoot and a half about Maybelle's darn tomatoes, but if they wilt or worse, she'll point a finger right at me. Don't need that. Heck, if an aphid lands on one of them, she'll say I put it there."

"It won't happen again," my mother said.

Who's she kidding? That dog is running all over the place like a maniac.

"Good. Because right now he's pawing through the compost heap they use for the plots in this area. Might want to rein him in."

My mother shouted to the dog, "Streetman! Come here!"

Nothing.

Again, "Streetman! Mommy is calling you!"

Like that's going to help.

"Fine," I grumbled. "I'll go fetch him." I meandered toward the large compost heap that was strategically placed equidistant from six large plots. The dog continued to paw through it and I was positive I'd be covered with yucky stuff when I went to grab him.

Streetman's head was buried inside the compost heap and I wondered why the fascination over bark, twigs, plant cuttings, weeds, grass clippings, rotted fruit and vegetables, and anything else organic that was tossed in there for good measure.

I took a breath and grabbed the little bugger under his front legs and pulled him out, expecting him to turn and snap, but he held fast to something in his mouth that I thought was a multi-pronged branch. *Good. Less chance of snarling and nipping.*

"I've got him," I shouted. Then Streetman turned his head and in that split second I knew why he wasn't about to release that branch from his jaw. Because it wasn't a branch. It was the skeletal remains of a hand, complete with small gold or bronze rings on one of the fingers.

"Call the posse!" I yelled as I charged toward the women. Herb, who was a few yards away, heard me and came running with Kevin at his heels.

"Did he bite someone?" Kevin asked.

"No one who's going to report it."

My mother rushed to the dog and stopped dead in her tracks. "Is that what I think it is?"

I nodded. "Uh-huh."

Then I heard Louise. "I got the posse on the phone. What am I telling them?"

"That's a skeletal hand your dog's holding!" Herb yelled.

No kidding.

"Never mind," Louise said. "They heard Herb. They're on their way. Maybe we should tell someone before they show up."

I looked around and bit my lower lip. "I don't think that's necessary. Gussie's on his way over and Barry isn't far behind. Give it five minutes and those preppers and hippies will abandon their plots to see what the ruckus is all about."

Streetman was still in my arms when I realized something. It was going to be impossible to extricate that hand from his mouth. Heck, he once held on to a shoe during a dance performance and nearly ruined the program.

"Mom! We'll never get the hand out of his mouth."

She crossed her arms and stared at her little prince. "Who wants to drive to McDonald's for a Big Mac?"

Chapter 6

"On my way, Harriet," Kenny said. "You can pay me later. I've wanted to sink my teeth into a double cheeseburger with fries all day. Anyone want to join me?"

Herb handed him a ten-dollar bill. "You're going through the drive-up. Can you bring me back a Quarter Pounder with cheese?"

"Make it two." Kevin also handed Kenny some cash.

As Kenny headed to the gate, I heard the sound of a siren and shuddered. It could have only meant one thing. The posse called the sheriff's office and it had to be Deputies Bowman and Ranston responding. They were the only ones who blared their siren as if it was a toy they had gotten under the Christmas tree.

In the meantime, my mother continued to coax Streetman into letting go of the hand but it was useless.

"Give it up," Lucinda said. "He's as bad as Leviticus when it comes to territorial possession. At least he's not going anywhere with it. He seems quite contented to sit over there and chomp on it."

"He'll destroy evidence," Gussie bellowed. "I heard what happened. Glad someone had the good sense to call the posse. Maybe they'll shoot a tranquilizer gun at him or something."

"Over my dead body! And yours!"

I never heard my mother raise her voice like that, and even the pinochle guys were taken aback.

"Easy, Harriet. Be careful what you say. Things have a way of coming back and biting. And I'm not referring to your dog, although it *is* tempting." Kevin stepped between Gussie and my mother just as the sheriff's car pulled up, followed by a Sun City West Posse vehicle.

Yippee. Bowman and Ranston. Can it get any better?

I wanted to shoot off a text to Marshall but I knew he had enough going on with Princess what's-her-name.

By now, the idyllic garden area had turned into a spectacle as all eyes were on Streetman—Ona, Anita, Gussie, Barry, Claudia, Thira, three pencil-thin women in cutoff jeans and peasant blouses, a scruffy-looking man with a long gray beard, and a woman who looked like a character out of Mother Goose with her polka-dot shirtwaist dress. And that didn't include our crew.

"No one make a move!" Deputy Bowman shouted. "I'm going to need names." Then he looked at Deputy Ranston, who immediately pulled out an iPad.

Without pausing to catch a breath, Bowman continued. "I need to know exactly what you found. The report says 'skeletal human hand.' Where is it?"

I stepped forward, waved, and pointed to the dog. Streetman had now positioned himself against someone's sackcloth-covered plot cage, his teeth firmly planted around the hand.

"All I see is the dog. I should have expected as much," Bowman said to me, "when the call came in. Why is it whenever a corpse appears, you and your mother's book club are inches away from it?"

"There's a corpse?" someone shrieked. "I just got here. I wondered why there were sheriff cars. Oh my gosh! A corpse. In our community garden. Who dropped dead?"

Ranston put his hands on his hips and narrowed his eyes at the crowd. For some reason, it made his toadlike appearance look even more comical than usual. "A hand! The report indicated a hand was found. A skeletal—"

"I'm not coming here anymore without my gun," one of the hippie women announced. "Someone chopped a body up in here."

"We don't know that," Ranston replied. "And it's skeletal. If any chopping took place, it had to be a long time ago."

If the deputy thought his response would be comforting, it wasn't. Gussie just *had* to put in his two cents. "It can take anywhere from a year to a decade. Depends on weather, soil composition, oxygen rates—"

"What are you? Some sort of forensic expert?" Barry walked toward Gussie until they were face-to-face.

"Nah, I just watch lots of crime TV and survival shows."

"For your information," Ranston said, "the sheriff's office happens to have an outstanding forensic lab and all determinations regarding the, uh, *finding*, will be made by them."

"Absolutely! Now where is this skeletal hand?" Bowman looked around, expecting someone to answer. Instead, a number of hands pointed to Streetman, who was still enjoying his newfound treasure.

"Don't tell me the dog's got it?" Bowman's face turned crimson. "That's your dog, Harriet. The little biter."

My mother drew her shoulders back. "Streetman does not bite. He may nip occasionally when he's stressed, or snap, but he's never bitten anyone to the point of drawing blood."

"Why take a chance?" Gussie's voice could be heard over the sound of a train passing by.

Just then, Kenny raced down the road with two brown paper bags. "I got the cheeseburgers and the dog's Big Mac."

"I didn't know someone was making a McDonald's run," Thira said, "or I would have asked for medium fries."

Sure. Why not? Maybe even popcorn for this circus.

Kenny handed my mother the Big Mac, and she, in turn, gave it to me. "You have better luck with him, Phee. You're younger and faster than the rest of us."

"I need my hands for typing and computer work."

"Then don't use the good one. Use the left hand."

"Maybe get animal control over here to lasso him." Gussie was adamant.

"No tranquilizer. No animal control. I've got it." I stormed over to the dog, waving the Big Mac in the air.

"Don't worry," Kenny called out. "I bought two. In case you ran into trouble."

Streetman let out a soft growl as I approached and clamped those little teeth of his tighter on the hand. I extended my arm and waved the Big Mac in the air, knowing he probably caught the scent of it the minute Kenny arrived. Still, he wouldn't relinquish his prize.

Then, he changed his mind and looked up, his nose breathing in the air. I knew I'd only have seconds to retrieve the hand while offering him the messy burger. That's when it dawned on me that I should have been wearing rubber gloves or at least put a napkin between the skeletal hand and mine. I turned and took a few steps back.

"What's the matter, Phee?" my mother shouted. "What's taking so long?"

"I need a napkin. Or a few of them."

"Don't worry about the dog making a mess."

"Not Streetman! I don't want to contaminate the evidence more than your dog did with his slobber."

Herb rushed over with a mouthful of fries and handed me a few McDonald's napkins. Not the sturdiest kind, but I couldn't be choosy.

"Thanks. Be prepared to grab him if he makes a run for it," I said to him.

"And have him bite me?"

"He won't. He's much too interested in the hand. Okay, here goes nothing."

I inhaled and strode toward Streetman for the second time. Again, I extended my arm and bent down to offer him the Big Mac. Too bad the *Guinness Book of World Records* staff wasn't on hand to record the speed at which he dropped the hand and simultaneously grabbed the hamburger and the hand. I couldn't believe that little mouth could hold both, but it did.

"Tell Kenny we need the second Big Mac," I yelled.

And just as Kenny came running with it, Streetman dropped the hand in favor of devouring the burger. It was now or never. *I better not lose a finger. Or worse.*

Moving like a Vegas blackjack dealer, I snatched the hand, but the dog was quick. As he jumped, mouth wide open to retrieve it, I threw it to Herb and shouted, "Catch it! You're on the men's slow pitch team!"

Kenny and Kevin stood inches away, their mouths wide open. Next thing I knew, Herb snagged that hand and stood wordless staring at it. With his green garden glove on, the skeletal hand looked like a Halloween decoration.

"You did it!" I rushed over, unaware that Bowman and Ranston were directly behind me.

"Did you remember an evidence bag?" Bowman shouted to Ranston.

"No need. The forensic crew just pulled in." Then he looked at Herb. "Mind holding that thing a few more minutes? No sense having it go from person to person."

Herb looked at his prize catch. "I'm no anthropologist, but this hand belonged to a woman. Check out the small linking rings on the fourth finger."

"It's a puzzle ring. Sometimes called a Turkish harem ring. They were really popular when my daughter was in junior high. Goodness, that's what? Over eleven years ago. She's now teaching up in St. Cloud," I said.

"Enough with the family reminiscing." Bowman looked at the hand and waved a lab tech over. "Got a prize for you," he announced to the lab tech. "It may be the tip of the iceberg. For all we know, skeletal body parts could be scattered all over the vicinity."

A loud shriek stunned us for a moment as Claudia reacted to Bowman's statement. "You mean to tell us you think someone chopped up a body and buried the parts all over here? Heaven help us! It could be more people. More people chopped up and rotting. What if one of them is under my potatoes?"

Barry, who had been otherwise occupied chitchatting, caught wind of Claudia's remark and thundered over to Bowman and Ranston. "What's this I hear about dead bodies buried in our agricultural garden?"

And with that, the speed record for rumormongering had just been broken.

CHAPTER 7

If rumormongering speed was fast, it couldn't compete with the speed of book club ladies' gossip. As Bowman and Ranston dealt with Barry, I heard Shirley's voice loud and clear as she approached us.

"Lordy! What's going on here?"

I looked and almost didn't recognize her. She was usually impeccably dressed but today she arrived wearing a tunic and jogger pants with calf-high boots. It didn't go unnoticed.

"Was there a wardrobe malfunction in your closet?" Kevin asked.

"Hush! I got Lucinda's call and then I called Gloria. She's on her way. And so are Cecilia and Myrna but they'll be a tad later. When I told Cecilia about the dog finding a dead hand in a pile of dirt, she said she had to sneak out some holy water from the church and sprinkle it around here. I didn't know what to expect so I dressed for the worst."

"I'll say." Kevin chuckled.

Shirley ignored his comment. "Someone tell us what's going on. All the details."

Bowman stood a few feet away and heard every word. "No one is to say anything. That's how rumors get started." He looked straight at Barry, then back to Shirley. "Harriet's dog found a skeletal hand in that pile of compost over there. Could be as recent as a year or longer than a decade. Forensics will make that determination."

"Excuse me, Deputy Bowman, but our team needs to cordon off the area, and sketch a preliminary map for visual signs of human remains. We'll move in a widening circle from the point of discovery." The lanky forensic technician wiped his forehead and waited for a response.

"You heard the man," Ranston shouted. "Everyone needs to vacate the premises now. Not fifteen minutes from now. Now. Right now."

"I'm not about to leave my precious lavender plants at the mercy of those skull diggers," the woman in the polka-dotted dress cried out. "If I have to sleep in my plot of land, so be it!"

"No one is sleeping anywhere!" Bright pink splotches appeared on Ranston's cheeks. "And they are not skull diggers, they're forensic lab technicians from the county."

A cacophony of voices continued as the crowd gathered closer to the detectives, who, by now, were showing signs of exasperation. Mainly Ranston's splotchy face and a slight twitch in Bowman's left eye.

"Listen up, everyone. This area needs to be cleared and we need to get your contact information. Do not leave the premises."

"The other deputy told us to go. He said 'vacate the premises.' So what is it?"

Bowman rubbed his eye and took a deep breath. "Everyone walk or drive to the front gate and stay there until you provide us with your name, phone number and address. Understood?"

"You think one of us stuck a skeletal hand in there?" The yet-to-be-identified man pointed to the compost heap. "We're not killers, we're farmers and gardeners."

"It's a matter of protocol. We'll need to follow up with questions."

"Does this mean the garden is going to be closed?" Gussie asked.

"Right now, only the immediate perimeters surrounding the area of discovery. Depending upon findings, things may change."

Amid the grousing, grumbling, mumbling and a few not-to-be-missed expletives from Barry, the parade of gardeners tidied up and made their way to the gate. My mother led her own charge with Streetman securely tucked in her arms and the book club ladies looking more like a Secret Service entourage than a bunch of senior citizens.

"If it wasn't for that dog of yours," Barry said to my mother when we reached the gate, "none of this would have happened. This is your fault!"

"Hey, it's no one's fault." Thira brushed some dirt from her forehead and glared at Barry. "Someone would have discovered it eventually."

"Or not. Now we're kicked out of our gardens for who knows how long. If I can't grow my stuff and keep having to buy vegetables, I'll send all of my receipts your way." Barry took a few steps toward my mother and the ladies but retreated the second Streetman let out a low growl and bared his teeth.

"Like I said, you better keep that dog away from here or—"

But Barry never got to finish. Because in that second, Bowman and Ranston's vehicle stopped short of bumping Barry into someone's tomatoes.

Both the driver's and passenger doors flew open as the deputies tromped over to the gate.

"Listen up," Bowman said. "We're going to do this in an orderly and sequential manner. Form two lines." He pointed to either side of the gate and continued. "As you approach one of us, give us your name and information. Then you'll be free to go."

Ranston motioned him aside and whispered in his ear.

"You'll also need to show us your rec card."

"What if we don't have it on us?" Barry called out. "It's not as if I carry that thing around with me all the time."

"Then show us your driver's license, and if you're not carrying that with you and you drove here, be prepared to get a ticket."

I watched as everyone pawed through their pockets, bags, and wallets to comply.

Then Ranston spoke. "If any of you noticed anything out of the ordinary in the past few days, please let us know. And if you happened to have noticed any odd or suspicious-looking people lurking around, tell us."

Odd or suspicious? That's the entire population around here!

My mother and her friends inched their way to the back of the lines and not the front. It seemed every time someone moved forward, they moved back.

"What are you doing?" I asked her.

"Shh. This is the best way to listen in on the conversations."

"Oh, brother."

One by one, the gardeners exited the property until only my mother and her friends remained. Bowman perused the group and waved them on. "No need to show a rec card. I know who you all are and I jotted down your names."

Shirley nudged my mother. "Lordy, that's awful. We've become regulars in the sheriff's office. Next thing you know, our photos will be on the walls."

Again, Bowman motioned us to the exit. "Thank you for your cooperation. Our office will contact you if need be."

The women took their time leaving but the men charged out of there with a clarion call for "a brewski at Curley's."

"Mrs. Kimball Gregory!" Deputy Bowman shouted. Then he walked toward me and lowered his voice. "This investigation is going to take a while. Didn't want to stir up the troops in here. Motley-looking crew if you ask me. Anyway, the lab guys are going to sift through that pile of dirt like nobody's business. Could be the hand was only the tip of the iceberg, or corpse. If we're lucky we may be able to identify it by more than one means."

"It's bone. I don't know how you can do that. I mean, other than identifying the origin of that puzzle ring."

"Fingernails. Had a case like this years ago in Phoenix. Not the actual fingernails. Those things fall off and decompose right away. But acrylic nails are different, and if that hand had acrylic nails, we might be able to learn more."

"Good to know."

"One more thing. We'll be notifying Williams Investigations on this if the questioning process becomes unwieldy."

"You'll be competing with a missing cat."

"Huh?" Bowman furrowed his brow and Ranston followed suit.

"I'm serious. Nate and Marshall are tracking down a stolen cat.

Probably one of the most valuable ones in the world. They're going to be tied up all weekend at the Cat Fanciers' Show in Phoenix."

"Tell them to lure it with a can of tuna, because my gut tells me that hand wasn't the only human remain to get planted in here."

Chapter 8

"What was that deputy talking to you about?" My mother literally pounced on me as we made our way to the parked cars. "You were chatting long enough. What did he tell you? What does he know? It's a psychotic killer, right?"

"Um, unless this is a sci-fi horror movie where the hand identifies the killer, there is no way of knowing who did it simply by looking at those bones."

"Does he think there are more?" Cecilia asked.

"I don't know. But what I *do* know is that the lab crew will scrutinize every molecule in that compost heap and spread the perimeter out. At least visually."

"How long will that take?" Lucinda looked around, as if waiting for an audience response.

Again, I responded with "I don't know."

"Well, I know one thing. I'm thirsty and Curley's bar is a stone's throw away." Herb's grandiose wave said it all—news of the skeletal hand in Sun City West's agricultural gardens was about to spread like a California wildfire. Only California wildfires have crews at the ready to put them out.

Since an actual body wasn't found, news crews didn't descend on the agricultural gardens. At least not right away. And by then, everything had turned topsy-turvy.

"I don't know about anyone else," my mother said, "but this has been very traumatic for my little man."

Very traumatic? He ate two Big Macs!

Then, in the same breath she added, "I have a nice peanut butter pie that I got at Betty's Rooste. If you ladies aren't doing anything, let's go back to my house. You, too, Phee. I'm sure Marshall is still working."

"Maybe for a few minutes. Just to wash up." By this point, I was positive I resembled a character straight out of John Steinbeck's *The Grapes of Wrath*.

Suddenly, Bowman bellowed, "Don't go spreading this around. No need to start a panic. Understood?"

Yep. In one ear, out the other.

Upon arrival at my mother's place, I immediately washed my face and arms before joining the gang in the kitchen/living room area. The women were already fast at work doling out slices of Betty's enormous peanut butter pie and reheating coffee.

"I'm glad the men went to Curley's," Gloria said. "They're like vultures when it comes to food. Especially cake and pie."

Just then, there was a knock on the door, and my aunt Ina burst in on the scene. "Good gracious, Harriet," she shouted. "Your dog found a dead body? Louis found out minutes ago from someone named Stan, who plays clarinet with him at those gigs."

My eyes literally rolled around in my head as my aunt continued. "Stan's wife has a plot of land there. She grows squash and beans. Said the county deputies were high-strung."

You think?

My mother motioned Aunt Ina further into the room. "It wasn't a dead body. Only part of one—the hand. With a ring on it."

My aunt stood still for a few seconds and then, "What kind of ring? Did you see it? And did you get a good look at the fingernails? They can be very telling."

"Well, they didn't tell much because they weren't there. It was just a skeleton. Grab a piece of pie, Ina, and all of us will chat."

My stomach was already in knots and I hadn't been in the house for fifteen minutes or so.

As the women made themselves comfortable on the couch and chairs, I walked toward my aunt and spoke. "According to the forensic technician, the hand and, um . . . the body, if they find one, could be anywhere between a year old and decades old."

"Tsk, tsk. I imagine the sheriff's office will be digging up all those garden plots." My aunt helped herself to the pie and put a spoonful in her mouth.

"Not likely. They would need real concrete evidence that other remains are there. Right now, they're concentrating on a perimeter search of aboveground places. Like other compost heaps, wood piles, shavings, things like that."

"So what are they going to do?" My aunt was persistent. And loud. "When word gets out, and trust me, it's probably on Facebook or Instagram by now, Sun City West residents will be rushing to hardware stores for security devices. And frankly, some of us in the Grand won't be far behind."

"Aunt Ina, we don't know the circumstances. That hand isn't recent."

"Aha! All the more reason for concern." My aunt stood in the middle of the room, took a deep breath and rolled her shoulders back.

Dear heavens, no! She's about to launch into one of her theatrical speeches.

"Think about it, ladies. That cold, steely skeletal hand didn't get there by itself. Some diabolical, menacing individual planted it there. That's how it begins. For all we know, that killer has lived in this area for decades.

Doing his or her nefarious acts with impunity."

"Lordy!" Shirley gasped. "He, and I'm saying *he* because I don't think a woman would have the strength to do such a thing, could be someone we see every day and say hello to."

"Or even sit next to in church." Cecilia looked at Lucinda and both of them widened their eyes.

"Relax, everyone. Please. Before you let your imaginations go wild. I know for certain that the sheriff's office will be questioning anyone who was at the garden area today. They'll also secure a list of the members of the agriculture club and will question them as well."

"What will that accomplish, other than to annoy us?" Myrna went back for a second slice of pie.

"They'll be gathering information that could lead them to the person responsible for disposing of the hand in the compost. Keep in mind, that person may not be the one who, uh . . . was responsible for the—"

"Go ahead and say it, Phee. For the murder of the person to whom that hand belongs. There. I've said it. Murder. There has to be a murder when a body part appears out of nowhere."

"That's wonderful, Myrna," my mother exclaimed. "It will be perfect for our next radio show. Now, if we can only think of cozy mysteries with detached hands. Or feet."

"Oh my gosh! I can think of one already. It's by Maisy Marple, *Boardwalk Body Parts,* a Sharpe and Steele Mystery." Cecilia nearly jumped out of her seat. "You can thank me later, Harriet."

"Enough about my sister's radio show. This is serious. First, a hand and then what? I know I don't live in Sun City West, but I'm right across Route 60 in the Grand. That's too close for comfort if you ask me."

"What are you suggesting?" Louise looked up from her pie.

"What we're best at—doing our own investigating."

"What? No!" I nearly choked. "You do your own investigating all right, but inevitably I wind up in the thick of it when you get yourselves mired under in precarious situations. And that's putting it mildly." Then I glanced at Streetman, who had positioned himself under the kitchen table with Essie swatting at his head. "And Streetman. Don't get me started on him. He's a regular terror train with teeth."

With that, my mother bent down under the table and snatched him in her arms. "My little gladiator happens to be an instinctive canine sleuth and a boon to the sheriff's office."

Is that what they're calling it these days?

"Moving along," my aunt said. "I have a plan."

And that's the exact moment when all sanity left the room. Too bad I didn't.

Chapter 9

I took a breath, tried to collect my thoughts, and then looked at my aunt. "What kind of a plan?"

"I'm glad you asked. Naturally the sheriff's office is going to question all of the people who were in the community gardens today, but I say we find out who they were and do our own digging."

"I guess that doesn't sound too bad. I mean, checking them out on Facebook and the clubs."

My aunt narrowed her eyes. "Facebook schmace-book! It has to be up front and personal. Once we get the names, we figure out who would be best to cozy up with them and eke out information. After all, isn't that what all good sleuths do?"

"Lordy, Ina. I'm not sure we're good sleuths." Shirley poured herself some coffee and took a sip.

"We'll come prepared. Once we get the names, we'll divvy them up for initial research. I'll ask Louis to put out his feelers as well. Those musicians can't keep their mouths shut. Then, we'll meet and figure out which of our personalities would be best suited to target the different gardeners."

"Good grief," Lucinda said. "That sounds like what people do on those dreadful dating sites." Then she looked at Gloria. "No offense, Gloria."

I rolled my eyes as my aunt continued. "We're not *dating* them, we're trying to find out if any of them were responsible for putting that hand in the compost heap. Or worse."

"Ina's got a point." Louise sliced another piece of the pie and took a bite. "Where do the men fit in?"

Suddenly an explosion of answers.

"They don't!"

"They'll mess things up."

"Herb will think it *is* a dating thing."

"They'll make it worse."

"I guess it's settled," my mother said. "This is a book-club-ladies-only investigation."

Until something goes wrong.

"We already know who some of the people are. Shirley, you have the best handwriting. Can you jot this down?" My mother reached for a pad and pen from the counter and handed them to Shirley. "I'll see who I can remember. Add names, everyone. We'll sort them out later."

"Thira something."

"Gussie"

"Barry. Everyone should know him."

"Ona and Aneta."

"Woman in polka-dotted dress."

"Scruffy-looking man."

"Those three really thin hippie women."

Shirley must have learned shorthand in high school because as soon as the names were blurted out, they were already on paper. She looked up and shrugged. "We may have trouble identifying the scraggy man and slender women, but we can start with the others. Maybe they'll know."

"Excellent!" My mother all but jumped in the air. "For once we're on top of the game."

"Uh, I wouldn't exactly say that, but, oh, never mind, Mom. Keep me posted. I've got to head home." I grabbed my bag and waved to the ladies. "Please don't blab about this until it becomes public knowledge, okay?"

With that, Gloria looked up from her phone and said, "It already is. It's on the Sun City West Gab About site on Facebook."

I made a mad dash for the door with all sorts of thoughts spinning through my head. The first was my mother's radio shows. I knew once Paul got wind of it, he'd ditch his fish-gutting talk and go directly for the whereabouts of the handless corpse.

On the drive home I tapped the screen and phoned my friend and confidante, Lyndy Ellsworth. I met Lyndy a few years back when I first moved to Vistancia in Peoria. We were young forty-something singles who connected immediately. Her husband had passed away unexpectedly, and she'd moved to this area to be near her eccentric albeit *wacky* aunt. Imagine my surprise to learn that her aunt also lived in Sun City West.

Working for a medical insurance company in Peoria, Lyndy immersed herself in work and shied away from dating. However, while helping Marshall and me track down a killer, she met Herb's softball coach, Lyman, and they've been together ever since. The guy fit the bill according to Lyndy: considerate, easygoing, athletic and a birdwatcher to boot!

"Hey, Lyndy," I said, hands-free. "I really need to let you know what's going on." *Thank you, Bluetooth.*

"Is it the skeletal hand? I just got off the phone with my aunt. Unbelievable."

"And then some."

For the next few minutes, I gave her all the details from start to finish.

"You've *got* to be kidding! Your mother and her friends want to track down the gardeners and conduct their own investigation?"

"Unfortunately, yes. You know what that means, don't you?"

"Yep. You and I will have to beat them to it before they make a mess of things. Golly, Phee, I'm no sleuth, but I have to admit, the last few times we did some sleuthing, it was pretty exciting."

"Nail-biting is a better term, but yeah. Listen, I'll keep you posted. I'm getting close to home."

"Okay, catch you later."

No sooner did I get inside the house when Marshall texted me: *Tip of the iceberg, hon. Will explain when I get home. I'll grab dinner on the way with Nate. Expect me around eight. XOXO.*

I texted back, *Shall do. Don't get clawed.*

It was now six thirty and I was exhausted. I nuked some leftover zucchini casserole and grabbed a Coke, pondering my next move. I wanted to help my mother out, especially since that group of women needed an adult in the room, but I felt as if they were jumping in too soon. Then again, what did I expect?

True, the discovery of a skeletal hand was unnerving, but without knowing *how* it was severed, all we had was speculation. For all anyone knew, the hand could have been amputated and somehow was compromised in the disposal process. Or maybe a farm injury. Or a workplace injury. Not unusual. Then, the darker theories, like a hatchet or butcher knife. I shuddered and took a shower to let the hot water relax me.

By the time I toweled dry and put on my sweats, Marshall arrived home.

"What a day! I'll hear meowing in my head all night."

"You want anything to nibble?" I gave him a kiss and he, in turn, hugged me.

"No, Nate and I had meatball subs. They'll stay in my stomach until morning. I'm so pooped, all I want to do is get comfortable and watch TV in the bedroom."

"Good plan. It requires company—mine."

When we settled in the bedroom I asked him about the progress on the stolen cat. He pinched his shoulder blades together and spoke. "It was arduous but we got a credible lead. Apparently, this kind of animal theft is not uncommon, but Princess and Queen Empress Trudalia had an around-the-clock surveillance system."

"And someone tampered with it?"

Marshall shook his head. "Nope. More of a technical glitch on the monitoring. We contacted Rolo and he's having one of his buddies look into it for us."

Rolo Barnes. Our office's cyber-sleuth with a penchant for the dark web and a skill set that rivals the FBI, CIA, Homeland Security and most likely the foreign agencies around the globe. He used to be the IT person when I worked for the Mankato Police Department in Minnesota, but left to start his own lucrative agency. To say he was eccentric would be like saying the ocean has water.

"Anyway," Marshall continued, "people have been known to use nontoxic dyes on animals to disguise them."

"That's awful. Tell me, what leads did you get?"

"The thieves are appearing at these cat shows under legitimate businesses but make their money on side deals involving exotic cats. Our source believes she will be shown at the Chicago Cat Fanciers' Show next weekend."

"Next weekend? And you and Nate are going?"

"Hon, this case pays more than months of other cases. Besides, we can't afford to lose this opportunity. We're already one step ahead. We've got the list of exhibitors, for lack of a better word, and Rolo's digging into the dark web for us to see who plays in the murky waters."

"I see."

"What about your day?"

"You won't believe it in a million years. I'll give you the CliffsNotes and then fill in the rest. Here goes: Streetman found skeletal hand in compost heap. Sheriff's office summoned. Streetman refused to give it up. Bribery with hamburger. Nearly became the next severed hand. Bowman and Ranston arrived. Forensic crew arrived. Investigation in its infancy. My mother and her friends are going to the extremes with this one."

"Is that all?" He laughed. "Poor Bowman and Ranston."

"Why?"

"Because this is one investigation they'll have to do without us. The cat caper trumps the severed hand."

"That sounds like a murder mystery."

"*That*, or the latest horror novel."

We spent the next ten minutes discussing the details and then decided to put it out of our minds and watch something mindless on TV.

"Do me a favor," I asked.

"Sure. What?"

"See if Bowman and Ranston can keep you and Nate in the loop on this. If nothing else, I can tell my mother that Williams Investigations is partnering. Even if it is in Illinois."

"I'll see what I can do. Once I tell Bowman that Harriet plans to snoop around with Streetman, he'll cough up information like a longhaired feline's spitball."

"You really have been at that cat show too long."

CHAPTER 10

It was a no-drama Sunday as far as my mother was concerned, but I attributed it to the fact that she and her book club friends hadn't a real clue as to where to begin. I figured I'd keep it that way.

Then Monday rolled around and Augusta couldn't keep a straight face when I told her about all of the drama at the agricultural garden plots. Nate and Marshall had already left to work on some of their smaller cases since they were flying out on Friday for Chicago.

"So the little bugger refused to give up the skeletal hand? Not surprising. Some breeds are like that. They latch on to something and good luck getting it out of their mouths. Surprised you escaped with all of your fingers."

"Yeah, me too."

"What do you know about the hand? Could you get a good look?"

"Not really. It had a slender puzzle ring on it so I'm pretty sure the rest of the body was a woman's."

"Don't tell me. Bowman and Ranston are on the case?"

"Uh-huh. The usual. The forensic team took the discovery to the lab for analysis, and right now it's a rumor-mill special."

"I'll bet. You said you saw a ring. Did you get to see what the attached wrist looked like? Clean cut or otherwise?"

"I don't know. I wondered myself. It could have been an accident. Or an amputation. Or—"

"I'm going for a bludgeoning with a hatchet knife. Now, if it was the Midwest, I'd suggest a corn shredder. Do you have any idea how many corn shredders have gobbled up limbs?"

"Ew! In any case, it was skeletal. Not recent. Maybe a year old. Maybe a decade. Anyway, you can only imagine the reaction from my mother and the book club ladies."

"I'm imagining their response. Next thing you know, those women will hatch a plan to find out where it came from and who was responsible."

I gulped. "The plan's already been hatched. At my mother's house. After we left the community gardens on Saturday. The good news is that they don't know what they're doing."

"Give it time. Then worry."

I walked into my office and booted up the computer. If nothing else, the routine of bookkeeping and accounting would keep my mind occupied. And it did, until Marshall texted me with the following message: *LOL, I was wrong. No need to ask B & R to stay in the loop. They already reached*

out. Asked if we could "assist" in between our cases. Talk to you later.
"Augusta!" I called out. "We're adding skeletal hand to cat caper."
"Is that supposed to be funny?" she shouted back.
I stepped out to the main office. "Must be the sheriff's office thinks there's more to their compost heap discovery. Marshall just texted me. We may be digging in the dirt and it won't be kitty litter."

As things turned out, Nate and Marshall were able to work in a few hours for the sheriff's office between Tuesday and Friday morning, when they flew to Chicago. No surprise, they got to interview Gussie, Claudia, Ona, Aneta, Barry, and Thira, while Bowman and Ranston concentrated on the only other piece of tangible evidence—the puzzle ring. Only it wasn't a puzzle ring. It was a 14-carat gold replica of a medieval gimmel ring.

Late Thursday as the four of us were about to shut the lights off and head out, Bowman faxed us the information from the forensic jeweler that the sheriff's office used. Augusta couldn't get over the fact that someone could make a career out of identifying the deceased from the jewelry they wore. Meanwhile, I had my questions about the ring itself.

"What's a gimmel ring?" I asked. "It sure looked like one of those puzzle rings we always see."

Marshall shook his head and tapped his cell phone. "According to this link on Safari, the gimmel ring is actually a betrothal ring that can have one to three small rings that interlink."

"Isn't that a puzzle ring?"

He shook his head. "The gimmel ring can be a puzzle ring, but a puzzle ring cannot be a gimmel ring."

"You lost me, Mr. Gregory." Augusta adjusted her tortoiseshell glasses.

"It's all in the meaning. The site I'm looking at says that Martin Luther married Catherine Bora in 1525 with a gimmel ring inscribed 'Whom God has joined together, Let no man put asunder.'"

"Well, someone put something asunder, ring or not." Augusta headed to the door.

"Was that jeweler able to ascertain the age of the ring?"

Marshall nodded. "Uh-huh. Late 1970s or early '80s. But that doesn't mean the skeletal hand is over forty years old. The deceased could have purchased that ring at an estate sale, or anywhere for that matter."

"What about an inscription?" I asked.

"Too well-worn. The jeweler uses a lab and they're in the process of using high-tech equipment to see if they can decipher the inscription." Then he turned to me. "Sorry, I can't head out right now. I've got a few more things to finish up here and I should be home in about an hour and a half. Want me to pick up a pizza on the way?"

I beamed. "Absolutely. Anything as long as it has pepperoni on it."

Augusta and I left the office and walked a few yards down the block to where we had parked our cars.

"Mr. Gregory and Mr. Williams never mentioned how those interviews went. I'm curious."

"I'm still trying to attach the right last names to the people. All I can seem to remember are Gussie Adams, Barry McGuire, Claudia Galen and Thira Tillwell."

"Wasn't there a Maybelle something-or-other? You mentioned she and Barry tossed barbs at each other before you tossed that hand to Herb."

"Oh my gosh! Maybelle. She must have slipped off the radar because no one mentioned her. I'll need to tell Marshall. Of course, there's not much he can do about it at this point except text Bowman. The flight tomorrow leaves at six a.m. and the men have to be at the airport at least two hours before for security and all that."

"I hope they catch a break and find that cat or they'll be globe-trotting around the world without having time to indulge in the local cuisine."

I laughed. "You're talking about Nate, remember? He'll find a way to indulge. I doubt either of those men are going to fly back to Phoenix without eating a deep-dish pizza and finishing it off with a Chicago hot dog."

"You got that right. See you in the morning."

When I got home, the landline was blinking and the caller ID registered my mother's name. Oops. I had turned off my cell phone so she probably got frustrated leaving messages. I walked to the landline and pushed the answering machine.

"Phee! Clean out your voicemail." *And hello to you, too, Mom.* "The rec center opened the community gardens yesterday. It was that or there would be a full-fledged revolt. Thira and Claudia already had posters made saying 'Don't Let Our Plants Die of Thirst.' Call me when you get this message."

I returned the call, but not until I had changed into my lightweight sweats and downed a bottle of Coke.

"What's this about dying plants, Mom? I thought the gardens had automatic watering like the houses do."

"Well, yes and no. Watering spigots, from a centralized system, are piped into each garden and it's up to the plot owner to set up their own watering plan. Mostly with PVC pipes and timers. All aboveground. That's what Herb set up for us. However, some owners hand water and those are the ones who were concerned their plants and crops would die. I mean, it's been a week. Seven days!"

"Yes, I know what a week is."

"I'm emphasizing, Phee. Emphasizing."

"So, uh, any plant deaths to report?"

"Fortunately, no. The polka-dotted-dress woman hand waters but her lavender plants only need about a half inch a week so she was fine. I saw her at Sprouts the other day."

"Anyone else?"

"Thira and Claudia have timers for their larger plots but they also hand water smaller plots that have legumes. So far, so good. But they're still not out of the woods."

"I take it the forensic crew is no longer poking around?"

"They did enough poking, prodding and even some digging. Very clandestine and circumspect if you ask me. Lucinda tried to make conversation with them but they ushered her away."

"Of course they did. They're conducting an investigation, not an outdoor coffee hour."

"Well, the forensic crew is gone but now we've acquired babysitters."

"Huh?"

"The posse was assigned to the community gardens. Two people are on duty here in shifts throughout the day. Louise said she feels as if she's back in grade school."

"They just want to make sure nothing else nefarious happens. You should be relieved."

"Relieved? They're unarmed! I'd rather have Myrna stroll around the grounds with her bear and pepper sprays."

"Uh, yeah. Speaking of Myrna and all, how far did you get with your snooping around?"

"You mean our *investigation*?"

"Yes, whatever."

"This is what we have so far. Gloria chatted with Mini-Moose at the bowling alley and found out that Gussie was a bigwig with Monsanto. You know, that gigantic bio-agricultural corporation responsible for those GMOs."

"Yeah, I know who they are."

"Gussie retired to Sun City West in the late eighties before the company merged with Bayer in 2018. From what Mini-Moose said, he was an up-front guy who just wanted to plant natural stuff the way they should be planted."

"Anything else?"

"It turns out that Thira Tillwell was a former model. Not a supermodel, but a model nonetheless. And you'll never guess who found out."

"Just tell me."

"Your uncle Louis. When your aunt gave him the details, he said he was acquainted with her. Thira's late husband played the baritone with

Louis on more than one occasion. Poor man died of a heart attack."

"So I take it there's nothing that points a finger at Thira?"

"Not as of yet. Now, Barry is another story altogether. Fired from Walmart as a greeter for insulting the customers when they came in."

I burst out laughing and held my hand over the receiver. "That still doesn't spell out potential . . . disposer of body parts on community property."

"He was also asked to leave a number of his HOA meetings for being disruptive. Turns out Louise saw his name on the list of homeowners in her HOA and made some discreet phone calls."

"No such thing as a discreet phone call in your group. Okay, did you unearth anything else?"

"I saved the best part for last, Phee."

"What? What best part?"

"Maybelle used to work at a butcher shop. Need I say more?"

Visions of a short, pleasant woman hacking away at animal limbs suddenly popped into my head. "I think you've gone off the deep end, Mom."

"The shop was in Sun City and they called her the cleaver woman."

Chapter 11

I stood in place and rubbed my temples. "The cleaver woman." Just what those book club ladies needed to hear. Next thing it'll be barricading windows and locking up the cutlery. My brain oscillated between laughing out loud and pulling my hair out. Not being able to keep this to myself, I phoned Lyndy.

"Sit down for this one," I said. "And beware the cleaver woman."

"The what?"

I explained that my mother and her entourage launched their latest so-called investigation and found out that Maybelle from the agriculture club used to work at the butcher shop in Sun City. They called her the cleaver woman."

"That was probably her job. Cutting the meat."

"You know that, and I know that, but the term *cleaver*, especially in my mother's circle, denotes a mad-maniacal killer."

"Oh, no. Now what?"

"No choice. We throw ourselves into the snoop-fest and find out about this woman. I'm sure she's a lovely lady who enjoys gardening and the only thing she cleaved was meat for the butcher shop."

"I'll call my nosy aunt and ask if she ever heard of her."

"Thanks. Meanwhile, I'll start a paper chase and see what I can find. Um, we may have to have boots on the ground at the community garden as well. And when I say *boots*, I mean don't wear any good shoes."

"Wouldn't dream of it. Talk to you later."

As soon as I got off the phone, I set the table in anticipation of a mouthwatering pizza. Then I made myself comfortable and pulled up the Sun City West Agriculture Club on the website, praying that there was a photo of some of the gardeners and that Maybelle would be in it. The one thing I needed was her last name.

The next hour flew by. I pulled up Facebook posts and newspaper articles until my eyes blurred. Then, in an act not short of a miracle—there it was! Maybelle Belgrade from Port Jervis, New York. She was showing off her tomatoes along with other gardeners for an article on "Tomatoes' Secret Health Benefits." It was written over seven years ago, but I imagined the health benefits hadn't changed, even though the folks in the photo sure did. Maybelle included.

At the time, her hair was reddish brown and wavy. It fell to her shoulders and looked almost as unkempt as Lucinda's. When I saw her that first day in the garden, her hair was mostly gray and chin-length. She wore a kerchief over it and resembled one of those peasant women who are always depicted in Renaissance art.

"I'm home with a hot pepperoni and mushroom pizza from Sardella's," Marshall called out from the utility room.

"Fantastic! I'm famished."

The two of us outdid the book club ladies while eating as we talked nonstop at the same time. At least we were on the same topic—the skeletal hand—and didn't bounce all over the place. I told him about the tidbits of information my mother acquired and he, in turn, said that, depending upon the results in Chicago, he and Nate would be more actively involved in the "hand case."

We both slept fitfully that night, which is always the case when one or both of us have an early flight the following day.

"Sleep on the plane," I told him when his Uber arrived at an ungodly hour to get him to the airport.

"For sure."

A quick kiss and off he went to Chicago, while I stumbled back to bed, hoping to nab some z's. A half hour later, having given up, I showered and outlined a plan of action to look into the severed hand. Not wanting to step on Bowman and Ranston's territory, I tried to figure out an inconspicuous way to approach it. *Tried* being the pivotal word.

"Got us cinnamon buns from Boyer's Café," Augusta announced the instant I stepped into the office. "I figured all you had for breakfast was coffee."

"You figured right. Thanks a million." I bit into the soft bun with its thick vanilla icing and then took a larger bite. "Yep, Marshall hightailed it out of the house in the dead of night. Boy, I hope they find Princess you-know-who."

Augusta grabbed a bun for herself. "It never ceases to amaze me how people can spend such an exorbitant amount of money on a cat. Heck, I grew up with cats. Barn cats and lots of 'em. They didn't cost us much and paid their own room and board by keeping the mice at bay."

"Speaking of paying, those clients have already sent us payment for expenses to date. Wish we could say the same for all of our clients."

"Maybe we should add pet retrieval as our specialty."

"Only if they locate that priceless hairless feline."

"Let's keep our fingers crossed. Anyway, it should be a relatively calm day. A few new clients are coming in to fill out paperwork because they didn't want to do it online. Other than that, business as usual."

"Don't say that. Whenever we say that, it invites craziness into this office."

Just then, Augusta glanced at the door. "I think we just did." She reached into a desk drawer and pulled out a can of Lysol just as Paul Schmidt breezed in. The aroma of fish and bait permeated the air in a nanosecond.

"Paul!" I exclaimed. "Uh, nice to see you. What brings you here?" *And please tell me it has nothing to do with my mother, Myrna, or the radio show.*

"I think I know where that severed hand came from. Since I don't have actual proof, I thought I'd run it by your husband and Nate. Those MCSO deputies would only tell me to come back once I could prove it."

Hmm, Bowman and Ranston aren't as obtuse as they may seem.

"Yeah, well, that's usually the case with these things."

Then Augusta spoke up. "Maybe both of you should chat in your office, Phee. Much more private."

I shot her a look and she grinned, holding on to the can of Lysol.

"Come on, Paul. We can talk for a few minutes in my office. Nate and Marshall are out of town on a case."

The sound of spray hitting the air was audible as I closed my office door behind us.

"Okay." Paul plopped into a chair and leaned back. "About a month ago, I was out fishing at Lake Pleasant and met up with a few guys from Whitman. Can't remember their names."

No wonder he's avoiding the deputies.

"Uh-huh. Go on."

"They were saying that one of the old graveyards in the desert up there had a few plots dug up accidently a few years back when a construction crew bulldozed the area. Lots of new development is taking place in that area. It's the next hot land market since it's between Wickenburg and Sun City West. The men reported it to the sheriff's office, but when they went to check, everything was back in order and that ended that."

"So you're thinking the hand might have come from one of those plots?"

"Yep. I do."

"If it's a construction crew for a developer, why would they remove a hand? And even more bizarre, why would they dump it into a compost heap in the Sun City West Community Garden?"

"Because maybe they didn't."

"All right. Now I am really confused."

"Think about it. Lots of hawks and owls out there. And vultures. Just suppose for a minute that the hand still had flesh on it. And what if one of those raptors or owls snatched it and dropped it in the agriculture garden?"

"And made a direct hit into the compost heap? What are the odds of that happening?"

Good grief! Am I really hearing this?

"Things like this have been known to happen. All I'm saying is that someone should look into that construction area and find out who's laying six feet under."

"Paul, most likely if there are any bodies—and usually they get relocated during construction—those bodies are six feet under a house. A house!"

"Fine. But share this with the detectives. They might want to look into it."

"I seriously doubt it, but we'll take it under advisement and keep you posted."

"Good. Everyone can thank me later. By the way, I can't wait for our next radio show to air. I might just run it by our audience."

Oh, heck no!

"Actually, I liked your original idea about gutting fish."

When I lie, I really lie, but someone has to stop him.

"Really? You think so?"

"Absolutely. It's a skill set everyone should have."

"Hmm, maybe you're right. Well, I've gotta get going. I've got my own fish in the cooler waiting to be gutted. Want any lake trout?"

"Um, not today. But thanks anyway. Have a good morning."

Paul waved to Augusta when I escorted him to the door and she immediately sprayed the air again. "What was that all about?' she asked.

"Raptors with good aim."

Chapter 12

It was a productive Friday in terms of accounting, and by four I felt as if I made up for all the interruptions during the earlier part of the week. Marshall texted me that they arrived safe and sound and were on their way to the hotel downtown.

Given the generous remuneration from the clients, they had booked accommodations in the same hotel that housed the Cat Fanciers' Show. Thank goodness for well-insulated walls. I told him about Paul, and when he finally stopped laughing, he told me to keep an eye on my mother because "Paul's explanation will pale compared to what the book club ladies come up with."

At a little before five, and not totally unexpected, my mother phoned with an invite I couldn't refuse. She, along with Lucinda and Louise, would be back at the community garden in the morning. As far as she knew, Herb and a few of his cronies would be there as well. The plan was to work until eleven and then pop over to Bagels 'n More, where they would meet up with the remainder of gossip central.

Curious as to their future sleuthing plans, since I knew my mother and my aunt would never be content with mere chitchat, I had to find out firsthand. And, with Marshall in Chicago and Lyndy tied up with Lyman, I figured a bagel breakfast would beat toast and coffee any day of the week.

"Will you be tiptoeing through the squash gardens, so to speak?" Augusta laughed.

"More like moseying around to gather my own intel before we meet up for bagels. To be honest, I'm waiting for the other shoe to drop."

"What other shoe?"

"Oh, my mother insisted all they would be doing is information seeking, but I know her better. She's brewing up a plan and I'm terrified of what that might be."

• • •

No surprise at all, I had a reason to be concerned. The following morning at a little past eight, I met her and Lucinda in the community gardens. They were chatting away at what they dubbed the next level as they waited for Louise to get there.

My mother had three trays of eggplant, tomato, and pepper transplants and had just donned thick gardening kneepads. She bent down and, using a small trowel, started to dig holes for the plants. Meanwhile, Lucinda, who handed her the plants, waved her hands in the air and kept shooing something from her face.

"Ew! Yuck!" My mother put the trowel down. "There are worms in the soil. Worms! And small grubs. No one told me about small grubs. I can't stand to go near them."

Meanwhile, Lucinda fought a battle of her own. "I hate these! I hate these. I can't go on like this. The small bugs keep hovering around the plants. I don't want to touch them."

I rolled my eyes and bit my lip. "Mom," I asked, "do those small flying bugs bother you?"

She looked up. "No, not really."

Then I asked Lucinda, "Are you afraid to go near the grubs and worms in the ground?"

She shook her head. "No. They don't upset me. Why?"

"Because you and Mom are getting nowhere. Switch places. You can dig the holes and my mother can hand you the small plants."

The women looked at each other as if an edict had come down from on high.

"That's a wonderful idea," my mother said. With that, she stood and switched places with Lucinda.

"I'll be back in a few minutes," I told them. "I think I'll mosey around the garden and say hello to people."

Ona and Aneta were planting basil around their tomatoes when I walked over. It appeared as if it had been rototilled not too long ago, making it easier for planting.

"It's good to get back in the garden again," Ona said. "There's nothing like homegrown tomatoes, especially the beefsteak ones. All of those hothouse tomatoes we get from the supermarkets are bland and tasteless."

"Yeah, I have to agree. Although the Campari tomatoes always seem to have a pleasant taste."

Aneta looked up. "If you can find them. I'm glad the varieties we plant are robust and juicy. I think it has to do with the soil. Our club is fortunate to own a decent rototiller. Anyone can use it."

"If they know how." Ona looked over her shoulder and kept working. "It's a good thing Joyanne was able to help us out with the back of our plot. She comes from a family of farmers from Kansas and she knew how to work a rototiller before she learned how to ride a bicycle."

"Um, yeah. That's certainly a skill that would come in handy." *If you plan to cultivate crops.*

"Ona and I have only hand-dug the soil. It's fine for smaller sections but when you're planting an abundance of something, the ground really needs to be tilled." Aneta grabbed a small bunch of basil cuttings and spread them out in the soil. "By the way, has your office heard anything about the investigation? Finding human bones in our garden is awful enough, but an entire hand?"

I shook my head. "It will take some time, I'm sure. I do know that they had a forensic jeweler look into the ring and Marshall told me that the hand will undergo DNA testing and carbon dating."

Just then, a loud scream pierced my ears and I recognized whose it was. Wasting no time, I charged back to the plot where my mother and Lucinda were planting their peppers and such.

"I thought it was a rock! A rock! But it's—Santa Maria!—it's the top of a skull! A skull! Santa Maria, it's a human skull top with holes where the nose should be." Lucinda stepped away from the garden plot and pointed to the ground.

"It looked like a large, round river rock," my mother said. "So I told Lucinda to keep digging around it and then toss it. When she reached in the ground to grab it, we saw teeth. Upper teeth! This place is a mine field for body parts!"

"Calm down, Mom. It's a skull. It's been underground for a while. Not as if you uncovered someone's recent body."

"And that's supposed to make me feel better? Look at poor Lucinda. She keeps crossing herself and muttering 'Santa Maria.'"

Wait until Cecilia gets here. She'll be dosing everyone with holy water.

If nothing else, Lucinda's screams brought the other gardeners to their plot—Gussie, Maybelle, Thira, and the polka-dotted-dress lavender woman. Only today it was a blue polka-dotted dress and not a red one.

"What happened?" Gussie shouted as he made his way toward us.

"Another body part." My mother's voice was almost as loud as his. "See for yourself. I refuse to touch it." Then she looked at me. "Phee, can you drive to the house and bring Streetman over here? I was going to bring him but I knew we were all headed to Bagels 'n More after planting and I didn't want him to get antsy."

"Then why do you want him here now?"

"He needs to sniff this skull before we call the posse and those deputies take over. He needs to get the scent. For all any of us know, this place could be strewn with body parts. He'd be able to ferret them out. He's making tremendous progress with the YouTube videos."

"What??" I had trouble trying not to overreact. "He's not trained for that sort of thing. If the sheriff's office wanted a dog to track something down, they'd engage a highly trained one from the Maricopa County K-9 Unit." *And one that isn't neurotic and doesn't snap.*

"Don't anyone touch anything!" Gussie shouted. Then he looked at my mother and Lucinda's plot. "Seems like you just got started. You know, there may be more bones buried next to those peppers."

"I'm certainly not about to find out." Lucinda tossed the trowel she was holding onto the ground and stood. As she did, chucks of dirt slipped off of her clothing.

"Leave it be and call the posse." Thira stepped over and put her hand on Lucinda's shoulder. "This has to be really upsetting for you. And you both are newbies, too."

Just then, Herb and Kenny thundered over. "What's this about a skull? I heard you all the way over by the sheds." Herb looked at Thira and sucked in his stomach.

"It had to have been there a while," I said. "According to what we were told, that plot of land was vacant for quite a while."

"Vacant from vegetables," Kenny said and laughed, "but not body parts."

"Will someone *please* call the posse? We can't stand around like this all day." It was the scruffy man I had seen on more than one occasion.

"Got it." I pulled out my phone, but just as I was about to dial, who should race toward us but Paul and Mini-Moose. They were doubled over, laughing hysterically.

"Finding more body parts is not a laughing matter," my mother said.

"Especially when they're Halloween decorations!" Then Paul laughed again. This time even harder. "Got you going, didn't we?"

"What?" Lucinda glared at the two of them. "The two of you planted a fake skull to scare the daylights out of us?"

This time it was Mini-Moose who couldn't stop laughing. "Yeah, we'll own up to it. When we found out about the hand, we couldn't resist burying a fake skull in your plot of land."

"That's the most sophomoric, childish thing ever!" Lucinda was adamant.

"Yeah, but it was really funny. We were watching from behind the plot of land over there with the shade cloth on the fencing." He pointed to a spot a few yards away.

I had all I could do to contain myself. "Good grief, I almost called the posse."

"Well, someone did. Turn around."

"Uh-oh," Herb said. "Your two favorite deputies just pulled in."

"Oh, no. Someone else in this group must have phoned them and they were in the vicinity."

I expected them to charge right over to us, but instead they turned in the opposite direction where Claudia stood, arms waving in the air.

Please don't tell me she found skeletal remains too.

Suddenly the men took off and ran to where Claudia and the deputies stood. I heard one of them yell, "Did you find the rest of the skeleton?" but it was Claudia's response that sent a cold shiver down my spine.

"It's Barry and he's stone-cold dead."

Chapter 13

Lucinda tossed the fake skull at Paul and, along with my mother and everyone else in creation, headed to where Barry's body was discovered. It took me a few seconds to process what was going on and by then, I was the only one standing by my mother's freshly planted peppers.

"Keep your distance, everyone!" Bowman shouted. "And stay put. Deputy Ranston will need your names and contact information. Now then, did anyone see anything suspicious?"

"Does a fake skull in Harriet's garden count?" Kenny whispered to Herb. Thankfully Bowman didn't hear him.

Meanwhile, Claudia stood three or four feet away from Barry, shivering as if it was the dead of winter. "I've never seen a dead body," she said. "Is it supposed to be blue? I may have nightmares."

"It's called livor mortis," someone shouted. "They all turn blue."

I rolled my eyes and waited for the deputies to bark more orders. I didn't have to wait long.

Bowman put his hands on his hips and addressed the crowd for the second time in less than two weeks. "Sorry to ruin your gardening but you will need to vacate the area until further notice. Like I said before, give your name and contact information to my partner, Deputy Ranston, and exit through the gate."

"We need to get our things," Thira said. "Coolers, bags . . ."

"Everything stays on the premises," Bowman continued, "until the forensic crew has completed its job." Then he looked at Ranston. "Did the office give you an ETA?"

I heard Ranston say, "They were right behind us," but I didn't see or hear any vehicles.

Meanwhile, I did hear my mother on her cell phone. "That's right, Shirley. Claudia found a dead body a few yards from where we were planting. What? . . . Yes, of course. Call Myrna and have her call the names on the phone tree. What? No, don't have her text. Half the women can't figure it out. Have Myrna tell them to hurry over to Bagels 'n More. We'll be on our way."

"I can't believe you had to call Shirley and the ladies. Now the entire community will be privy to this information in a matter of minutes. You were all going to meet at Bagels 'n More anyway. Couldn't it have waited?"

"And have them find out from someone else? Absolutely not."

"Hey, Harriet," Herb called out. "We'll be joining you. I just got off the phone with Wayne. Our entire pinochle crew is coming."

Just then, the forensic crew's vehicle pulled up to the gate.

"Hold up, everyone!" It was Bowman again. "One more thing. Listen up! Not a word about the identity of the victim. I know some of you couldn't help but get a look, but until an official identification is made, this information cannot be shared. Do I make myself clear? Anyone who shares this information will be cited."

"For what?" someone said.

"Interfering with an official investigation." Bowman moved his head back and forth, ensuring that he made visual contact with everyone in the immediate area.

No one said a word until all of us had exited the community garden. When we were a good ten or fifteen yards away, Gussie called out, "From now on, it's Blue Barry and not Bad Barry."

I grabbed my mother's arm. "Don't you dare use that on your radio show."

"How can I? I'm not supposed to say his name."

"Good."

Next, I searched the crowd for Paul and told him the same thing. "And don't be cryptic about it, either. Like referring to blue bass barries or crappies, or whatever those fish are."

"Geez. That's no fun."

"Good. Keep it that way."

Before heading to Bagels 'n More, I shot Marshall a quick text: *Barry's body was found in the community gardens a little bit ago. B & R on scene. How's the cat caper going?*

He texted back, *Keeping us moving. Not much time to text. Will try to call later. Any signs of a struggle? Blood, etc.*

I replied, *Nope, he looked peaceful, but blue pallor.*

Then: *Rigor mortis. Sets in 2–6 hours after death, gone in 12. XOXO*

Smiling, I gazed at my phone. Not many people, I'm sure, are sent hugs and kisses in the same message as details on rigor mortis.

The next text I sent was to Augusta with the same info. Her response was short and sweet: *Thought they were planting tomatoes and peppers. LOL*

As I was about to send my final text to Lyndy, she beat me to it: *Crazy aunt called. Dead body in the community gardens. Weren't you supposed to be there?*

Instead of texting back, I phoned her with the details and suggested we meet for a swim the following morning since she'd be going out with Lyman tonight. We agreed on nine with breakfast at Panera afterward. Then I tucked the phone into my bag and drove to gossip central.

Lo and behold! Aunt Ina and Uncle Louis were at the huge oval table ushering me over. Apparently I was the first one from the garden to arrive, but only by a few seconds. My mother and Lucinda were right behind me, hands waving and mouths wagging.

"Another body, Ina!" my mother said. "Well, a full one this time. Not a hand. What's the special today?"

"Brisket on hash brown bagel with home fries."

How anyone can mention a corpse in the same breath as the special of the day was a talent that only ran in my family.

As I sat down, Shirley and Cecilia arrived. They were followed by Gloria, Wayne, and Kevin. Then Myrna announced herself while reaching for a complimentary mini-bagel.

"Who are we missing?" I asked.

"Look no further," my mother replied. "Herb, Paul and Mini-Moose decided to join the party."

Thankfully the seats on either side of me were occupied by my aunt on one side and my mother on the other. Last thing I needed was to be regaled by Paul with more of his fishing photos.

"Are you going to order the kippered herring today, Louis?" my aunt asked.

"I think *I* will," Paul answered before my uncle could utter a word. "Fish is brain food, you know."

I looked at him and kept my mouth shut. Not an easy feat.

The poor waitress assigned to our table approached us as if she was about to have an encounter with a wild boar. "Will this be on one check?" she asked. A chorus of "no's" and "separate checks" followed. I guessed she was new to the job.

After what seemed like an eternity, with Cecilia and Gloria changing their minds every few minutes, the waitress was finally able to get our orders. Thankfully Bagels 'n More places carafes of regular and decaf coffee on the larger tables so we didn't have to go through that scenario.

"Well," my mother said, "now that the food order has been taken care of, we need to ask ourselves this one question."

"Who murdered Barry?" Mini-Moose asked.

"Lordy, we don't know that the man was murdered. He might have succumbed to the heat." Shirley poured herself some coffee and tore open a packet of sugar.

Herb shook his head. "Claudia said the body was blue. That meant rigor mortis set in. According to *CSI*, that happens after two to six hours. It wasn't hot out so early in the morning so I doubt it was heatstroke."

Then Kevin spoke up. "Did anyone get a good look? Any blood? Bullet wounds? Throat slit? Knife to the stomach? Limbs missing from an

Planted 4 Murder

animal attack?"

"Lordy, Kevin," Shirley said, "I'm about to eat lunch."

I knew this would turn out to be a never-ending conversation and yet, I stupidly joined it. "You all realize that a determination is made by the coroner following a postmortem. Then there's toxicology screening, X-rays, bloodwork, you name it. And only the coroner or medical examiner can make the determination as to cause of death. No sense speculating."

Paul leaned across the table and shouted, "You're right. That's why we should move on to who killed him."

"Wait!" I nearly choked on the mini-bagel I bit into. "Didn't you listen to anything I said?"

"Yeah, yeah. Cause of death . . . blah, blah . . . But we don't need cause of death to figure out whodunit."

I am never going to complain about Bowman and Ranston again.

"Um, I think you do. Without the pertinent information, it would be difficult to pinpoint a killer."

"You're saying he was killed?"

And in that instant, down the rabbit hole I went. Faster than Alice.

Chapter 14

"For once, can we please leave things to the deputies?" Wayne asked.

"That's easy for you to say," my mother responded. "You're not growing crops like the rest of us."

"Crops?" I nearly choked. "Mom, you're growing a few peppers, tomatoes, and what? Zucchini?"

Next thing I knew, Paul turned his attention to my mother and Myrna. "Our combined radio show is a lifeline to the community. I say we dangle some informational bait and see who responds."

A lifeline? More like a lead sinker.

"Uh, what did you mean by 'informational bait'?" I clenched my fists and waited for his response.

"Just a few open-ended questions. There's no harm in that."

I narrowed my eyes and fixed them on his. "What kind of open-ended questions? Give me an example."

"Fine. Here goes: 'If a dead body, belonging to a loudmouth bully, was found in our community gardens, do you think a fellow gardener did it?'"

"That's not an open-ended question. It's a lead-in question and one that will get all of you in hot water. What happens if people phone in and give you names? Then what?"

Paul puffed out his chest. "Then I'd say we were off to a good start as far as an investigation was concerned."

I reached into my bag and handed him a business card.

"What's this?"

"The name of a bail bondsman our office recommends." Then, to my mother and Myrna, "Don't even think about it."

Just then, the three threadlike hippie women approached our table. The tallest one, with her long gray hair that was parted down the middle, spoke first. "What a scene at the garden. I still can't believe it. Of course, it doesn't surprise any of us. It was only a matter of time before Barry got what was coming to him."

"You mean because he was so belligerent?" Lucinda asked.

"Belligerent, conniving, obnoxious, selfish . . . hmm, what words am I missing?"

The curly haired petite woman answered. "Unhinged, unpredictable, and unpleasant. And any other 'uns' you can think of. When I find out who was responsible, I'll chip in for their defense attorney."

I widened my eyes and didn't say a word.

"So," the first woman said, as if we were talking about the weather and not a possible murder victim, "do all of you have plots?"

"Only our friend Cecilia, and that's through her church," Myrna said. Then she studied the looks on their faces. "Oh. You mean *garden* plots."

Lucinda gave her a sideways glance. "Only Herb and his buddies over there and Harriet, Louise, and me. I'm Lucinda. We're new to gardening. Mostly we read mystery novels and talk about them when we're not eating."

"The three of us are mainly into vegan cookbooks. It's wonderful to discover a new recipe." She turned to another woman. "That *Fun with Fungi* recipe book was a delight." Then, she looked back at us. "Forgive me. I'm Joyanne and these are my friends, Marlie and Tunnie."

The usual introductions took place. Not that it mattered. I knew that in a matter of seconds, no one would remember the names. Myself included. A chorus of "nice to meet you" followed. Then Joyanne spoke again. "As we were leaving the garden, we asked how long it would be cordoned off and the deputy said at least two days. I hope not longer. We hand water so it's very concerning in this heat."

"Tell them why we do hand watering, Joyanne." It was the other thin woman, who hadn't spoken until now.

"You tell them, Marlie."

"Because someone cut our water lines last year. Maybelle told us she was positive it was Barry. He said our water overflowed and created a muddy mess. We couldn't prove anything, though, and we didn't dare make an accusation for fear he'd retaliate."

As they spoke, I couldn't help but wonder who else got on Barry's bad side. "Were anyone else's PVC pipes cut last year?"

The women shook their heads. "No, but Barry and Gussie got into a big brouhaha over cigarette smoking in the garden. Well, over the cigarette butts to be precise. Gussie was insistent they belonged to Barry but Barry told him to go pound salt. That didn't go over too well."

"What do you mean?" By now my interest had been piqued.

"The following day, Gussie arrived to the garden with a gun on his belt and Barry went straight to the administration building to file a formal complaint. Next thing anyone of us knew, the management plastered that huge sign on the gate that reads 'No weapons or firearms allowed.' Not that it mattered. Lots of folks have concealed weapon permits so they basically ignored the sign. Gee, now I'm wondering if Barry was shot."

I shrugged. "We'll all know soon enough. No sense conjuring up our own theories." As soon as I said that, I made it a point to look directly at my mother.

Thankfully two waitresses arrived with our orders and the three thin women headed over to secure a table near the windows.

"Lordy"—Shirley leaned over to get my mother's attention—"watch out for gunslingers, Harriet. Look at their ankles. They always hide the guns there. And the two of you as well." This time she motioned to Lucinda and Louise.

"Whose ankles should I be looking at?" Herb laughed.

"Never you mind." Shirley inhaled the aroma of her garden veggie omelet with cheese and moved a forkful to her mouth.

"Right now, this whitefish with cream sauce is the only thing on my mind. Ask me about guns and murder later." With that, Paul stuffed a giant spoonful of the flakey fish into his mouth and swallowed it without chewing. It was an image that I feared would remain in my brain for weeks.

The next ten or fifteen minutes were comment-free. The only sounds were cutlery clicking on the plates and the occasional flow of coffee as it left the carafe. Then, the cacophony began again.

"Do you think Gussie could have done it?"

"What about Maybelle? They were at each other's throats."

"I wouldn't put it past those three spokeswomen for Jenny Craig."

"Louise! That's so snarky. And I agree, by the way."

Then, the worst. Lucinda gasped and looked at my mother. "Remember that first day when Barry complained about Streetman peeing on Maybelle's tomatoes? Everyone heard him. And you, too, Harriet. Oh no! What if those deputies think *you* had a motive for murder?"

"Whoa!" I held my hands in the air. "Let's all give it a rest before we get indigestion. My mother may have had a motive—no offense, Mom—but there's also means and opportunity."

"No offense taken. I will do anything in my power to protect the reputation of my little gladiator."

It was one of those moments when I was glad that I never suffered from a gag reflex. "Good, let's enjoy dessert and let the deputies deal with Barry."

It was a mountain of cheesecake, chocolate mousse, pumpkin spice cake, apple cobbler and cinnamon buns. I prayed the sugar fix would lull them into a stupor for a while but I was wrong. Our delightful meal ended with a plan to meet at one of the Beardsley ramadas in the morning to "plot a course of action."

"Don't look at me," I said when I stood to pay my bill at the register, "I plan on sleeping in."

Too bad no one heard me.

When I arrived home, it was almost three and still blistering hot in a summer that seemed to have no end. I tossed my clothes into the laundry basket and put on my bathing suit. I knew the pool would be crowded at this time of day on a weekend, but I didn't care. As long as I was in the water, it didn't matter.

A lovely eighty-eight-degree water temperature greeted me and I remained in the pool for over an hour and a half. When I got home, the red light on my phone was flashing, and not only that, but I had a few voicemails as well, along with two text messages.

I immediately tapped the text from Marshall: *Will call later. In the thick of things. XOXO*

It was sent about the same time as my swim and pretty much sounded like business as usual. I texted back: *I'm here. XOXO*

The next text was from my aunt Ina and it was barely decipherable. Usually she pens a long and detailed epistle but for some reason this time she texted: *On U r TV I thk U r Frm*

I read it aloud twice but all I could figure was that there was something on TV from someplace she found interesting. I deleted it and made a mental note to call her tomorrow.

Next, the voicemails, beginning with Augusta's. "Turn on your TV, Phee, and call me. Big ruckus in Chicago. Cat hair flying!"

Without wasting a second, I tapped the remote, but it was a commercial for replacement windows. I moved to another channel. Another commercial. This time for crepey skin. One more try and again, a weight-loss commercial. I decided to wait it out and listen to my mother's message on the landline.

"Phee! Where are you? Oh, never mind. Turn on the TV. There's a situation at that cat show in Chicago. It's all over the news. I could have sworn I saw Nate and Marshall chasing after someone. I didn't see their guns drawn. Call me."

If I never see another commercial for windows, skin, or weight loss, it will be too soon. I went back to my voicemails and tapped Shirley's. Looking back, I should have listened to Lyndy's message first in order to process what was going on, but everything moved so fast.

"Lordy, Phee! The Chicago cat show is all over the news. It's a melee. All I see are zoom-in shots of cats. Maybe they got loose. Isn't Marshall there?"

I wondered if that's what his text meant when he'd written *in the thick of things.*

Shrugging, I played Lyndy's message just as the weight-loss commercial ended and the two anchors for one of our local stations came on. They bantered about an "unlikely shake-up at a prestigious cat show" just as Lyndy's recorded voice came over loud and clear.

"Marshall's on national news with Nate! It didn't go down easy but they caught a few players and one of the kingpins in an international exotic cat smuggling operation. Right under everyone's noses at the cat convention, or whatever you call it, in Chicago. The footage shows them chasing after the guys along with the Chicago Police Department. Call me!"

At that moment I had at least five calls to return but all I cared about was Marshall and Nate's safety. I envisioned cat clawing and some scuffles with the "players." Finally, the bantering by the news anchors morphed into the actual reporting and I was able to watch the video of Nate and Marshall racing through the convention hall like a pair of high school sprinters.

I tapped Augusta's number in a nanosecond. "Oh my gosh," I said. "Does this mean they found Princess what's-her-name?"

"I'm not sure. I think it's too early to tell. Nate texted that he'll text me later. Some help that was."

"I know. Marshall said he'd call. At least it appears as if they're all right. I really hope they found that million-dollar feline."

"You and everyone in the cat community, according to what I've been watching. But what the heck. Let's celebrate anyway. I'll bring donuts Monday morning."

Just then, another commercial hit the air and, of all things, it was for canned cat food. I took it as a good omen, but boy, was I way off.

Chapter 15

"I'm exhausted, Augusta," I said Monday morning as I finished the coffee I held in my hand and searched for a K-Cup to brew another. "It was phone tag all day yesterday as that cat show was still in full force. This time with more police backup to ferret out the remaining smugglers. Marshall wasn't able to speak with me for more than a few seconds until after eleven. By then I could barely keep my eyes open."

"Mr. Williams texted me around the same time but it was mostly a series of emojis and I couldn't figure out if he had a stomachache or won the lottery. By the way, I got us a super assortment of BoSa donuts. The new pumpkin flavors are in!"

"Terrific. Thanks. Okay, here's what I could piece together. Nate and Marshall, with behind-the-scenes help from Rolo, were able to uncover a cat cartel, for lack of a better term. They had enough evidence to nab the ringleader with help from the Chicago Police Department."

"Shouldn't that be the other way around?"

"Uh, yeah. It should be, but it wasn't. Our guys led the charge and when all was said and done, a valued sphynx was in their possession and not trafficked to the highest bidder."

"That's wonderful! They found Princess and Queen Empress Trudalia."

"No, they didn't." I took a sip of the freshly brewed dark roast and reached for a strawberry-filled donut.

"I don't understand."

"They found Sir Sidney Melville, a tricolored feline whose net worth rivaled Elon Musk's. He was stolen in Toronto eight or nine months ago and a number of international agencies have been on his tail, so to speak, ever since."

"Did the perpetrators confess to having stolen the cat we were paid to find?"

"According to Marshall, they were arrested and questioned. Admitted to the thefts they made but were adamant they were not in the same cartel as the one that most probably nabbed Princess and Queen Empress Trudalia."

Augusta bit into a jelly-filled roll and wiped her lips. "I feel like a balloon that was just deflated."

"Deflated but there is a bright side. The wealthy owners of Sir Sidney have already wired money into Williams Investigations for returning their 'precious little furball.' Nate spoke to them on the phone, and according to Marshall, when they found out Sir Sidney was rescued, they carried on worse than my mother with Streetman."

"How much money?"

"Let's put it this way, we're all going to have one heck of a Christmas bonus. Rolo, too. Unfortunately, the chase is still on for the case we signed up for."

"Don't tell me it's another cat convention."

"The biggest one in the west and the guys can drive there if that's what they want to do."

"Las Vegas?"

I nodded. "This coming weekend. The Chicago PD was pretty sure they'd be able to provide some info for our guys since these so-called cartels seem to operate in full knowledge of one another even though they deny it."

"The weekend, huh? That means they can pick up on the smaller cases as well as—"

"Don't say it: Help Bowman and Ranston with the latest episode of *What Lies Beneath*."

I thought Augusta was going to spit out the mouthful of coffee she'd just sipped.

"Dirt digging or fur flying, either way it'll keep this office on its toes." She smiled and turned to her computer, but not before adding, "Let's turn on the noonday news in a bit and see if Williams Investigations made the headlines."

As it turned out, we didn't need to wait for the noonday news. Not with an abundance of news apps and a local grapevine that could play telephone like nobody's business.

My mother was the first to regale me before I even had time to get into my chair. And on my cell phone, no less.

Her voice was enthusiastic and one step below downright loud. "Myrna has Apple News on her phone. Nate and Marshall are famous. They're being dubbed the cat duo. Have you seen any of this? They kept showing footage of a wild chase and all sorts of things getting knocked over in the convention hall. This is a bigger deal than I imagined. Go figure. From now on, Essie doesn't leave my sight. She can join Streetman in the stroller."

"Uh, she usually joins him in the stroller, Mom."

"This time it will be with a GPS tag on her collar." Then, like a magician's quick slip of the hand, she changed the subject. "Did your office find out anything about Barry's death yet?"

"No. It's only been two days. Two days! You know that the coroner's office needs to do a preliminary autopsy and then the toxicology report. No one expects to hear anything for a few days and the complete tox report is usually two weeks."

"We got an email update from the rec center. Other than the section where Barry's body was found, the rest of the garden will be open. It will also be monitored by posse volunteers and a full-time deputy. Unless of course they're needed elsewhere. Oh, and get this—the rec center had the nerve to tell us that until further notice, no pets are allowed."

"That sounds about right. Face it, your little man could contaminate the crime scene with all his digging, and who knows what else."

"If it wasn't for Streetman, there wouldn't be a crime scene. Well, the first one, anyway."

"Indeed. Tell me, are you headed there tomorrow?"

"Yes. Just for an hour or so in the morning before it gets hot. Honestly, September is the worst month of all. Heat and humidity. The only thing missing are the Mankato mosquitos. Before I forget, Herb's going too, along with Lucinda and Louise. We want to finish planting our zucchini. Everything else is in."

"Just steer clear of the cordoned off area. I know how you and your friends operate."

When the phone call ended, I had momentarily forgotten about the cat convention news, but a half hour later Shirley called to let me know that "a relatively unknown investigative agency out of Glendale, Arizona, was credited for rescuing a priceless feline."

Then Paul called. But with a different reason. He heard on the news that our detectives would be pursuing leads in Las Vegas for the other priceless cat and had a brainstorm. He offered to join them and "follow the cleaning crews into the rooms with fish entrails to lure out any cats that might be hidden there." I pulled myself together and told him I'd pass along the word.

If that wasn't enough to rattle me, the call from my uncle Louis cinched it. No stranger to the Las Vegas entertainment scene, my uncle offered his services as well. Since he knew many of the musicians who performed there, he figured he'd join one of the gigs and do his own snooping around on the cat case. He also mentioned that my aunt was going to host a *Pride and Prejudice* reading at the house for her literature group next weekend and he "wanted to get the heck out of there."

When I was finally able to tackle my spreadsheets, Augusta announced that it was time for the noonday news. By then, we could have delivered it ourselves.

• • •

Nate and Marshall caught the red-eye back to Phoenix and arrived bleary-eyed the following morning. A quick shower and shave, preceded by two cups of coffee, and Marshall got into the office only an hour and a half after me. Nate was already there, but only by a few minutes.

Augusta and I got the complete rundown from them, including details on "the final train stop in Vegas before the Cat Fanciers' circuit ends for the year and won't resume until February."

"I guess it's a now-or-never sort of thing, huh? Not that I want to put pressure on you or Mr. Gregory," Augusta said, "but I don't remember such a tight timeline."

"Thanks for reminding us." Nate laughed. "Frankly, we're in better shape than most of our missing client cases. Rolo was able to connect with a few of his dark web sources and we're pretty certain that a major deal will be made at the Optimum."

"The Optimum? That's where you and my husband will be staying? Didn't the president of the United States stay there a month or so ago for a meeting with some oil sheiks?"

The men nodded while Augusta's jaw nearly hit the ground.

"Relax, hon, our lodging is being paid for by our client. Too bad we won't have time to enjoy the amenities like those herbal spas or fancy lobster dinners."

"Phee can always run you a hot shower and pick up an order of fish and chips." Augusta could barely keep a straight face. "Oh, and speaking of fish, I bet she's dying to tell you the latest offer from our favorite pescatarian."

"Paul?" The look of fear on Nate's face was priceless. "What did he want?"

I grabbed Marshall's wrist and squeezed it. "To accompany you and lure out cats with fish entrails. Please don't ask me to go into details."

"At this point, the only place I want to go is into my office." He gave me a quick hug and made an even quicker exit, along with Nate, who made a fast retreat to his office as well.

Chapter 16

With the cat caper on hold until the weekend, Nate and Marshall were summoned into the investigation regarding Barry's untimely demise, which was officially deemed a homicide the following morning. So much for a fun-filled hump day.

The postmortem had been completed as well as a preliminary tox screen. Cause of death was deemed nicotine poisoning but other lab screenings were still in the works.

"At least it wasn't a bloody mess," my mother said when she phoned to relay the news around lunchtime. She heard it on the midmorning report along with a "boring discourse on the dangers of smoking and trying to quit."

I assumed the nicotine poisoning had something to do with Barry's smoking habit, but according to my mother, it was quitting that did him in.

"How do you die from going cold turkey on smoking?" I asked her. "I thought that was reserved for hard drugs or alcohol."

"One would think so, yes, but he used a nicotine patch. The amount of nicotine that leached into his system at once was what killed him. The pulmonary specialist they interviewed on Fox explained it pretty well."

"How did they determine it was foul play and not an overdose?"

"The other expert, some forensic technician from the county, said that it would be rather unlikely that Barry would tamper with the patch. He knew what to expect from the delivery system for that substance. Plus, they looked at tissues from his body as well as conferring with his primary care physician. It was murder, all right. Pre-calculated murder. Thank goodness none of us are smokers."

I rolled my eyes. "Um, did they mention how you go about tampering with a nicotine patch?"

"You make small cuts in it, almost indiscernible. They allow the drug to get into the body rapidly and—Shazam! —you're dead."

"Shazam?"

"It was the best I could think of, Phee. Whoever wanted him dead knew his habits and knew what to do. At least it's a relief for all of us."

"A relief? What do you mean?"

"Whoever did it must have had it in for Barry. Not a random lunatic who'd be stalking the gardeners."

"Uh, I suppose. Anyway, you can get a good night's sleep knowing the community is safe from mad lunatics."

"And we can get on with our planting. Lucinda was worried that the soil might have been contaminated, and Louise thought maybe it was the water. The water is always to blame for something."

"Uh-huh. Well, I need to get back to work. Catch you later, Mom."

I had a blissful few hours before Nate and Marshall returned to the office in order to drop the other shoe. And while nicotine poisoning was the initial cause of death, there was one more. And that one, if my mother found out, would keep her awake for a fortnight.

"It's a timeline tie!" Nate announced when he stepped inside the office. My office door was ajar and I heard the exuberance in his voice. "This is a first for the county and for us."

I could make out Augusta pestering him with questions but couldn't discern what she asked. Curious, I left my seat and walked to her desk, not even bothering to come up with an excuse, like needing a Coke or coffee.

"Hey, kiddo," Nate said, "guess you overheard me."

"Overheard but not understood." I looked around, expecting to see Marshall, but he had already made his entrance and was now in his office, taking a call from someone at the county lab.

Nate took a swig of Coke from a can he'd just popped open and shook his head. "Looks like our favorite farmer, or gardener if you prefer, met his end with a combination of nicotine and potato poisoning. The latter was discovered in the bloodwork."

"Potato poisoning?" Augusta stopped fidgeting with her glasses and looked straight at Nate. "What'd he do? Binge out on French fries? Because if that was the case, I would have thought Paul would have beaten him to it with all those fish and chips dinners he eats on Fridays and any time in between."

"Not fish and chips, or fries. More like Solanum tuberosum." Nate narrowed his eyes for a few seconds.

"What on earth's that?" she asked. "And remind me to substitute yams and rice from now on."

"It's potato plant poisoning that happens when someone inadvertently consumes those green sprouts that appear on the outside of the potato. No need to stop eating them, just use a potato peeler before you cook them."

"Those little green tubes can kill you?"

"According to my notes from the lab, they can. Hold on." Nate fished around in his pocket and removed a crinkled sheet of paper. "Okay, ladies. It says here that solanine is a toxic glycoalkaloid."

"Glycoal . . . what?" I half expected to hear a longer discourse, but thankfully Nate put it in terms for us to grasp.

"A toxic substance. It can kill you in ten to thirty minutes if you ingested enough of it. The lab tech I communicated with said that chemists know how to create compounds that can be administered to the victims without their knowledge."

"Either that, or make a darn good potato salad that would call for lots of second helpings." The small laugh lines on the sides of Augusta's lips grew until they reached the crease line from her nose.

Just then, Marshall joined us. "Nothing like playing a game of 'Which came first?' The chicken or the egg? Nicotine can kill between five minutes and six hours. And both substances are dependent upon amounts administered as well as the body's response to it."

Augusta brushed her hands together. "Dead is dead if you ask me. But here's the real question. That is, if you want my opinion."

Nate and Marshall looked at each other and simultaneously rolled their eyes. "You'll tell us anyway, Augusta, so go ahead."

"I think that guy got under more than one person's skin. Remember *Murder on the Orient Express*? I'll wager if we wait around long enough, the forensic lab will discover additional substances or maybe even the pinprick of a needle . . ."

"You're saying there was one murder but more than one murderer? Silence that thought, Augusta, or my mother and her friends will go off the deep end. And just when she started to return to normalcy."

"It's logical, Phee. Why on earth would someone go to the trouble of sabotaging a nicotine patch, only to find a way of getting those solarium spuds into the guy's system?"

"Solanum. And I tend to agree with Augusta." Nate studied the crinkled paper again and sighed.

"It still boils down to gumshoeing, hon. We may know *what* killed the guy and maybe how it was administered, but motive plays the strongest role. And to get to that, it's old school all the way."

"I know. More interviews with the gardeners, picking up on what they say and don't say, and then following hunches."

"You see?" Augusta said to the men. "Phee should be gumshoeing alongside you."

"*No!* No, she shouldn't!" I took a step back and pinched my shoulders together. "I should be reconciling accounts and starting on estimated taxes. In fact, I hear a spreadsheet calling."

The three of them laughed as I headed back to my office, but I knew without a doubt that I'd be embroiled in this case whether I wanted to be or not. It was only a matter of time, and that seemed to move at a faster pace than my mother's gossip line.

• • •

Thursday morning, Nate and Marshall paid a visit to the rec center's admin building to delve into any complaints registered against Barry by anyone in the Sun City West community. MCSO had arranged to have Williams Investigations take over that part of the investigation as well as "anything deemed necessary as per circumstances." That left a pretty broad scope.

When the men returned to the office at a little past eleven, having started before eight, I expected to hear that they were buried under a mound of verbal abuse complaints as well as disturbing the peace, and possibly littering, as a result of Barry's cigarette habit. What I heard instead took me off guard but didn't seem to surprise Augusta.

Nate handed her another one of his notorious crumbled sheet notes, this one on the back of a paper menu from a taco shop in Sun City. "These are the notes from the written complaints."

"I'll piece it together, Mr. Williams," she said, "and run it by you." Then she looked at Marshall, who offered her a cockeyed grin.

"Thanks but I'll type up my own notes." He pointed to his head and his grin grew larger. "Anyway, I met with facilities and club director since that office handled situations that required temporary loss of privileges."

I immediately thought of Streetman and how often he was placed on probation from the dog park. Words like "unwanted amorous advances toward other dogs" and "peeing on people's legs" sprang to mind and I tightened my lips.

The men sauntered off to their offices and I asked Augusta to tell me what was on that crumpled paper. She looked around and whispered, "Ona and Aneta Zlatkova reported a theft eight months ago. They were positive Barry had taken a full cup of tomato seeds from 'the old country' that their uncle Santi brought to the United States."

"Is that all?"

She shook her head. "Oh, heavens, no. I'm just getting started."

Chapter 17

"I need another cup of coffee for this." I grabbed a McCafé medium roast, and once it was in the Keurig, motioned for Augusta to continue.

"Thira Tillwell reported that Barry carried a four-inch knife everywhere he went and used it as his 'all-purpose gardening tool.' She said she saw him dig up plants with it and use it to cut off bread slices. And that's not the worst! He used it as a toothpick after eating."

I cringed. "Did the knife fall under the no-weapons category?"

"Nope. The complaint was listed as 'posing a threat.'"

Only to his dentist.

"What else?"

"Here's a doozy. This is from Claudia Galen. That was the woman who discovered the body, right?"

"Uh-huh."

"Okay. This was only four months ago. She said she observed Barry messing with the water timers in one of Gussie's plots. And that's not all. She said she saw him wash his feet with Gussie's water."

"Why didn't she tell Gussie?"

Augusta shrugged. "Why doesn't anyone do anything logical? There's more."

I rubbed my forehead and took a sip of my coffee. "Go on."

"This one is actually from Barry. Mr. Williams underlined it."

"What does it say?"

"He was convinced that someone by the name of Racine was growing marijuana behind her lavender plants."

Hmm, must be the polka-dotted-dress woman.

"I thought growing marijuana was legal in Arizona."

"Six plants per person and only in an indoor, enclosed space, as per Proposition 207."

"How do you know that?"

"It's a side note from Mr. Williams."

"Oh."

"Is there anything else?"

"Are you kidding? This is enough to launch a small soap opera."

I laughed and went back to the work that awaited me on my desk. Nate and Marshall had a brief meeting with the deputies and touched base with a few of the gardeners, while it was business as usual for Augusta and me. At a little past four, a cc of a fax addressed to Bowman and Ranston came in from the county lab.

"Hey, Phee," Augusta called out when she saw what had been delivered. "The forensic jeweler was able to ascertain the inscription on the ring. And guess what—it's a triple gimmel. At least it was supposed to be. One of the rings is missing."

I stepped out of my office and took the paper from her and read it. "Where's Vanna White when you need her? According to the fax, the inscription was laid out so that each ring had a part of the message. The lab was able to identify minuscule notches where all three rings fit together."

"Yep. Find the missing ring, find the killer."

"Did you take that from *Lord of the Rings*?"

"No. That would have been easier. No one at the lab pieced together the fragments of the inscription but we can give it a try. I'll enlarge the photo."

A few minutes later, Augusta and I studied the letters, but it was alphabet soup as far as I was concerned: *isavet eta dra ov on*

We tried to rearrange them as if it was an anagram but couldn't.

"Don't feel bad," Augusta said. "The folks who are supposed to know this stuff couldn't do it either." Then she sat bolt upright and flattened her hand on her chest. "Howdy do, I bet that third ring isn't on a corpse or another severed hand. I bet it's sitting in broad daylight on someone's finger."

"My gosh, you're on to something. I really hate to say this out loud, but this is the kind of thing my mother and her band of merry chit-chatterers could focus on at the garden without getting into trouble. You know as well as I do, if I leave them to their own devices, it could be a disaster."

"I suppose there's no real harm in that. Hmm, maybe they'll discover why the corpse hand had two rings on it instead of three."

"According to what Bowman told Marshall, the forensic jeweler noted that gimmel rings usually represent engagement, wedding, or another milestone, such as the birth of a child. The bride, or wife, accrues the rings at those intervals. We can always ask Rolo. He's a wealth of obscure information."

"Yep. Giving and receiving. I'll send him an email. It's not an emergency."

A few minutes later, Nate and Marshall returned, the sweat dripping down their cheeks. Both were chugging giant Polar Ice drinks with no intention of stopping soon.

"Warm out there, Mr. Williams and Mr. Gregory?" Augusta asked.

A few nods and they kept slurping their drinks. Finally, Marshall spoke. "The inclusivity of primary and secondary poisonings seems to be a touchy point for the sheriff's office. They're taking our approach—hands-on investigation and interviews. We'll work all day tomorrow and then fly to Vegas on the eleven fifty-one flight on Southwest."

"You know where to find us," Augusta said. "By the way, we got a fax regarding the gimmel ring."

Nate finished his last swallow and tossed the cup in the trash. "Ranston mentioned it but it wasn't a priority. Full corpse out-trumps skeletal hand."

"Sounds like a good title for a horror movie." I chuckled.

"Oh, it's a horror movie, all right, kiddo. Your husband and I will look into it when we get back on Monday."

I didn't say a word about inviting my mother to step in, and neither did Augusta. Needless to say, when work resumed the following day, two distinct investigations were underway. The professional one that consisted of our office meeting with individuals for timelines, facts and anecdotal information pertaining to the late Barry McGuire, and the "snoop" and "gawk" one that relied on moseying around the ag plots and accidently bumping into people.

And while Marshall and I didn't have much time to chat, the opposite was true of my mother and me. It was a little past nine that Friday night, and both men were at the airport awaiting their flight when I phoned her.

"It's a terrible TV night, Phee. I was just about to call you. Herb left a little while ago. He stopped over to drop off some paper goods he picked up at Costco for me. While he was there, he ran into Maybelle, who told him that the women won't have any more heart attacks walking into the community gardens now that Barry's gone."

"Huh? I don't understand."

"Barry was the club's treasurer and he would always hide behind the big barrel at the gate where that giant clump of bushes are. He'd jump out at people when they came in and he would demand they pay their ten-dollar yearly fee if they hadn't done so."

"Wow. Talk about zealous. You don't suppose he scared the daylights out of someone to the point where they—"

"Murdered him?"

"I was going to say 'tried to give him indigestion with potato poisoning.'"

"If so, they gave him more than that."

"Listen, the reason I called was that I may have a *project* for you and the book club ladies if you think you could be discreet about securing information."

"Honestly, Phee. I'm about as discreet as they come. I wish I could say the same for your aunt and Myrna, possibly Louise, too, but as far as the other women are concerned, they are about as guarded and circumspect as could be. Especially Cecilia. She would have made a great spy in the armed forces. All they'd get from her would be name, rank, and serial number. Oh, and maybe some holy water sprinkled on them."

"Good to know."

I spent the next six or seven minutes delving into the cryptic message found on two-thirds of the gimmel ring, before telling my mother exactly what I needed her to do. When I finished, her response was clear and to the point. "Piece of cake!"

"Uh, do you know how you'll go about it without grabbing people's hands for a look-see?"

"Of course I do, but I'll need Lucinda. I'm not about to touch dirt after the last time. Those worms and grubs were horrible."

"It's *soil*, not dirt, and they live there. They aerate the soil."

"Fine. They can do it without me. I'll deal with the aboveground plants. And I'll ask for assistance. That way I can look at people's hands without them realizing what I'm looking for."

"Whatever you do, don't gasp if you think you see a gimmel ring on someone's finger. Act nonchalant."

"I wasn't born yesterday."

"Fine. Are you planning on going there tomorrow? It's Saturday."

"I know. And yes. Early. Then brunch. No excuse for you not to join us."

I'll think of one.

"Okay, good. I'll chat with you in the morning. Thanks, Mom."

"My pleasure."

The way she said "my pleasure" made me wonder if she had something else up her sleeve, but instead of worrying, I spooned out some strawberry ice cream and called it a night.

Chapter 18

The landline phone all but blasted me awake at six fifteen. Unfortunately, the caller ID was on the machine in the kitchen, but I had a pretty good idea of who would be at the other end.

"You missed the excitement, Phee!" My mother's voice was breathy and loud. "Gussie chased two of those ne'er-do-wells off of the property. Up and down most of the lanes—Fennel Flats, Garlic Grove, Asparagus Avenue, Lettuce Lane, and Clover Court. They all but toppled over Santi Campanola's vines. When the vagabonds got to the gate, they climbed over it like mountain goats and took off running down the block. We called the posse, but by the time the dispatcher picked up the line, they were out of sight and most likely on Bell Road."

"Ne'er-do-wells? Vagabonds?" I was still working through my thought processes at that hour and for some reason all I could picture was a scene from one of those black-and-white movies from the Great Depression where hobos rode the rails from town to town. Apparently, I wasn't too far off.

"Ona and Aneta think it's quite possible one of those 'rail-riders' was the person who dumped the skeletal hand into the compost heap. The train yard is right next to the rear of the gardens and it's an easy jump from that caboose or whatever it is they've got docked over there into our garden. Even Myrna could do it."

"Seems a bit far-fetched to me. I mean, if one of those people was in possession of a skeletal hand, they could have unloaded it anywhere. Or tossed it off a train rather than climb over a fence to a community garden, seek out a compost pile, and stick it there."

"Aha! You just answered your own question."

"What? Come again?"

"What better hiding place than that? No one would suspect them."

"No one even knows who they are! Um, if that's all you wanted to tell me, I'm going to try to get another half hour of sleep. It's my day off."

"I didn't get to finish what I started to tell you."

So much for that extra half hour . . .

"What?"

"Gussie thought Ona and Aneta may be right. Later on today, when the rail workers leave that compound of theirs, he thinks some of us should poke around and see if there's anything suspicious over there."

"Suspicious as in body parts?"

"He didn't specify."

"He didn't have to. Look, whatever you do, don't go over there. It's way too dangerous."

"It's a rail graveyard. Not the active train tracks. They're a good thirty feet away."

"If Ona and Aneta are so concerned, suggest they call the sheriff's office with their theory."

"The sheriff's office is just going to dismiss it and tell them that they need ironclad evidence. That seems to be the words of the day for Bowman and Ranston."

"That's how law enforcement works. On evidence. Not thoughts that waft through someone's head."

"Uh-oh. Now Gussie's getting into it with that scruffy-looking man whose name none of us knows. If you'd like, I can record what they say. My phone is right here and they're really loud."

"No, I don't need to hear—"

And then, like it or not, I heard.

"If you had a complaint about my weeds, you should have taken it up with me, not chopped down my asparagus plants."

"I didn't chop your plants. I don't even like asparagus. And whoever did it probably thought they were part of your weeds. Weeds are not allowed. You get fined for having them."

"News to me. When I got here yesterday, all I saw were clippings and your rear end walking down the path. Pretty hard to miss your rear end, Gussie."

"At least I know what a razor looks like. And if you must know, I always walk down the path. It's where my plots are. Besides, you were gone for a few days. It could have been anyone who did that."

"Oh, drat!" It was my mother's voice.

"What? What happened?"

"Nothing. They got to the end of Peapod Patch and their voices got jumbled."

"Never mind. Whatever it is, stay out of it."

"Oh, believe me, I will. I'm not getting between that scruffy man and Gussie. Say, ask your husband who that man is. They interviewed everyone."

"Mom, I—. Never mind. Catch you later. And stay away from the trains."

I glanced at the clock and it was now ten minutes to seven. So much for extra shut-eye. It was now extra coffee time. At least my mom didn't bug me about joining her crew for another one of their notorious breakfasts at Bagels 'n More. But in hindsight, it would have been a better option than the invitation she dropped in my lap a half hour later.

"Sorry to bother you, Phee, but with Ona and Aneta's take on the hand disposal, and then the dustup between Gussie and the scruffy man, I forgot to tell you that the agriculture club is holding a special meeting tomorrow afternoon at one, even though it's Sunday. I quote, 'We must discuss the unfortunate events plaguing our halcyon gardens.'"

"Halcyon gardens? Who used a word like that?"

"The president, Racine Rachel. Gussie's term expired and she was voted in this year."

"Okay. Enjoy your meeting."

"Phee, you *have* to come. One of those attendees could be Barry's killer. Not to mention all the information you'll be able to glean for Williams Investigations. You can unobtrusively take notes on your cell phone while pretending to text. It's the latest skill on the Hallmark Channel Mysteries."

"I'm not sure I'd—"

"Well, of course you can always go back to Cindy Dolton at the dog park. She seems to have a good grip on the unsettling events around here."

"The dog park again? With Streetman? That's extortion."

"It's information gathering."

"What time did you say this meeting was?"

"At one. In the lovely ramada in front of the small office building as you come in to the gardens."

With Marshall gone for the weekend and the looming threat of the dog park, I bit my lip and acquiesced. "Only this one time. Understood?"

"You won't regret it."

"I already do."

And while the start to my day was not exactly as relaxing as I envisioned it would be, the rest of the day was rather pleasant. I did housework, laundry and got in a quick midmorning swim before making one of our favorite Crock-Pot dishes—Mississippi chicken roast, a spinoff from the famous pot roast dish.

At a little past three, Marshall texted me to let me know that my uncle Louis had joined the investigation but didn't say much more than that. In fact, he used the emoji with the zipped-up lips. I sent back one with wide eyes and he replied, *Later.*

"Later" came all right, but it was from my aunt Ina and it took me a good few seconds to realize she was speaking in English and not in tongues.

"Talk slower, Aunt Ina, I don't understand what you're saying."

"Louis! Your uncle! He exposed—"

"He exposed himself?"

"No! The cat smuggler. Got a tip from the bassoon player and had the man cornered near the blackjack tables at the Optimum, but two thugs

arrived before Nate and Marshall could get there. They escorted the man out."

"*Escorted* as in 'working with him,' or *escorted* as in 'wanting a take in the cat action'?"

"I don't know. Louis ended the call."

"If he calls again, let me know. I'll try to reach Marshall."

It was now a little past five and the text I sent Marshall still said "Delivered" and not "Read." All sorts of horrific scenarios played out in my mind and I kept tapping the news apps on my phone, but there was nothing about the Cat Fanciers' Show or anything else trending in Las Vegas.

Finally, at a few minutes before eight, Marshall called.

"Sorry about the radio silence but it seems we're after quite the elusive cat-napper. Your uncle had connections in this city that dated back to the Rat Pack. He located the thief but none of these criminals work alone. Two of his henchmen made sure the guy slipped away."

"Oh, no. You were so close."

"It's not a done deal. Louis is working another angle and Nate and I are pursuing the leads to his whereabouts. Don't worry if you don't hear from me. We're okay but this chase most likely won't end with the cat show."

"What's that supposed to mean?"

"A longer time in Sin City. We haven't heard from Bowman and Ranston so we figure everything is stalled for now."

"Everything on *their* end. The garden club is meeting tomorrow afternoon to discuss the series of unfortunate events."

"Uh-oh. Is that the politically correct way of saying they plan to do something outrageous along with your mother's crew?"

"Nothing surprises me anymore, but I'll find out firsthand."

"Firsthand? Why?"

"It was the lesser of two evils. At least I know when I walk in the garden area, it will be soil I'm stepping on."

Chapter 19

When I arrived at the ramada Sunday afternoon, at least fifteen people were seated on the benches, chairs, and the floor as if it was a yoga class. Gussie, Claudia, Ona and Aneta were to the right and Herb was a few feet away with Kevin and Kenny. I supposed it was a slow sports afternoon on the TV or the guys would have been couch potatoes instead of sitting around with the folks who cultivated the real ones.

The tall hippie woman with the long, straight gray hair walked over to Ona and Aneta, leaned until her face was obscured by her hair, and whispered to them. For a second, her mannerisms reminded me of junior high, when secrets only lasted until the next bell rang.

My mother hadn't yet made her grand entrance and I prayed it would be without her precious "fur-babies." A few seconds later, Lucinda appeared, her hair flying in all directions. She was talking with Thira, and when Herb spotted them, he immediately ushered them to the remaining seats on the bench next to him.

The woman whom I presumed was Racine stood adjacent to the wall that separated the ramada from the little office. She was clad in a purple polka-dotted pinafore, and I was positive my guess was correct. I mean, how many people have a wardrobe that consists only of anything polka-dotted?

As she shuffled through a handful of notes, my mother and Louise arrived and quickly sat near me on the wobbly wooden chairs. Before my mother had a chance to talk, Racine cleared her throat.

"Good afternoon, everyone. Thank you all for coming at such late notice. As I mentioned, this is a special meeting to discuss the unfortunate events that have befallen our beloved agricultural garden club. Now, I know some of you wish to deviate and address the two burning issues that came to the attention of the club, but I must remind you that those agenda items will be forthcoming at our regularly scheduled meeting."

"For goodness sake, Racine, just address them and get it over with." Gussie stood with his hands crossed and surveyed the ramada.

"What are the two issues?" I whispered to my mother. Unfortunately, my voice carried.

"A stinking dress code and an edict for organic gardening." Again, it was Gussie.

"I don't see why we need a dress code," Thira said. "It's not as if we're going to a garden party. We're planting and harvesting. Not sipping tea and eating crumpets."

"I agree with Thira," Ona added. "I want to be comfortable while I dig and plant."

"Weren't there health issues involved?" Claudia waved her hand in the air and continued. "Like *some people* who walk around here barefoot. That's an invitation for all sorts of insect and scorpion bites. And fungus."

The scruffy-looking man who had the altercation with Gussie stood and pinched his shoulders back. "Going barefoot on the ground allows the earth's energy to enter our bodies and sustain us. And it shouldn't fall under a dress code. It's healthy living at its best."

"It's downright disgusting if you ask me," someone shouted. "Almost as bad as going bare-chested when your T-shirt gets too sweaty."

"We didn't ask you," someone else shouted back. "As far as I'm concerned, we can all go bare-chested in this humidity. This is an equal opportunity club."

Racine clapped her hands and glared at the group. "Enough! These agenda items are not up for discussion at this time."

"I don't think they should be up at all." This time it was one of the pencil-thin hippie women who spoke. "Especially that proposed rule for organic gardening only. This isn't a commune. It's a community garden. And who proposed that item anyway? I must have missed that meeting."

"It doesn't matter," Racine said. "If you're insistent, we can look back at the minutes. Maybelle should have them on her computer since she's the secretary."

All eyes turned to Maybelle, who shrugged.

"Now then," Racine went on, "we need to address what brought us here in the first place—the grim discovery of a skeletal hand in the compost heap and Barry McGuire's dead body near Claudia and the Zlatkova sisters' plots."

"Whose plots?" someone asked.

"Ona and Aneta," Racine whispered. "The Zlatkovas."

"Oh," the voice mumbled.

"What's there to address?" the scruffy-looking man asked. "Sounds like it's pretty clear to me."

Racine inhaled and held it until I thought she'd turn blue. "I'll tell you what we need to address, Orvis. We need to address how we are going to deal with it."

Orvis. The scruffy-looking man is Orvis.

Then Racine launched into what could best be described as an elementary school teacher instructing his or her students how to comport themselves in the hallways.

"To begin with, we must face facts. Our otherwise peaceful garden has now become the center of nefarious behavior."

"Is that the newest word for murder?" someone called out.

Racine ignored them and went on. "We can no longer think of this area as safe until the perpetrator or perpetrators are apprehended. Therefore, starting tomorrow everyone needs to leave the garden area an hour before dusk. We cannot afford to incur another tragedy."

"Says who? You?"

Racine took out her cell phone and replied. "This is from the administration office. I received it right before I sent everyone the email about our meeting today. It reads, 'Effective on Monday, all gardeners are to leave the agricultural area one hour prior to dusk. We are forwarding everyone a copy of the sunset times as taken from the Weather Channel so there can be no question as to when dusk is. Keep in mind this is for everyone's well-being until further notice.'"

"What about dawn?" Maybelle asked. "Does it say anything about dawn?"

Racine shook her head. "No. Now then, I have something I would like to add. It's not required but it should be."

A series of moans and grumbles followed, including those from Herb, Kevin, and my mother.

"I suggest, beginning tomorrow, we move to the buddy system. No one works in the garden without a buddy or two. If there is a killer in the area, or heaven forbid, among us, he or she would be less likely to seek out another victim."

"Good grief, Racine!" Gussie shouted. "Are you suggesting one of us is a serial killer?"

Racine clasped her hands together. "I'm suggesting we act responsibly, that's all. And while I cannot enforce my prudent suggestion, I strongly urge all of you to follow it."

More groaning and one "oh, brother."

"Have we heard anything more from the sheriff's office?" Thira asked.

Silence.

"I haven't," Racine said, "but that doesn't mean they haven't made headway with these, um, *situations*."

"That's a new word for it," Orvis said. "But I know someone who might have." He pointed to Gussie and added, "Why don't you tell them what you were doing in the railroad yard back there?"

Gussie shot Orvis a look. "I was doing what all of us should have been doing—scoping it out to see if there was evidence of foul play."

"Was there?"

"Not that I could tell. But I did find out one thing. The sheriff's office combed the area too. That's what the railroad workers told me before they asked me to get out of there."

I turned to my mother and kept my voice low. "I doubt he was asked. More like *escorted* out. Aren't you glad you didn't go there?"

I expected some sort of reply, but instead my mother shot her hand in the air and announced, "Does anyone know if the sheriff's office sifted through the compost heap where my Streetman found the hand?"

A series of responses toppled over each other.

"Not that I know of."

"Ew! Who wants to do that?"

"Do you think there are more body parts?"

"I say we find out for ourselves."

"Leave well enough alone."

"If they thought it was worth sifting through, they would have sifted."

"Since when do they think ahead?"

And finally, "That pile is taller than last time. I say we do it in the morning."

Unfortunately, that last remark was followed by a chorus of "Yes! Tomorrow. At dawn."

I don't know who offered that up, but next thing I knew my mother poked me and said, "Too bad you have to work."

And just when I thought the meeting had wound down to the point of bringing it to a close, one of the three thin hippie women added her two cents.

"We haven't talked about Barry's murder. I think that's far more urgent than a bony hand."

"What are you proposing?" Racine furrowed her brow and sighed.

The woman was about to say something but stopped in her tracks. I glanced around the ramada to see if anyone gave her the stink-eye or something but I couldn't tell. Finally, she said, "Never mind. It'll get sorted out."

With that, Racine concluded the meeting, but not without reminding everyone that they are to leave an hour before dusk.

More grumbling, including Herb's familiar voice. The seven of us—my mom, Lucinda, Louise, Herb, Kevin, Kenny and me—all ambled to the gate when the thin woman, who brought up Barry's demise, called out to us.

"Hold on! I need to speak with you."

She was by herself but turned around as if to check and see where her friends were.

"I'm Joyanne. My friends and I have been gardening here for over a decade. Listen, I know you're all new and that's why I know none of you would have a reason to murder Barry. But that can't be said for the rest of this gardening community."

"Racine was right," Lucinda said. "It *was* one of us. My gosh—I could have been sitting next to a killer."

"Then thank your lucky stars." Herb laughed. "You escaped without a scratch."

Joyanne bit her lip and continued. "I need your help to find out who really murdered that louse."

"Um, if he was a louse, why would you exert yourself to find out who was responsible?" I tried to sound genuinely interested and not snarky, but I wasn't sure how it came off.

"Because Barry was my ex-husband. No one knows, but once they find out, all eyes will be on me."

"What is it you want us to do?" *As if I don't already know.*

"Help me figure out who did it before the sheriff's office takes the easy way out."

"Um, why would they do that?"

"Because I quit smoking a month ago and I use nicotine patches, too."

"What about your girlfriends? Do they know?"

Joyanne responded in a whisper, "One of them might be the murderer."

Chapter 20

In a nanosecond, my mother responded with a sentence that will go down in infamy. At least as far as I was concerned.

"My daughter might be able to help. She works for Williams Investigations in Glendale."

Joyanne immediately lit up. "That's fantastic! I could really use a private investigator."

"I'm not—"

"What my daughter started to say is that she works in a different capacity but is well-versed in uncovering the facts."

I grabbed my mother by the elbow and ushered her off to the side. "Excuse me, Joyanne. Please give us a moment."

Behind me, I could hear Louise, Lucinda and the men all chatting at once.

"What on earth were you thinking?" I narrowed my eyes and glared at my mother.

"That we've just found a shortcut into finding out who was responsible."

"What shortcut? I can't go around impersonating a detective."

"I never said you were a detective. I said you were 'well-versed' with these sorts of things."

"It's a matter of semantics. She thinks I'm a private investigator. When she finds out I'm a bookkeeper/accountant, who knows what she'll do."

"Right now she needs your help. Worry about it if she asks for an invoice."

"Oh, brother. And tell me, why am I doing this?"

"Because Joyanne may know more about Barry than two counties' worth of sheriff deputies. And if we ever expect to find out who double poisoned him, she'd be a good person to start with."

"You owe me. Big time."

We walked back to where Joyanne stood and I handed her my card. "I need to be up front. I'm their bookkeeper/accountant."

"Oh my gosh! A detective and a bookkeeper! Does this mean a higher fee?"

I turned to my mother and gave her "the look" before I responded to Joyanne.

"Um, no. My mother and her friends garden here and I want them to enjoy their pastime without fear."

"It's not a pastime," Herb shouted from a few feet away. "It's survival.

Some of you may not pay credence to those impending solar flares, but I do."

"Solar flares?" Joyanne had a strange look on her face.

"It's a long story. Listen, call me and we can meet privately." I said the word *privately* out loud so my mother and her entourage wouldn't get the idea that this was going to be Twenty Questions with the ex-wife of a murder victim.

Joyanne thanked me and raced off to where her girlfriends waited, just outside the gate.

"Strange friendships," Lucinda remarked. "She thinks one of them might have poisoned her ex and yet she's palling around with them."

"Nothing surprises me anymore." I responded to Lucinda but made eye contact with my mother as I did.

"Don't know about you ladies, but the men and I are going to DQ for ice cream. It's too early for beer and too late for coffee." Herb looked at us and waited for a response.

"It's never too late for ice cream," Lucinda said. "What do all of you say?"

Fifteen minutes later, I found myself at a large rectangular table eating a soft ice cream cone as everyone yammered about the meeting and about Joyanne's relationship with the late Barry McGuire.

Suddenly my phone vibrated and it was my aunt. "Phee, do you know anything about baccarat?"

"Uh, no, Aunt Ina. Why?"

My mother's ears perked up. "Aunt Ina? What's going on?"

"Is that your mother's voice I hear? Where are you?"

"At Dairy Queen. We just left an impromptu agriculture club meeting. Why do you want to know about baccarat?"

"Your uncle is at a baccarat table. Wanted me to convey a message. I don't understand it, but maybe you will."

"If it's about baccarat, I won't, but go ahead."

"Fine. He said 'Martingale system in play. Banker's in on the heist. Once he folds, we can move on.' Then he hung up."

"Hmm, I don't know what a Martingale system is, but I think I understand the rest of it. The banker at the table has info on the whereabouts of that princess and queen empress cat. If he or she loses to Uncle Louis, then my uncle will be privy to info leading to the cat."

"Don't tell me the rest. If you uncle loses, we'll be eating cat food instead of filet mignon."

"I wouldn't worry." *Of course I would. Who am I kidding?* "Uncle Louis knows what he's doing."

Just then, Herb shouted, "Who's playing baccarat? I heard that. It's one heck of a game to win. Almost impossible odds."

"Did Herb say something? I recognize his voice, too."

"Nothing important. He wanted to know if pumpkin flavor is back yet. Said it was impossible to find."

"Oh. Tell him to wait another week or so. Call me if you hear anything from Marshall."

"I will. And don't worry. They're in a casino, not on a high-speed chase." *Yet.*

On my drive home, a text came in from Marshall. At least I didn't need to decode it: *Will be in Vegas at least for another day or so. Louis saved us some time. Who doesn't he know around here? Don't worry. We are on the move with not much slowdown. XOXO*

I'd been around my uncle long enough to know that he was calling in his markers in order to snatch up clues regarding the whereabouts of that cat. And if I knew my uncle, it wouldn't take him too long.

I phoned Augusta the second I got home to let her know what was going on since she'd have to rearrange schedules and appointments for the week.

"Already figured as much," she said. "Mr. Williams sent me a short text but I was one step ahead. We're all set until Thursday. What else is new?"

When I told her about the agriculture club meeting and my venture into deceit and impersonation, she laughed. "I'm glad you don't work for a neurosurgeon."

At a little before midnight, another text came in from Marshall: *Banker folded. Your uncle traded chips for info and tickets to Cirque du Soleil. Cat's in the bag if we're fast enough.*

I figured it was too late to call Aunt Ina and besides, all I could really tell her was that her husband excelled at baccarat. As for the show tickets and Marshall's last comment, my take was that Princess and Queen Empress Trudalia was somewhere on the set of Cirque du Soleil. I only prayed it wouldn't involve flying theatrics on a tightrope. The Canadian show that gained so much popularity in Las Vegas didn't use live animals, so I doubted the cat would be in any danger. Still, it was my husband and my boss that I worried about.

• • •

No news the following morning, but that was to be expected given the nature of Marshall's job. Augusta greeted me at work with a selection of apple cinnamon bear claws from a bake shop near her house and a box of pumpkin-flavored K-Cups.

"Fall is next week. It's as if pumpkins and cinnamon exploded everywhere. Any news from Mr. Gregory? All I got was a text at five a.m. from Mr. Williams. Two words: *We're okay.*"

"I know. Marshall's was a tad more detailed at midnight but not by much. Here, read it for yourself." I handed her my phone and waited while she perused it.

"Hmm, could be anything, but my guess is that someone in that show has the cat."

I nodded. "At least it's the usual 'track down the info' and not dangle from a rope fifty feet in the air."

"Unless that's what they have to do to get the information."

"Great. Now I'll have that image in my mind all morning."

"Tell me, did your new client tell you when she'd make an appearance?"

"Not a client. Exactly. More like a miscommunication from my mother resulting in a, um, well, more like a . . ."

"Just spit it out! An investigation by a not-so-private unlicensed investigator."

"Yeah. That. And I'm pretty sure she'll show up any time now, thanks to my mother."

As it turned out, I didn't have long to wait for Joyanne. She made her entrance shortly after I completed the recent pile of invoices that were taking up space on my desk. Wearing wedge heels, jogger pants and a gauzy top, she looked more like a carefree retiree than the Mother Earth image she exuded at the agricultural gardens.

Augusta announced her arrival via the office phone and I stepped out to greet Joyanne. Augusta peered over her tortoiseshell glasses as Joyanne rushed toward me, speaking a mile a minute.

"Thank you so much for seeing me. I hardly slept a wink. And every time the phone rang or I heard a car on the street, I was convinced it was the sheriff's office with a warrant for my arrest."

"Whoa. Slow down. I doubt any of that is about to happen. Come on, we can chat in my office."

I caught Augusta rolling her eyes and turned away so I wouldn't laugh.

"Would you like some coffee? Or water?" I asked when we were both seated.

Joyanne shook her head. "I'm fine, thanks."

"Okay, then suppose you start by telling me what makes you think that one of your friends was responsible for your ex-husband's death. But before you do, let me reassure you that the sheriff's office does not have concrete or circumstantial evidence to point to you as his killer. Lots of people try to quit smoking and nicotine patches are sold everywhere. No prescriptions are needed. Don't let your imagination go wild."

"I'll try. This goes back to last April but I'll tell you everything I know. Tunnie, that's the woman with the shoulder-length hair who always wears a flower near an ear, used to have the garden plot next to Barry's. She was cultivating dahlias for an exhibition in Phoenix. Anyone who knows anything about growing those flowers knows that they grow best when the days are warm and the nights are cool. But with heat-tolerant varieties and light afternoon shade, they should do well. Tunnie made sure that happened by using shade cloth in addition to mulching them because their feeder roots are shallow."

I was dumbfounded. "Wow. You seem to know a great deal about this."

"Only what Tunnie told us. She was so passionate about this that she carried around a list from the Dahlia Society of Georgia."

If I wasn't flabbergasted prior, the Georgia list made up for it. "All right. Tell me how Barry entered into this."

"He killed them. Every last one of them."

"How? Why?"

"He poisoned the soil. Short and simple. And all because of an idiotic clause in the bylaws that stated the plots are to be used for growing crops. Tunnie got permission from the prior club president, who has since moved back to Michigan, but that wasn't enough for Barry. He literally pitched a fit. When Tunnie first noticed her plants dwindling and shriveling, she thought maybe it was the heat since the days were getting warmer. But then, Orvis told her that he saw Barry messing around with the soil in her plot when she wasn't there."

"Uh-oh. I can see where this is going."

"Tunnie took soil samples to a private horticultural lab in Cave Creek and found out that herbicides were used to an extreme, resulting in plant death. She confronted Barry but he told her to go pound salt and grow something edible. That's when she told him it wasn't over and she'd see to it he'd get what he deserved. After that confrontation, she started a small potato patch."

"Hmm, I can see where this is going."

"Oh, it's going all right. Were you aware that Tunnie was the salad maker for a local restaurant in Sun City West? If I have to give you the name, I will, but I don't want the word to spread or it might hurt their business. Potato salad was her specialty and she made a few varieties."

"Are you saying you think she used the potato tubers in a salad that Barry ingested?"

Joyanne nodded.

"Um, wouldn't he have been suspicious if she gifted him with potato salad? Or worse yet, brought it to a public function where anyone could have partaken?"

"Tunnie's smarter than that. Want to know how I think she pulled it off?"

Before I could respond, Joyanne presented the theory like a seasoned prosecutor at a high-profile trial and I was left with my mouth wide open.

Chapter 21

My brain worked overtime to digest everything she'd said, and I tried to look nonchalant as I responded.

"So, uh, you believe Tunnie used her own homegrown potatoes, since they would have a higher potency than the store-bought ones."

"That's right. Those supermarket potatoes are mainly shipped from Idaho and sit around forever. That's why they look ancient before you even boil, bake, or fry them."

"I see. Well, getting back to Tunnie . . . are you telling me that she brought her homemade potato salad to the gardens and handed out small containers for everyone to take home?"

"Yes."

"And Barry's was tainted?"

"No. That's the beauty of it. If it was ever questioned and that salad came under the scrutiny of the lab, it would be harmless."

"Come again?"

"I think Tunnie rubbed the moisture from those tubers onto Barry's coffee cup when he wasn't looking. He always left his high-octane coffee laying around. Trust me, no one would go near it."

"Except a killer."

"That's right. If anyone suspected anything and actually went through his fridge, all they'd find is yucky ancient potato salad that might make you gag, but not take your last breath."

"Joyanne, is there any way to prove this theory of yours?"

"Maybe."

"From Barry's coffee cup? Was it a special one that could be found in his house?"

"Hard to say. He used throwaway paper cups from Starbucks and McDonald's. But I don't know what he drank out of at home."

"That's not helping. If we can't find the coffee cup, it would be impossible to prove."

"Not really. Tunnie lets her laundry pile up in her garage until it resembles the Andes Mountains."

"I don't follow."

"Her gardening gloves. Forget the coffee cup and go for the gardening gloves. They're probably laden with that toxin. She has tons of gloves and never reuses them. Always takes a new pair. I bet she's got those culprits in her laundry pile, just waiting to be thrown into the washer with the rest of her things. Housekeeping is not Tunnie's strong suit. When she rubbed the tuber onto the cup edge, the poison must have gotten onto the fabric."

"Are you suggesting breaking and entering into Tunnie's house to find them?"

Joyanne looked around and smiled. "Not exactly the house. The garage. It's the only way. And I would suggest sooner than later. Eventually Tunnie's going to need to refresh her underwear. Everything gets sweaty in the heat."

Ew!

"I thought you and she were friends. Along with Marlie."

"We were, but I have a nagging feeling Tunnie knows that I know and that she'll do something to make sure I don't rat her out."

Like her laundry?

"Um, isn't that what you just did by telling me?"

"To you, not to the sheriff's office. And if you could find those gloves and if they had traces of potato spud poisoning, no one would dare glance my way."

"What you're asking is against the law."

"So is murder. And right now, I might very well be the next victim."

"Aren't you being a tad dramatic? After all, it's only a theory. A good one, mind you, but a theory nonetheless."

"That's because you don't know Tunnie's background the way I do."

And here we go. I have now entered Lucinda's world of Telemundo.

I offered Joyanne some coffee but she declined. Understandable, given what she had just said.

"All right, I've got some time. Tell me what you know."

"Tunnie shared this with Marlie and me a couple of years ago when we learned how to make Long Island Iced Tea. Let's just say a little bit opens up your lips like the town crier."

I kept still and motioned for her to continue.

"When Tunnie was in junior high school, she was failing French and knew she wouldn't pass the final exam. She had a D average but with the final, it would have most likely been an F."

Please do not tell me she murdered her French teacher.

Again, Joyanne looked around the room as if someone was lurking behind a chair. "Tunnie's only option was to make sure her teacher didn't show up with those final exams."

Oh my gosh. She did *murder the French teacher.*

Next thing I knew, she moved her chair closer to mine and whispered, "Tunnie had an A-plus average in chemistry."

That cinches it. Most poisoners are chemists.

In a hushed voice, Joyanne said, "Tunnie put sorbitol in her hot cocoa the day before. Sorbitol is a laxative and it gave her teacher the runs the next day. The final exam was canceled and the grades were averaged. Tunnie got promoted and no one was the wiser. Don't you see? This is her MO. That's the term, right? Modus operandi."

"Uh, yeah. That's the term all right."

"And that's why I'm worried. But you can't breathe a word of this to the sheriff's office or I'll be joining Barry."

"There must be another way around this."

"I doubt it. Listen, if I didn't think it was a viable plan, I never would have asked you. It's easy-peasy too. Tunnie's house is one of the few houses that has a side door into the garage and there are oleander bushes in front so you can't really see the door. She keeps a spare key under a hideous blue garden gnome a few yards away near some bougainvillea bushes. Plus, I would make sure Tunnie was nowhere near her house during the time you went over. Believe me, if there's any way you can locate those gloves and have them tested, it would put everyone's mind at ease. Especially mine. And like I said earlier, I'm willing to pay whatever your office fee is."

Office fee? That was the last thing that crossed my mind. "Joyanne, you unloaded a truckload of information and speculation in less than an hour. I need time to process all of this. And unlike what you see on TV, breaking and entering is not something we do." *As a rule.* "I'll get back to you soon."

"Please make it soon. Her laundry day has to be coming up."

But my court date doesn't need to.

"Let's talk first thing tomorrow. I'll call you."

"Thanks. I knew you'd understand."

When Joyanne left the office, I clasped my hands and pressed them to my lips. If what she said was true, Tunnie wasn't merely a gardener. She was a burgeoning poisoner.

I went straight to the Keurig machine and didn't even bother to rifle through our selection, resulting in Dunkin's pumpkin spice. Augusta glanced over and shook her head. "Must have been a doozy of a client meeting."

"She's not a client. *Exactly.* And she wants me to go digging through someone's laundry to find poison on garden gloves."

"Backtrack, please. I'm usually pretty good at piecing stuff together but this time I'm at a loss."

While I waited for the K-Cup, I gave Augusta the lowdown, including how Tunnie managed not to fail French. She rubbed her chin and then leaned back. "Hate to say this, Phee, but that woman may be on to something. I mean, what other evidence has anyone uncovered? And that close-knit group of gardeners or planters, or whatever the heck those people go by now, sure do know each other's habits."

"So you think I should sneak over, find the key and fumble through a mountain of wash?"

"It doesn't exactly spell danger, although I'd be wearing gloves too."

"Augusta, this sounds exactly like the kind of thing my mother and those book club ladies would do, not me. Thank goodness they don't know anything about it."

Lamentably, I spoke those words too soon. Way too soon. At a little before noon, my mother called and could barely get the words out of her mouth.

"I'm at the manicurist with Shirley. She chipped a nail and mine needed to be refreshed but that's not why I called. Marlie, the skinniest one of those 'never left the seventies' women, is yapping it up with Maybelle right behind me. They don't know we're here because the salon has these giant ferns on a pony-wall that separates the areas. They used to have this ugly lattice thing but replaced it and redesigned the area so that it would afford more privacy."

"Slow down. I really don't need to know about the layout to your salon."

"Shh. That's not why I called. Shirley and I overheard a very telling conversation between those two women. I'll make this short and sweet. We need to get into Tunnie's house. She's the third party in that group of 'no-meat-on-your-bones' women."

"What?"

My mothers' voice dropped so that she was barely audible. "Tunnie may have poisoned Barry and the proof is in her laundry. It's not like we have to sift through a bloody mess. She didn't stab him."

"We? No 'we.' '*We*' are not doing this."

My mother continued as if she hadn't heard me. "They all get up before dawn and traipse down to the agricultural plots. That's when we need to strike."

"Strike? We're not at war. And there is no *we*. Look, I have to get back to work. Let's chat later. And don't set up any sort of soiree in the meantime. Especially if you plan on calling Aunt Ina."

"Boyer's Café is on your way home. Meet Shirley and me there at six. We'll talk. It's Monday. They always have their cappuccino brownies on Mondays."

"Yes to the cappuccino brownies, no to rummaging through Tunnie's laundry."

"We'll talk."

The worst two words ever uttered—*we'll talk*.

For the second time that morning, I went straight to the Keurig and wound up with decaffeinated hazelnut. *Thank you, Mom.*

Chapter 22

Augusta nearly split a gut when I told her about my mother's eavesdropping and her subsequent plan to get into Tunnie's garage and root through her dirty laundry to find the incriminating evidence of murder.

"I feel as if the odds are stacked up against me," I moaned. "Joyanne will plead with me, my mother will badger me, and worse yet, the book club ladies will all call me, one by one, to ask me to step in so that they can return to normalcy."

"They have a 'normalcy'?"

I rolled my eyes. "In their world, yes. I suppose."

"So what are you going to do?"

"I'd say wait it out but that never works. It's like ignoring one gray hair and the next thing you know you're checking out every L'Oréal and Clairol product on the market."

"Not this gal. But I get your point. It's like weeds. You find one and it turns into forty by the next day. Listen, you can stick to your guns and say no, but face it, your mother won't give up that easily. Hey, you know her better than I do."

"Even so, I know her band of merry troublemakers, beginning with Myrna and my aunt Ina. And she always seems to wind up taking them with her on these so-called reconnaissance missions."

"Good grief—your aunt! Didn't she wind up suffocating some fish? And getting trapped in a museum?"

"Don't remind me. And Myrna. She got caught under someone's back fence. Heaven help me. It just gets worse and worse when I think about it."

"I'll take that as a yes."

"I know the guys will be at Cirque du Soleil tonight so that would mean I'd better do the deed tomorrow morning. Yikes. I can't believe I am actually considering this."

"Look at it this way, if you *do* find evidence of poisoned gloves, then the deputies could haul in Tunnie as a bona fide suspect and then all that would be left is the severed hand."

"Evidence has to be acquired with a search warrant."

"Hmm, these technicalities are so annoying, but I'm sure we could come up with a reason for Bowman and Ranston to get one. Let me think on it."

"Sure. Think. I've got to get back to account reconciliation. Much more fun."

I started for my office when suddenly, it was as if someone punched me in the stomach. "Oh, no! Oh, heck no!"

"What? What's the matter? Did you stub your foot or something?"

"No. Worse. I just remembered something. My mother is training Streetman to become a scent detection dog so she can get him registered as a service dog. It's a big step up from emotional support dog." *And ten steps up from annoying, snapping chiweenie dog.*

"Uh-oh. I know where this is headed. You think she'll bring him to Tunnie's garage to sniff out the laundry."

"Not *think*. I *know* she'll bring him there. My only choice is to do it alone."

"What time did you say those women go to the agricultural plots?"

"At dawn."

"Sounds good to me. Call if you need me. This farmgirl is always up before the roosters."

"And this city gal is always asleep and looking at the inside of her eyelids."

I phoned Joyanne an hour or so later and told her I'd agree to checking out Tunnie's garage. What followed was a garble of words going a mile a minute. To say she was animated would have been an understatement.

"Oh my gosh, Phee! That's fantastic! Oh my gosh. Oh gosh. Okay, I'm texting you her address and all the related information I can think of. Be sure to wear gloves. You don't want a concentrated amount of that stuff getting on your hands. Not that I think the skin absorbs it, but who knows?"

"No worries. It's a protocol we always follow. Trace evidence and all that."

"Not fingerprints?"

"Not easily discernible on gardening gloves. Which reminds me, how would I know which ones were used? I doubt I could smell anything."

"Uh, gee, that's a good point. I would imagine they'd smell like potatoes. Maybe separate out the gloves and sniff them. If you're not sure, take all of them. Hmm, maybe that's not such a good idea because you'd have to get back in and return them. Better just sniff. I'm sure potatoes must have a smell."

Suddenly, Streetman's burgeoning skill was looking better and better. Still, I hadn't lost my mind.

"Okay. I'll think of something. Anyway, I've got work piling up."

When the call ended, I stared straight ahead and chastised myself for jumping into something headfirst. Then, I took swift action.

"Lyndy? It's me, Phee. Call me the second you get this voicemail."

I didn't have to wait long.

"What's up? Are you okay? Did anything awful happen?"

"No, no. Sorry to worry you, but I need your help. How good is your sense of smell?"

"My sense of smell? I suppose it's as good as anyone else's. I can smell cigarette smoke from a block away as well as cigars, garlic, and freshly baked bread. Why?"

"Because it's going to come in handy if you can help me out."

Lyndy didn't utter a word for the next minute or two as I gave her the rundown on Joyanne's theory and more importantly, my mother's brainchild to have Streetman do the investigating with his nose. Her response was nothing like I expected.

"Fine. What time? And I have to be at the office by nine, just so you know."

"You're the best, Lyndy! The absolute best!"

"You'd do the same for me, only I can't imagine a scenario where I'd ask someone to sniff out poison."

We agreed to meet at the Starbucks on Grand and Reems at five in the morning and take one car. Then we'd drive over to Tunnie's house in Lyndy's car, and park it on an adjacent street just in case a neighborhood nosy-body was looking out their window.

"We'll have to work fast," I said. "I've got my mother on hold, but it won't last that long."

"Got it."

Having a good friend is one thing, but having one who's willing to get a desk appearance ticket for breaking and entering is a rare gift.

And just as I began to feel as if I was in control of the situation, I remembered the Boyer's Café chat with my mother and Shirley after work. Too bad I never mastered a poker face. But maybe they wouldn't notice if they were otherwise occupied eating brownies.

• • •

"Good luck, Phee," Augusta said when the workday ended and we locked up. "I'll be sure to have victory donuts here in the morning for you."

"Victory, sympathy, whatever . . . but thanks, Augusta."

I expected to see my mom and Shirley at Boyer's, but lo and behold, Aunt Ina and Myrna were there as well. Already munching on a platter of brownies and who knows what else. I took a breath as I passed the window where they were all seated and walked inside to join them.

"We have to act fast, Phee," my mother said. No "hello." No "make yourself comfortable," just "we have to act fast."

"Um, nice to see everyone. I'm going to get something to eat and I'll be right back."

With my order for chicken salad and a small iced tea in play, I returned to the table like a prisoner awaiting his or her sentence. But rather than putting it off, I took the direct approach.

"I know why we're all here and yes, what my mother and Shirley overheard today was quite enlightening, but think about the consequences." Then I looked at my mom. "And yes, yes, Streetman is probably becoming very well-versed with smells." *What a liar I am!* "But he's still quite new at it and as such, could easily make a mistake that could prove to be an embarrassment for all of us." *Not to mention that the dog himself is an embarrassment at times . . .*

"Hmm, that does make sense, but all of us can smell, too. Isn't that right, Ina?" my mother asked.

My aunt crinkled her nose as if she was a contestant on the *Million Dollar Question*. "I can smell exotic aromas and pungent aromas. Also noxious odors. At one time, I could discern the varied scents of rose petals, but breathing this dust-filled air has compromised my once potent skill."

"I'll take that as a no." I shrugged my shoulders and looked at the other ladies. "Face it, none of us have that kind of ability to detect a potato spud smell on a gardening glove. My suggestion is to somehow plant this idea in Bowman and Ranston's heads and let them get a search warrant and bring in a highly trained K-9 dog."

Silence.

"Okay," I said. "Here's the deal. All of you refrain from this DIY endeavor and I'll make sure to convince the deputies to take action."

The women looked at each other and nodded.

"We'll be praying for you, Phee," Shirley said. "Those two are not the easiest to contend with."

I smiled. "Don't worry. I can handle it."

Liar, liar, liar. I am the worst liar going. And I got away with it, too. I had better be pushing the victory button in the morning.

Chapter 23

In retrospect, I should have known better. My mother never acquiesces so quickly. And without an argument, no less. Had I not had so much on my mind regarding the ring-finger hand, Marshall's cat chase and Barry's murder, I would have realized I had been duped.

I'd gotten a brief text from Marshall at a little past one stating: *Closer than ever. Don't worry. Am on the ground. Not a tightrope.* I figured if there was more to it, Augusta would have called or texted, regardless of the hour.

At three forty-five Tuesday morning, I showered, dressed, grabbed some coffee and a Trader Joe's mini apple pie before taking off for the Starbucks on Grand. Too bad Lyndy and I would be gone before they opened.

True to plan, we ditched my car at the far end of the lot and jumped in hers for our escapade at Tunnie's place. Before Lyndy parked, we drove past Tunnie's house and pulled over to make sure she'd be on her way to the agricultural garden. Fortunately, we didn't have to wait long. Tunnie's garage door opened and out came a beige SUV that veered right, oblivious to the silver one we were seated in a few houses down.

"I'll wait a sec and then park on the other street," Lyndy said. "We can walk fast."

And walk fast, we did. No need to worry about time at the gym. I got in my morning exercise for sure.

When we got to Tunnie's house, I wasted no time locating the key under the garden gnome by the row of bougainvillea. Using the flashlight from my iPhone, I unlocked the side garage door and closed it behind us.

"Holy mackerel!" Lyndy stepped over a mound of laundry that blocked the path to the washer. "And I think *I* let stuff pile up. This makes my house look like Martha Stewart lives there."

"Yeah, it's more than I bargained for. We'd better start rooting." I handed her the evidence gloves we use and both of us put them on before making a move. "We're going to need a brighter light than the security light she's got in the garage, but I don't want to turn anything on or someone might think Tunnie's still here."

"How about if I hold both of our phone lights and you can start. Just toss the gardening gloves into another pile and we can sniff them out when we're done."

"Sounds like a plan to me."

What we didn't count on was the fact that no one can hold on to a flashlight, no matter the size, without shaking it. It was like performing surgery with a strobe light.

"Anything that remotely resembles a glove is getting tossed into that pile," I said.

Within minutes, the glove pile started to resemble a small hill. And that's when Lyndy and I heard the unmistakable sound of someone at the side garage door.

"Rats," I whispered to her. "Tunnie's back. She probably forgot something but didn't want to drive in. Hurry and hide behind those freestanding cabinets over there."

We moved so fast that I was worried I'd stumble and fall over something. I heard a rattling sound at the side garage door and turned stone-cold when I recognized the voice.

"You won't need to take out that lock pick you bought on Amazon, Harriet. The door's open."

Harriet? Lock pick? Amazon? Oh, rats!

"We can get up, Lyndy," I said. "And welcome our guests—my mother and Myrna."

As I brushed off some dust from my clothes, Lyndy nudged me. "Your aunt's here, too. Along with Shirley."

I aimed my cell phone light at the crew and walked toward them. "Don't touch anything." Then I took a closer look at my mother.

"I can't believe it! You brought the dog!"

"Of course I brought the dog. Who else is going to sniff out the poisoned gloves? Luckily, Streetman hates potatoes."

"Mom, I asked you to stay home."

"The same could be said for you."

"I brought Lyndy, not a militia."

"Four people is not a militia." She looked at Shirley and my aunt. "Is it?"

"It doesn't matter. We're all here and we might as well continue where Lyndy and I left off. Maybe one of you can keep watch at the door."

"I'll be happy to do that," Shirley said. "I don't like dark places with mice and insects."

She was at the side door before I could respond and Streetman was rooting and jumping through the laundry before I could stop him.

"Mom! What if he pees on it? Put him on a leash or—Oh, no—he just lifted his leg! So much for a scent-detecting dog. Yikes! Now he's rolling around in the laundry! He's probably destroyed any possibility of identifying a scent."

"We don't know that. I say we find the glove and sniff it for pee. If it doesn't have any, we can put it in a separate pile and put the ones that were compromised in another pile."

"Compromised? That's a nice way of putting it."

As Lyndy and I approached the laundry, the odor was unmistakable. "I think it's too late, Mrs. Plunkett," she said.

With my own gloved hand, I reached into the pile to grab a floral gardening one. "Ew. Soaking wet. This is *not* going to work. And we can't very well leave a pile of pee-saturated clothing here. Tunnie will think a raccoon or coyote got inside. Which, by the way, may have been better. Streetman is tearing some unmentionables apart. Look!"

My mother immediately scooped up the dog with one hand and some laundry with the other. She tossed the laundry into the washing machine, and for one wishful moment I pictured the dog getting washed instead.

"Shouldn't you separate the whites from the colors?" my aunt asked.

"There's no time. We've got to separate the pee from the material."

My aunt tapped my mother on the shoulder. "Harriet, don't you think Tunnie is going to get suspicious when she comes home to find out there's a load of laundry in her washer?"

My mother shook her head. "Relax. Tunnie will think she put it in the washer and forgot. This is Sun City West. People do stuff like that all the time. Louise told me her next-door neighbor took the garbage out in her babydoll pajamas and when she bent over, Louise saw that the woman didn't have underwear on. We've got an excuse. We're seniors, after all."

"Excuse or not, this is horrible," I said. "We better get out of here before Tunnie gets back or someone shows up."

Suddenly, a car pulled up to the garage. Thoughts of being fingerprinted by Bowman and Ranston immediately sprang to mind.

"I guess I spoke too soon. I think it's too late for that."

Just then, Shirley called out, "Someone's just using the driveway to turn around. I peeked."

"Okay, we need to leave now. All of us. Where did you park? And please don't tell me right in front."

"We took Shirley's big Buick and it's a few houses down," my aunt replied.

And then, the unthinkable. Streetman, having had his fill of rollicking in dirty laundry, sniffed the air and went directly toward some crates that were stacked up in the corner of the garage. One good push from his head and ka-bang! The first crate toppled over and with it dozens of potatoes. All sizes. All shapes. And all of them with tubers.

"Aha! She's been cultivating poison all this time," my mother said.

"She's been stockpiling potatoes, for heaven's sake." I went to upright the crate to return the potatoes when I realized that they were not the only thing Tunnie had been cultivating.

"Um, I don't think potatoes were her main interest."

"What do you mean?" Lyndy walked to where I stood and started to pick up some of the potatoes. Then she saw what I saw. "It says Dalstrong Gladiator Series Meat Cleaver on the side of the sheath. Take a look."

I picked up the meat cleaver and read the other side of the sheath. "Yeesh. It even comes with a nickname—the Obliterator."

"Are you thinking what I'm thinking?" Lyndy asked.

And then, everyone crowded around as my aunt shouted, "We found the murderous killer of the body that belongs to the hand with the ring. The wrist was severed and I bet Tunnie did the severing with that obliteration knife of hers. That's why she hid it in the potatoes."

"Lordy, that woman's a poisoner and a knife-wielding maniac. Ladies, I am running back to my car. Running."

With that, Shirley took off like a world-class sprinter and didn't look behind her. My mother called out from the open side door, "Meet us at Bagels 'n More. I'll have Phee drive us."

"First we get these potatoes back in the crate," I said, "and put the crate back where it was, including the Gladiator or Obliterator, or whatever you call it. Then check the wash. Then out of here."

Oddly enough, the five of us wasted no time getting things in order and getting ourselves out of there and hustling around the corner to Lyndy's car. Shirley was on her own for at least a block.

"I hope you don't mind dog hair," my mother told Lyndy.

Lyndy took a breath as we reached the car. "Nah. It beats everything else we've come across."

As she drove down the block, I turned to my mother, who was crammed in the backseat with my aunt, Myrna, and the dog. "Not a word of this," I said. "Until we can figure it out."

"I'm one step ahead of you," my aunt said. "And I may have a plan."

"Gun it," I said to Lyndy. "And drive us off the nearest bridge!"

Chapter 24

"Are you sure you don't want to join us for a quick coffee at Bagels 'n More?" my mother asked me.

"We've got to get to work. It's almost eight."

"Don't worry, the four of us will flesh out my plan while we have breakfast." My aunt turned to my mother and added, "The only kink in the armor will be Louis if they get back too soon from Las Vegas."

"Hold on a sec, Aunt Ina." *And don't flesh out that plan. Flush it down the toilet.* "Whatever you do, don't act on anything yet. Tossing ideas around is one thing, but going full-blown Rizzoli and Isles is another. And speaking of my uncle, do you have any word on him? Last I heard was a text from Marshall around one this morning. He said they were getting close."

My aunt shook her head. "Not yet, but when Louis is entrenched at a roulette wheel or poker table or whatever gambling games he plays, he loses all track of time. Sometimes days."

Wonderful.

"If I hear anything, I'll let you know."

I leaned into the car and made sure to look at everyone. "Please, if you do come up with a plan, put it on paper, not in action. Okay?"

"Honestly, Phee," my mother said as she stroked Streetman, "you worry too much."

Had it been Cecilia, Louise and Lucinda in the car and not Shirley, Myrna and my aunt, I wouldn't have been as concerned. They seemed to be the more reasonable ones in the group. But today's entourage spelled disaster with a capital D. First, the impulse control. None of those ladies had any. Then, the penchant for drama. Theirs was Academy Award material. I stiffened my shoulders and stepped away as Shirley moved the Buick forward. Two blocks later and the ladies got into her car. Dog hair and all.

A minute after that, Lyndy waved them off and rubbed the back of her head. "We've got time for a quick coffee. McDonald's is right across Grand. What do you say?"

"Egg McMuffin. Let's go."

"Any chance the women will change their minds and go there?"

I shook my head. "Not a chance. Dogs aren't allowed inside, and after a disastrous experience with Streetman at the outdoor seating, they removed it altogether."

"Seriously? They removed the seating?"

"Sure did. No more outdoor chairs."

"What did he do?"

"Do you want the alphabetized list?"

"Nah. Just spout off."

"Got loose. Jumped on patrons' laps and stole their burgers. Knocked French fries on the ground and ate them. Took small ice cream cone from a baby in a stroller. Also licked her face. Peed on empty chairs. Had issue with someone's leg and peed on that, too. My mother had to cough up more money to compensate those people than paying for a cruise."

Lyndy burst out laughing. "McDonald's it is."

Two sips of coffee later, and a few bites of my Egg McMuffin, a text from my mother appeared.

"Ugh. Now what?" I said out loud. "They've been gone what? Five minutes?"

I looked down and read it out loud. *"Louis is getting a tetanus shot at the ER near the Bellagio. The hospital called your aunt to find out when he last had one."*

"Do you think that means they found the cat?" Lyndy widened her eyes and took another sip of coffee.

"Who knows? No one in my family seems to be able to communicate directly. It's as if I need an interpreter to get through the day."

Just then, another text came in. It was from Marshall and it was an attachment with one image. I immediately pulled it up.

"Holy cow! It's my uncle holding a hairless cat with a gold collar. He seems to be squirming."

"The cat or your uncle?"

I showed the photo to Lyndy.

"That probably explains the ER visit. Cat scratch fever maybe."

"Keep your fingers crossed it's Princess and Queen Empress Trudalia."

Then another text. This time from Augusta: *Your uncle's gambling paid off. They ransomed the cat. Owners are flying into Vegas today on the first flight they can get. The guys are tied up with police and paperwork. The text Mr. Williams sent me said they'd be back tomorrow if all goes well. How did your mission go?*

I texted back: *My mother showed up with Streetman.* I followed it with a series of angry emojis and a thumbs-down. Then I added: *If you text the guys, tell them to come back sooner.* I put a smiley face and a laughing one after the word *sooner.*

"That's great news, Phee," Lyndy said when I read her the text from Augusta. "The round-the-world cat chase is over."

"I know, but the butcher knife in the potato crate means another chase is on the way. And my mother will want to lead the charge."

"How do you think it got there? Seems an unlikely place for someone to stash a murder weapon. Unless they were —"

"Set up?"

"Exactly. But by who? It couldn't have been Joyanne or she would have directed me to the food storage crates instead of the laundry. I'll have to tell her that I was unsuccessful but I'm not saying a word about that discovery."

"Too bad you didn't have time to pull it out from the sheath to see if there was blood on it."

I shook my head and took another bite of my McMuffin. Then I replied, "Even the most amateurish killer would have sense enough to wipe the weapon clean. Of course, those forensic techs can pinpoint the most minuscule evidence of blood. Still, we'll never know. It might not be a weapon at all. It could be a Christmas or birthday gift Tunnie hid for a boyfriend. Joyanne said she was single."

"You're certainly the optimist."

And just as I thought today's crime-solving venture had reached its conclusion, the most frightening of all texts came in from Shirley: *I am in the ladies' room. Harriet doesn't know I am writing to you. She and your aunt think we should go back to see if there's blood on the knife.*

I texted back one word in all caps: *NO!* Then, because I didn't trust my mother, I phoned her and told Lyndy while I waited to be connected.

"I believe the cat has been found but that's not why I called. Tunnie should be getting home any time now. Whatever you do, stay away from her house."

"Did Shirley call you?"

"She didn't have to. I can read your mind. Listen, the guys will be getting home tomorrow from Las Vegas and I have every intention of telling them what happened. The deputies are running those investigations, not us."

"We still haven't heard your aunt's plan."

"Whatever it is, tell her you'll take it under advisement. I've got to go, Mom. Maybe watch the news or something. Uncle Louis may be on it with the cat."

When I ended the call, Lyndy shook her head. "Got to hand it to you, Phee. You can maneuver around a situation like nobody's business."

"You've met my mother. I've had lots of practice."

When I got back to the office, Augusta couldn't wait to pepper me with questions about my undercover escapade in Tunnie's garage. I gave her the complete rundown, leading right up to our current situation.

"You *do* know what that means, don't you? If not, let me clue you in— a worse plan is developing like a hurricane in the Gulf of Mexico."

"I'm trying not to think about it. At least the guys will be back tomorrow so they can diffuse any whackadoodle idea that pops into my mother's head. I can't believe they located the cat. I can't imagine how it wound up at Cirque du Soleil."

"Underhanded dealings with one of the producers, from what little I could find out from Rolo. Between him navigating the dark web for us and your uncle's gambling prowess, Mr. Williams and Mr. Gregory slipped into motion like David Copperfield during a performance."

"One thing for sure. I'll be ecstatic when they get back. Meanwhile, I need to break the bad news to Joyanne. Not sure how's she's going to take it, but I can imagine."

"Hey, you did your best. Who would have predicted your mother would show up? And with that chiweenie to boot!"

"I need to get the image of Streetman peeing on the laundry out of my mind. Catch up in a while. I'd better get going."

A minute later, I booted up my computer and dialed Joyanne. Her voice was as exuberant as ever. "Tell me you found the glove! You *did* find the glove, didn't you?"

"Joyanne, there's no easy way to say this—the evidence got tampered with. It's been compromised."

"Compromised? How?"

"Um, let's just say it's in the wash." *And technically, I am not lying.*

"Oh, no. I'll just have to be on my guard, that's all. If Tunnie thinks I suspect her, I could be next. Um, while you were in her garage, did you notice anything suspicious?"

Like a hidden cleaver designed to cut through bone?

"Suspicious?"

"Like wrappers for nicotine patches in her trash. Tunnie is one of those people who always has a backup plan."

"Nothing out of the ordinary." *ABunch of people store butcher knives with their spuds.*

"I need to sleep on this. I've got to find a way to expose her."

"You're *that* sure she's responsible for Barry's death?"

"Yes."

"Keep in mind, there may be two killers—the nicotine patch and the tubers."

"Or one determined assassin."

Chapter 25

It was a little past three the next day when Nate, Marshall, and my uncle's plane landed. And while Uncle Louis took a limo home, our guys Ubered straight to the office. Unlike other ventures of the sort, they looked rested and energized.

"We did it, hon," Marshall announced when they charged in. I rushed toward him with a giant hug. Thanks to Augusta, who had her eyes glued to the street, I was all set to greet them.

"Tell us how you did it, Mr. Williams," she said. "The news had a short blurb with Phee's uncle holding a cat that looked like it was about to attack him."

"About? That thing *did* attack him! Priceless or not, that feline was extremely ill-tempered. Until her owners arrived. Then it was all purrs and snuggles. Go figure."

Nate explained how Uncle Louis gambled his way to information regarding the location of Princess and Queen Trudalia backstage at Cirque du Soleil. At least their exploit didn't involve any tightropes but it did involve skirting around the performers, and at one point, almost winding up onstage as the three of them played hide and seek until they found the cat.

Augusta rubbed her temple and looked at them. "Bet you're both glad to get away from ferocious felines and back to old-fashioned murder and body part cases."

Nate grimaced. "Don't remind me. Bowman and Ranston have been texting nonstop. We're being called to our county consult duty first thing tomorrow with a few of our usual cases sprinkled in."

"No more cat chases?" I asked.

The men looked at each other and Marshall responded, "Yes and no."

"Huh?"

"There's a cartel-like business that targets pedigreed cats and dogs. The network is more complex than anyone realized, but the FBI is tied up with human trafficking, not pets. The animal welfare leagues are working on it, but they need help. Given our success with two major cases, a number of agencies reached out to us. Right now, we don't have anything on the horizon, but that could change."

Augusta propped her elbows on her desk. "Do me a favor, gentlemen. Solve the dead body in the garden first, along with the severed hand out of nowhere. Phee's mother has reached a new level of . . . hmm, how can I put this delicately?"

And then, the men responded.

"Snooping?"
"Yenta-ing?"
"Nosy-ing around?"
"Breaking and entering?"
Augusta nodded. "Yep. All of the above."
I bit my lower lip and offered up a smile. "It's not as bad as you think." Then I glanced at Augusta. "Fine. It's worse. Much worse. Thank goodness you're both back!"

The rest of the day raced by as the men played catch-up while Augusta and I concentrated on what we were paid to do. And just when I began to think Nate and Marshall, along with the deputies, would pick up where my mother left off, she called.

"Herb just went home. He must have gotten a whiff of the pumpkin pie I picked up from the Homey Hut. Anyway, you don't have to worry about us going back to Tunnie's garage."

"Good."

"That's because we need to do something else."

Oh, please! Someone shoot me now!

"What? What have you got to do now?"

"First, let me explain. Herb and Bill were at Curley's bar last night for free chicken wings with every purchase of a draft. Or was it a free draft with every purchase of the wings?"

"It doesn't matter. Just get on with it."

"Fine. Orvis was there and he told Herb that Barry was poisoned by chewing on an unlit cigar. According to Orvis, Barry gummed cigars when the urge to smoke a cigarette got too strong. I suppose nicotine patches don't do the entire trick."

"And how did Orvis know that the cigar was poisoned?"

"Because he overheard a conversation the day before Barry's body was discovered. He was in the men's room at the garden. The women's stalls are right on the other side and only thin plank board separated them. He heard everything."

"What did he hear? What did Herb tell you?"

"Keep in mind that Orvis had been drinking."

Wonderful. A really credible source.

"Okay. Okay. Now tell me."

"Orvis heard the woman say, and this isn't verbatim, 'Glad he used to smoke like a chimney and chews like a cow. Made it so much easier. Now all we have to do is sit back and wait.'"

"What did the other woman say?"

"That's all Herb knows. But don't you see? This still doesn't let Tunnie off the hook. For all we know, she could have been one of the women in the stall. This piece of information just moves our investigation to a new locale."

"What new locale? The women's restroom?"

"Don't be flippant, Phee. Our investigation needs to move along."

"Our investigation? This isn't our investigation. The men are back and they're meeting with Bowman and Ranston first thing in the morning."

"That's perfect. We can get on with phase two this afternoon. When you get out of work."

"There *is* no phase two."

"There is now. It's a perfectly benign plan."

"Listen, I have work to do. Please refrain from phase two. I will call you later. Okay?"

"Okay. And then you can thank me. Or Herb."

I pressed my fingers right above my nose and took a deep breath. Then, I stepped outside my office and walked to Augusta's desk. Before she uttered a word, I told her about Herb's encounter with Orvis and the new cigar scenario.

Augusta wasn't surprised. In fact, it was almost the opposite.

"A cigar, huh?" she said. "Reminds me of the sausage death a few decades ago in Plattville, a stone's throw from Iowa, where my cousins lived. Anyway, the local judge was found dead in his chambers having consumed a sausage roll. No visible signs of tampering, and it took forever for the lab back then to figure out that the thing was stuffed with more than toss-away pork parts."

"Ew!"

"The murderer seasoned it with wisteria seeds. Fatal for sure. Since sausage usually contains fennel, sage and cloves, the judge probably thought the seeds were supposed to be there. Anyway, the sheriff's office decided to check out the judge's freezer since it was a homemade sausage roll and not from a restaurant."

"And?"

"They found tiny pinpricks where the seeds were thrust inside the casing. The murderer wasn't about to take any chances and poisoned the whole lot of them."

"The wife?"

"Nope. The refrigerator repairman's nephew, whom the judge had sentenced for fifteen years on a robbery."

"And what does this have to do with a cigar?"

"Think about it. Someone could have easily poked tiny holes into the cigar and added poison. Real easy with a syringe."

"I wonder if my mother is thinking the same thing. And without benefit of your sausage story."

Planted 4 Murder

"Looks like you'll be tackling phase two after all."

"The only thing I want to tackle is Marshall's dirty laundry."

"You'll have plenty of time for that, but my curiosity is getting piqued. Call your mother back and find out what she has in mind. Face it, it's the only entertainment around here."

I gave Augusta "the look" and retreated to my office. Five minutes later, I phoned my mother.

"Okay," I said. "What's phase two?"

"I knew you'd come around. Orvis told Herb that Barry always hid a cigar or two in a ziplock bag under a mound of dirt in the back of his garden plot. Not likely the forensic crew knew about it. All we have to do is find the dirt and dig it up. Then look for holes in the cigars."

"And suppose we find the holes. Then what? March over to Bowman and Ranston's office and plop the cigars on their desks?"

"Don't be ridiculous. We figure out a way to make Bowman and Ranston re-dig up the cigars and test them. Then we tell Nate and Marshall."

I remained still as I tried to process what she had just said. It almost seemed logical.

"Phee? Are you still there?"

"Uh, yeah. I don't like this idea but when did you want to snoop and dig around in Barry's plot?"

"At dusk. Everyone's gone by then. And how hard could it be to find a mound of dirt?"

"Dusk turns into nightfall pretty quick. And it's all dirt, even when illuminated by a flashlight."

"Then we'll have to be quick. I had Shirley check the sunset times. It's around six. She wasn't sure if we wanted civil sunset or nautical and got confused by the chart."

"Six is close enough. I'll meet you over there."

Augusta gave me the thumbs-up when I told her, but I wasn't so sure. The only plus side to all of this was that Marshall told me he and Nate would be working late to catch up and that he'd be happy eating peanut butter and jelly for dinner. Yay for small favors.

When I left work at five, I drove straight to the agricultural plots. Wedge heels and all. My mother, Shirley, and Lucinda were waiting for me by the gate.

"Everyone's gone home," Lucinda said. "We've got the all-clear."

"And don't worry about any of us getting poisoned from touching those cigars. We came prepared with gardening gloves. And I have a pair for you, too, Phee." My mother handed me an ugly pair of gray gloves and I slipped them on.

"Thanks."

Then, without wasting another minute, we walked over to Barry's plot. Only someone else was already there. I saw the dark figure from a distance and held out my arms to block my mother and Shirley, but Lucinda was already a few steps ahead of us.

Then, she saw what I did and immediately spun around, waving for us to duck into the nearest plot and crouch down on the ground. Trampling over someone's carefully tendered plants, we huddled together and waited.

An instant later, the slender figure of a woman ran down Lettuce Lane and out of the community garden before any of us could identify her.

"I don't think she was looking for incriminating evidence," Lucinda said. "It could have been a homeless person looking for food or a place to sleep, and we might have scared her off. I mean, if we could see her, maybe she saw us."

"We better not waste any more time." I stood and dusted myself off. "The sun is starting to set already."

And with that, we made our way to Barry's plot, flashlights at the ready, just in case.

Chapter 26

"Oh, no," I said as we approached. "With all of this subterfuge, we forgot about a shovel or even a trowel."

"Barry had lots of them strewn all over his plot. That's why I didn't mention it." Lucinda tried to get her hair to stay behind her ears but it was useless.

My mother picked up speed as if this was a race and beat us to the plot. "Lucinda was right. It's a regular mine field of gardening tools. All we need to do is find the likely spot."

Oh, brother. The likely spot.

"Herb said it was a mound on the back of the plot." She rushed inside and, taking out her own phone, shone a light on it, even though it was pretty visible in the sunset sky. "Aha, right in plain sight. And it looks like someone started to dig it up."

"Probably the woman who ran off." Lucinda put on her gardening gloves and was the first to approach the mound. "I don't want to destroy the evidence so I'll use one of those trowels. Whoever was here first got a good start but it doesn't look like she found anything. Boy, talk about good timing for us."

The three of us bent down and Lucinda began to dig. To make it easier, I pointed my phone at the ground and my mother did the same with hers. Seconds later, Lucinda announced, "I hit something hard. I hope it's not a big rock. Herb said the cigars were supposed to be in a Ziplock bag. Good grief. I can't believe Barry went through all this trouble to chew on something disgusting."

"Dig around it," my mother said. "That should loosen it."

Lucinda continued and much to our astonishment, she unearthed a small wooden cigar box.

"It came right out," she said. "I'll put it on the small table over there where he's got all those jars and bowls."

I looked around to be sure we were the only ones excavating where we shouldn't have been. "There's no lock on it but wait! Put on our masks in case there's something in the air that could be dangerous. Lately nothing surprises me."

Lucinda lifted the lid and sure enough, there were five new cigars, all labeled Montecristo. Along with them was a disgusting chewed one with a short nub.

"Okay, we found our prize," I said. "Now what?"

My mother looked around as if Union or Confederate spies were everywhere. "Now we do something that would give Bowman and Ranston a reason to find these cigars."

"Like what?" I shuddered at the possibilities.

"Give me a minute. I can't be expected to come up with something at the drop of a hat."

"You've had all day, Mom!"

"I have an idea." Lucinda looked around and shook my mother's arm. "How fast can you drive to Walmart?"

"What?" My mother and I replied at the same time.

"Walmart. Halloween decorations are already out. Buy one of those fake bloody hands and we'll put it over the spot where we dug. We'll leave a threatening note near it."

"Lucinda," I said, "they'll think it's just a prank. Besides, the gardeners will see it before Bowman and Ranston even get here. But I may have another idea in a similar vein. We rebury the box and get an anonymous message to the deputies that says, 'I poisoned Barry's soil.' They'll have no choice but to check things out. And that mound is pretty obvious."

"What do you think, Harriet?"

"Working in that detective agency is paying off for Phee."

I rolled my eyes and gestured for the box to be returned to its hiding place. We exited the gardens as the last of the twilight skies turned dark. Shirley was still at the gate eyeballing her phone. "I was about to call you."

"Did you get a good look at the woman who ran out of here?" my mother asked. "You were supposed to be keeping watch."

"What woman? I didn't see any woman. Oh, Lordy! Tell me it wasn't a ghost."

I walked to where she stood and looked around. "I can guarantee it wasn't a ghost. Look over to your left. That part of the fence is chain-link and it goes right into someone's backyard. Whoever was trampling around in Barry's plot must have exited from over there. See? It wouldn't have been the first time. The top of the chain-link fence is bent. It's been climbed over before. Lots of times, I imagine."

"Come on, Shirley," my mother said. "Lucinda and I will tell you what we found."

"Can you tell me over dinner? I'm famished. And we're right across the road from Texas Roadhouse or Outback."

"I have to get home, ladies. But before you leave, let me reiterate what I said earlier. I will get the anonymous message to the deputies. Do not, under any circumstances, mess it up. Okay?"

"Honestly, Phee, you're becoming so bossy."

"It runs in the family."

As I walked to my car, I overheard Shirley say, "What anonymous message? And forget waiting until we get to the restaurant. Tell me now what you found. Unless it was another hand. Then I don't want to know."

I unlocked my car and jumped in before the women could begin their cigar saga. Then, I pondered over how on earth to get an anonymous message to Bowman and Ranston. As I headed out of Sun City West, one name came to mind, but I needed a burner phone to reach him.

No sooner did I get home and change into jeans and a top when I heard Marshall's car pulling into the garage. I rushed to the kitchen, took out a Trader Joe's ham, gruyere, and caramelized onion flatbread from the freezer and put it in the air fryer just as he opened the door.

"Something smells good," he said.

"It'll be ready by the time you get comfortable. I also have some broccoli and carrot salad."

"Great. I'll fill you in on the latest updates."

"Uh, yeah. Me too."

A few minutes and bites of flatbread later, I said, "Why don't you start?"

"No problem. Well, okay, two problems—Bowman and Ranston, but that's to be expected. First of all, the deputies and the forensic team checked Barry's house and car. They didn't find anything that would bring us closer to finding out who murdered him."

"Any next of kin? Greedy relatives?"

"Only an ex-wife and she's also got a plot with the agriculture club. Joyanne McGuire, although according to Ranston, she went back to her maiden name—Valk. Trust me when I tell you the deputies will be grilling her like a steak."

"Um, yeah. About that, there's something you should know. Well, lots of somethings." I bit my lip and smiled. "She approached me at the garden. Terrified she'd be a suspect."

"Right now, she's the only one with a traditional motive."

"Traditional motive?"

"You know, ex-wife and all that. Plus, she used to be a smoker. And with a little poking around, the deputies found out she used nicotine patches to quit the habit."

I started to say something but Marshall continued. "It's hardly credible evidence. Zillions of people use them, but it just adds more Pick-up sticks to the pile."

"And speaking of piles, there are two of them I need to tell you about—laundry and dirt."

"I left that much dirty laundry before I went to Vegas?"

"No, not you. Tunnie. And I don't know who left the dirt."

"I must have been gone way too long or you've been hanging around with the book club ladies way too much. I am completely befuddled."

"You won't be for long. Here goes."

I watched the expressions on Marshall's face as I wove through the details of the Tunnie garage escapade and the reason, aka Joyanne, behind it. Then, while I still had the momentum, I launched into cigar stub excavation. When I finally finished, all Marshall said was, "Oh."

CHAPTER 27

Next thing I knew, he burst out laughing. "Honestly, in the deep recesses of my mind I somehow knew you'd get tangled up. You can't help it. It's that kind heart of yours combined with a penchant for investigating. Toss in your mother's wacky women friends and well, what can I say? I'm just glad nothing awful happened at night in the garden."

"Um, actually, it was more like dusk. Early dusk."

"Dusk. Night. It's the same thing. We have no idea what lunatics are lurking about."

I do. The book club ladies. And Herb.

"I figured there'd be safety in numbers. Plus, all those Screamer devices they have. Anyway, I need to figure out how to get our favorite deputies to mill around in Barry's plot."

"I think I can help you out with that. With all the interviewing we've been doing, I'll pass on the word that 'rumor has it Barry may have been poisoned by chewing on a laced cigar tip.' Then I'll let it slip that he was observed hiding his stash in the back corner of his plot. That should send them snooping around."

I threw my arms around him and gave him the tightest hug ever. "That's a relief. It'll also get my mother off my back, even if it's only for a little while. I'm still stymied at who the woman was that we saw sneaking out of Barry's plot and disappearing. I'll ask my mother to stroll over to the chain-link fence in the morning with Lucinda or Louise and see if they spot anything that the woman could have dropped."

"Good idea. Bowman texted us a short while ago. He's sending a forensic update on the severed hand for us to look over in the morning. I'm not sure it will yield much, but you never know. Anyway, let's finish eating and make up for lost time."

"Absolutely!"

• • •

While Marshall and Nate studied the forensic report the next morning before conferring with Bowman and Ranston, I presented my latest course of action to Augusta during our break.

"Let me get this straight," she said. She propped her chin on the back of her hand and eyeballed me. "You want to create an 'extended link' murder map of the agriculture club's players."

"That's right. Sort of like a friend of a friend of a friend. The direct connections don't seem to be giving us the information we need. But suppose for a minute that someone was friends with gardener A, who happened to be related to gardener B, who happened to have been a business partner with gardener C, who lost a major business deal, causing gardener B to lose his or her investment. Then it would give gardener A—"

"A reason to poke his eyes out with a fork? Good grief. That scenario is worse than the ones they used to use on standardized tests."

"I'm just going to look for the not-so-obvious connections. At least it's a paper and pencil project and not traipsing around into goodness knows where."

"Okey-dokey, keep me posted, Sherlock. By the way, are you the least bit curious about that forensic report on the hand? I made a copy for our files."

"What? Of course. Show me!"

Augusta pulled out a paper from her files and handed it to me. "It's strewn with a lot of medical mumbo-jumbo but I know the word *arthritis* when I see it. That hand was arthritic. *Really* arthritic. Whoever's body it belonged to was no spring chicken."

The report was only two pages and I read it twice as Augusta worked at her desk. She paused for a second and turned to me. "Read over that part about contradictions on the 'point of dislodging.'"

"I did. According to this, what was first deemed a clean cut is not so clean after all. The language is a bit confusing. Evidence is suggestive of industrial machinery but it doesn't rule out a sharp meat cleaver."

"Read the next paragraph again."

"I did. It said, 'Notwithstanding, an accidental encounter with a sharp surface, given the appropriate amount of force, could yield the same or similar result.'"

"Yep. Someone could have slammed that body onto something really sharp and the hand got the raw end of the deal. I'm thinking one of those workbench saws that half the men in Sun City West have in their garages."

"Or the metal shop. Some of their machinery is downright scary. I was in there once with my mother and Shirley. Shirley bought an outdoor metal art decoration for her patio wall. A giant sun with a huge smiling face."

"Really?"

"You're not saying 'really' because you're interested in Shirley's wall art. You're saying it because you think we should find out if any of the gardeners are also in the metalwork club."

"Harrumph. I didn't think I was that obvious."

"You are. And you had a good idea. I'll add it to my mother's list. She's the one with all the free time, not me."

"Now you're making sense."

I might have been making sense but I should have factored in the hoopla that would go along with my mother's snooping. Beginning with checking out the chain-link fence area. Shortly after Augusta and I talked about the forensic report on the hand, my mother called to let me know she had a lovely conversation with the woman whose property butted up against the chain-link fence.

"Iris, that's the woman's name, planted a thick row of oleander to hide the hideous chain-link fence. She told me all about it this morning when Lucinda got her sweater caught in one of the links."

"How'd she get her sweater caught? I thought you were just looking on the ground."

"She needed to see the other side and thought she'd climb up a few notches. She said she used to do that all the time when she was in the sixth grade."

"The sixth grade? That's over sixty years ago."

"Lucinda is still nimble. Unlike Myrna or your aunt."

"Never mind. What happened?"

"Iris was outside watering some flowers when she heard us and walked over. By then, Lucinda had extricated her sweater. No damage."

"Uh-huh."

"Anyway, the three of us got to talking and Iris saw a woman rush through the back of her yard. She said the woman trampled her flowers and knocked over a potted plant on her patio. Her motion sensor light came on in the yard and Iris happened to be at the kitchen sink, so she looked out the window. She thought it was maybe a coyote but was taken aback when she saw it was a woman."

"That's terrific. Did she get a description or call the posse?"

"Dark clothes. And a hoodie. She couldn't see the woman's face."

"That figures. What about the posse?"

"She didn't call them because the woman scooted out of there too fast. She said the only thing she saw, and it was just for a split second, was one of those reflector emblems on the back of the hoodie."

"What kind? What color? What shape?"

"She said it looked like a gang insignia."

"A gang insignia?"

"That's what she said."

"Do you think she could sketch it for you? Wait! No! I have a better idea. Listen, Marshall is going to plant a seed in Bowman and Ranston's collective heads so they'll scope out Barry's buried cigars. That keeps us out of the equation. No sense putting us in by having the woman make a sketch for you. I have a better idea."

"What?"

"Pay Iris a visit. Bring her something nice from the Homey Hut or

Bagels 'n More. And ask her to please go to the posse office and report the incident for their files. Have her tell them she thought the emblem was a gang insignia and that she and her neighbors are worried about gang members infiltrating the neighborhood. The posse will have no choice but to have the sheriff's office look into it. And when they do, it will put us one step closer to finding out who that woman intruder was."

"Are you thinking it was a gang member, too?"

"Oh, heck no! I'm thinking it was either a designer label or a team logo. Football, baseball, ice hockey, basketball . . . you name it. Half those logos are pretty intimidating, especially if you don't follow sports."

"I don't know who the better family detective is. You or my Streetman."

"I'm about to gag, Mom. Anyway, visit Iris, okay?"

"I'll call Lucinda and Louise and get back to you later."

"Sounds good. Um, there's one more thing. In all of your prying around, see if you can find out if anyone in that close-knit agriculture gardening club is also in the metal club. If not, see if you can get a list of club members from the rec center."

"Why? What do the gardeners have to do with the metalworkers?"

"There's a slight, um, very slight, chance that the hand was severed by a piece of machinery in the metal club."

"What? Now we have a metal club killer?"

"No! That's not what I said. The forensics lab is trying to determine how the hand was severed from the rest of the body, that's all. The subject of machinery came up when Augusta and I talked about it, that's all. I figured while you were out and about, you could check our theory."

"So there's no metal club killer?"

"No. None that we know of."

"Honestly, Phee, you put my hairs on edge sometimes."

Look who's talking.

"I guess that means you'll do it."

"It will take time and that means I won't have as much to devote to my little prince."

Oh no. I know where this is going.

"Okay, okay. I'll take Little Lord Fauntleroy to the dog park."

"Plan on Tuesday, if not sooner. And think of everything else you can pry out of Cindy."

"Oh, believe me, I won't miss the opportunity. Thanks, Mom. Catch you later."

When the phone call ended, it was as though I returned to earth following a lunar landing. It took me a good minute or two to reconcile what I had asked my mother to do. Then, another minute to pray she wouldn't mess it up.

Chapter 28

"I did it, Augusta. I just unleashed the kraken." I staggered to the Keurig and made myself a dark roast.

"Just your mother or the whole book club?"

"It will wind up being the entire club, but for once I'm delegating the investigating."

I went on to tell her about our conversation and the caveat that went with it—Streetman in the dog park.

"It could be worse, Phee. Herb could call for another one of his powwows."

"Ugh. Don't remind me. I need to wipe that thought out of my head entirely or I'll wind up with hives."

"Funny you should mention that. Hives, that is. Got a text from Mr. Williams. Seems Bowman wound up with a severe case of hives that he blames on stress. Or a possible food allergy. Or both. That means our guys will need to hustle on their minor investigations in order to focus on those two county ones."

"I think the real dilemma is not knowing if one or two murderers were involved in Barry's death."

"Would it really be two murderers if the first poison did the job and the second was just icing on the cake?"

"I honestly don't know. From what Marshall told me, our forensic lab is conferring with university research labs to see if a timeline determination can be made. Not that it makes a difference. There's at least one killer out there. And one targeted victim. I suppose that's comforting in a bizarre sort of way. Not a random killer unless the severed hand holds a few surprises."

"It doesn't or we'd know. Rolo follows up on all information like that hand. If other severed hands were discovered across the United States, we'd be looking at a whole new scenario."

"Your words are like comfort food for the soul, Augusta." I broke out laughing and returned with my coffee to my office.

And while the forensic labs seemed to move slowly in the next two days, the pace in our office didn't. Nate and Marshall were in and out of here juggling their routine cases with miscellaneous follow-up interviews for Bowman and some generalized gumshoeing, for lack of a better word. One good thing, though. With Bowman nursing his hives instead of giving them to everyone else, Ranston arranged for the forensic crew to scour Barry's garden plot and "find those stinking cigars."

It turned out to be a lucky break for us, but it also opened a new can of worms. It was a Saturday work morning for me and I had just returned to the office following a donut run. Augusta waved a paper in the air and announced, "It's a fax from the lab. I took a picture of it and texted it to Mr. Williams and Mr. Gregory. Here, read it for yourself."

She helped herself to a French cruller while I perused the message. "Holy cow! The short-chewed nib didn't match the brand of the unused cigars. Those were Montecristo ones and the lab identified the stub as Oliva Connecticut Reserve."

"Keep reading," Augusta said in between bites of her cruller. "That's not all they identified."

"Yeah, I see it right here—Solanum tuberosum. Potato poisoning. Oh, goodness, they also did a saliva DNA on the stub and it was Barry's. You know what that means, don't you?"

"Sure do! Now we're up to three murderers or one very, very determined person."

• • •

When Monday morning rolled around, Bowman was back on the job and feistier than usual. He sent two deputies to deliver letters to the active members of the agricultural gardening club, informing them to report to the posse office the following morning for questioning regarding "a new finding in the Barry McGuire case."

Naturally my mother was one of them, and when the deputy arrived around ten with the request, she literally flew off the rails and onto the phone.

"Phee! Do you hear me?"

"Of course I can hear you. The entire office can hear you, and I'm in my own office with the door closed." The last time I heard that hysterical voice was when Streetman managed to push open the screen to the patio door and jump into the UPS truck parked next door.

"Please don't tell me the dog got out."

"It could be worse. We are all being summoned to the posse office tomorrow. Now what?"

"Calm down. I believe I know what this is about and you have nothing to worry about. In fact, you're the one responsible for it."

"What?"

It took me a full five minutes to explain what had ensued regarding the cigars we found. But instead of relief, my mother fumed. "Those deputies should have sent me a thank-you card. Or better yet, a box of chocolates or maybe a nice plant. You should have warned me. I can't talk now. I have to let Lucinda and Louise know. And Shirley. Oh, and Herb. He can tell his buddies."

"Fine. But don't get too carried away."

"Carried away? I've seen episodes of *Death in Paradise*. I bet they're going to round up everyone and point to the killer."

"I seriously doubt that. Remember, we have evidence but nothing that links it to a specific person."

"Aarugh. What are Nate and Marshall doing in the meantime?"

"Reviewing notes and evidence at the posse office. Face it, this latest discovery set them back, not forward. They now have a third timeline to contend with in order to determine which toxin killed Barry. As far as Bowman and Ranston are concerned, they're not about to point a finger at anyone right now."

"Well, I'm pointing mine. And I dare not tell you which one."

I shuddered when the phone call ended, but I had to admit, it was my fault for not informing her. My mother simply cannot handle the unexpected. Both she and my aunt have to orchestrate everything or they implode. I only hoped it wouldn't deter her from paying a visit to Iris regarding that logo on the hoodie, and asking around to see who might also be in the metal club.

Then, the guilt set in. I wondered if I had piled too much on my mother. I rubbed the back of my neck and did what I always did when things got too stressful. I turned to the one thing that was rock solid in my life—mathematical calculations that gracefully appeared on my spreadsheets. Give me an Excel worksheet any day of the week and I'll take solace in numbers and figures.

An hour later, when I had eased into my workday, Augusta called out, "Get out the Lysol! Paul Schmidt is approaching the front door. I can see him out the window. He's with a scruffy-looking man. They better not be showing up with fish or bait."

I saved my work, took a breath, and walked to the door. "Don't overdo it, Augusta." Then I glanced at the door. "On second thought, an extra spray can't hurt. And the scruffy man is Orvis from the agriculture club. This could be a lucky break."

"No, a lucky break is if a sinkhole appears at our entrance."

"Hi, Paul! Hi, Orvis," I said as they walked inside the office. "What brings you to Glendale?"

"My civic duty."

I wanted to tell him we weren't law enforcement but I let it go. Paul waved at Augusta, who nodded and busied herself with the computer. "Orvis here finally sobered up, and when he did, he remembered whose voice he heard in the bathroom stall at the ag garden." Then Paul turned to Orvis. "Isn't that right, Orvis?"

Orvis scratched his shoulder and looked around. "I *said* I recognized the voice but not the one in the bathroom stall."

"What do you mean? What voice? You told me you recognized it."

"I did, Paul. I recognized the voice all right. It was Gussie's. He was right outside my stall and said, 'Hurry up, Orvis. Got to drain the monster. Glad this isn't one of those so-called family stalls where we have to share them with the women. Sounds like Maybelle is yakking over there with someone.'"

"Okay," I said. "So Orvis didn't recognize the voice, but Gussie did. Is that right?"

"Best to my recollection." Orvis nodded.

"And Gussie thought it was Maybelle."

Again Orvis nodded. "That's what I recollected."

"I told you Orvis would be a big help. That's why we rushed over here."

"Thank you. That really *is* a big help." I reached for a tissue in my pocket and feigned blowing my nose. I didn't know how much longer I could handle the odor of fish entrails and whatever else Lake Pleasant gifted Paul and Orvis with.

"Is there a reward if we catch Barry's killer?" Orvis asked Paul.

"Just the joy of doing your civic duty," I said and smiled. "Anyway, I'd hate to hold you up from whatever you've got planned."

"Just checking out bait shops."

"Well, thanks again." I maneuvered them to the doorway and rushed to hold it open. "Have a great day!"

Paul looked a little dazed but once outside, shouted, "You too!"

When I closed the door, Augusta reached for the Lysol.

"You're right," I laughed. "Can't spray enough for germs."

Chapter 29

When I awoke Tuesday morning, I remembered that it was the day I had agreed to bring Streetman to the dog park. *Agreed* in the general sense; *negotiated* would be more accurate.

"I'm grabbing a quick shower," I called out to Marshall. "I forgot I'm taking my mother's precious cargo to the dog park in exchange for her tracking down information for us."

He laughed. "Saves us payroll. Is it about the woman who ran out of Barry's plot in the dark?"

"Uh-huh. I wanted my mother to visit Iris, that's her name, and insist that she report what she observed to the posse. Then there's the not-so-small matter about the hand. It could have been the result of contact with the kind of machinery found at the metal shop. I told my mom to ask if anyone in that gardening group was also in the metal club. I said 'pretend you're interested in purchasing a piece of metal art. Easy-peasy. Nothing to raise any eyebrows.'"

"Mark my words, hon—if she finds someone and we can link them to the severed hand, that would be spectacular. Then again, she may just special-order a piece of metal art that resembles the dog."

"Ugh. By the way, I'm going to use my break and lunchtime to stop by the posse office during the Bowman-Ranston inquisition today and see if I can chat with Maybelle. If what Orvis said was true, she may indeed be the person who had it in for Barry."

"You think she'll let down her guard with you?"

"I can try. Intimidation from the deputies can only go so far. What's on your docket other than the smaller cases?"

"Working on timeline specificity as well as deeper background checks on some of the agriculture club members. Don't mean to upstage you, but Nate and I have already mapped out an extended link into the relationships among the group. Now you can practice what you do best—extracting information without anyone knowing it."

"You give me more credit than I deserve."

"Hardly." He tossed the covers from the bed, stood and threw his arms around me. Then it was off to the shower and the dog park.

Cindy Dolton was in her usual spot by the fence with Bundles a few feet away. Streetman charged over, sniffed Bundles and promptly peed on the nearest rock before darting to the other side of the park.

"Hey, Phee, I wondered when you'd pop back over here. Not that I gleaned a whole lot of information since we last talked, but what I did find out is worth hearing."

"Good, because those two mismatched crimes at the agricultural gardens are far from being solved. Everything seemed to have tentacles."

"You've probably figured out that some of the gardeners work in close-knit groups. The hippies and the doomsayers. A few of them have dogs and come here to vent after they finish up at their plots. I keep a low profile but an open ear."

"What did you learn?" I turned for a brief second to check on Streetman and so far, so good.

"There's been some friction lately with Marlie and one of the women she gardens with, Joyanne. Marlie has a pom-chin and sometimes blows off steam when she shows up. I don't know Joyanne, only by secondhand knowledge. Anyway, Joyanne was supposed to help Marlie with some cuttings but 'left her high and dry' last week. Marlie's words, not mine. Then, Marlie saw her with Ona and Aneta at Starbucks' outside patio when she left the garden that day."

"Maybe she was more in the mood for coffee than work."

Cindy shook her head. "It was the second time that Marlie played second fiddle to those two sisters. And according to Marlie, Joyanne's been acting rather suspicious lately."

"Did she say how?"

"Uh-huh. She said Joyanne appears to be eavesdropping on everyone when she pretends to be on her phone."

"How would she know?"

Cindy laughed. "Because the phone was upside down."

"Yeah, that is suspicious. Tell me, what do you know about Ona and Aneta? The sisters from Macedonia."

"They've lived here over ten years. When they first came, they had a wolfhound and I'd run into them from time to time. I believed they lived with their mother because there were always three of them walking the dog. Back in Macedonia, the family ran some sort of a business and did their own gardening for fresh fruits and vegetables. I haven't seen them in well over a year and figured the mother must have passed on. She was the one with that striking dog on the leash."

I turned again to check on Streetman and he had stopped to clean his paws. Then, he proceeded to do his business a few feet away. Just then, my phone vibrated and I excused myself to answer the call. I was positive it was my mother, but instead it was a frantic Joyanne.

"Someone broke into my house this morning, Phee. The sheriff deputies are over here right now. I heard the intruders smash a window and hid under my bed. Then I remembered I had an Echo Dot device and had Alexa make the sound of a siren. That scared them off but I am not sure if they took anything. I wouldn't be surprised if Tunnie found out I suspected her of killing Barry and wanted to give me a warning."

"Oh my gosh. How awful."

"The deputies asked me to see if I was missing anything. How am I supposed to know? You never know if something is missing until you need it."

"Let me know if the deputies find anything. Maybe one of the intruders dropped something."

"Thanks. I won't be at my plot today. This is way too upsetting."

"I understand."

"I told Marlie and Tunnie what happened and both of them sounded shocked over the phone. Then again, it could have been good acting on Tunnie's part."

"Okay, just don't do anything rash. I'll touch base with you later."

"What was that about?" Cindy asked. "I couldn't help but overhear you."

"A break-in at Joyanne's house. They smashed a window but she didn't think they stole anything. She used her Alexa to scare them off."

"She was lucky. Lots of really unhinged people around lately."

As soon as she said that, I knew I'd have to let my mother know ASAP. Otherwise, by the time the news reached her, the break-in would be more like the aftermath of a category 5 hurricane.

"Thanks Cindy, I appreciate you keeping me informed. I'd better get going before Streetman becomes unhinged."

We both laughed and I headed out once I tidied up after him.

...

"How was my little prince and what did you find out once you spoke with Cindy? And before I forget to tell you, I popped by Iris's house this weekend with some of those mini-pies from the Homey Hut. And guess what? She *did* report the incident to the posse. She said she had a nightmare about that scary-looking insignia."

"Good. It may turn out to be an important piece of these investigations."

Streetman proceeded to bump Essie with his nose, and next thing I knew the two of them chased each other into the bedroom.

"I hope he wasn't too rambunctious in the dog park. You know how he gets."

I tried not to roll my eyes. "Your prince was fine but there's been some friction between Marlie and Joyanne, and Joyanne seems to be palling around with the Zlatkova sisters more than with Marlie and Tunnie." I paused to catch my breath and then continued. "I know. It sounds so junior high. But this isn't—Joyanne called me to tell me her house was broken into this morning. She's okay. She used her Echo Dot to scare the intruders off."

"How many intruders? A gang? Maybe the woman with the gang insignia from the other night is one of them. And maybe they've targeted us."

"Whoa! Slow down. No one has targeted you. And I seriously doubt it was the woman from Barry's plot. Most likely random burglars. Still, make sure your house is locked and that your security alarm is set at night."

"I have Streetman and my Screamer. Oh goodness. I need to let the book club ladies know what happened. I don't want to wait until we see each other at the posse office. I already know what the deputies are going to tell us. There might possibly be a third nutcase killer on the loose or one really determined lunatic."

"Good. Then there won't be any surprises. I've got to get going. I'll talk to you later."

"Will you be at the special meeting with Bowman and Ranston?"

"No, I'm not a paid investigator. But I do plan to drop by to try to talk to Maybelle."

"I'll call you after."

"I know."

"Do you want to give Streetman and Essie kisses before you leave?"

Not particularly.

"No time. Kiss them for me."

I was out the door and in my car before she could grab one of her fur babies. Then it was off to the Starbucks drive-through on Grand and Reems before heading to the office.

When I walked in, Nate, Marshall, and Augusta were doubled over laughing. Augusta waved a fax in the air and could barely contain herself.

"What's so hysterical?" I reached for the fax just as the three of them answered in unison.

"The Los Angeles Raiders."

CHAPTER 30

"What's so funny about a football team?"

The three of them kept looking at each other and laughing. Finally Marshall spoke. "Not the team—their insignia. It's what that lady saw on the back of the hoodie. The face of a man with a patch over one eye and two crossed swords behind the helmet he wore. Not a gang insignia! It's the logo for the Raiders."

"Obviously the woman doesn't watch football." Augusta started to laugh again. "Or shop at any major clothing stores."

"At least the book club ladies won't be perseverating over gangs infiltrating the area," I said. "And the good news is that everyone can be on the lookout for a hoodie with the Raiders logo on it."

"Yep," Augusta added. "A hoodie with the Raiders logo. Not that there aren't a million of them floating around. Along with the hats."

"But not necessarily in the agricultural gardens." Nate rubbed his chin and retrieved a cup of coffee from the Keurig that had just brewed. "If the woman who was in Barry's plot is a fellow gardener, then chances are she'll be sporting that hoodie again. After all, she has no idea that she was spotted wearing it as she trampled flowers in someone's garden. Ranston and Bowman may get lucky and she'll be at the office along with everyone else today, hoodie and all."

"I'll be on the lookout today," I said. "I'll be over there as well to chitchat with Maybelle. Maybe I'll spot it."

I didn't hold out any great hopes but something had to give. We had way too many clues and way too few links. I knew that all it took was one good link to connect to the other and voilà! But what would it take to make that first link?

At midmorning, when I was about to head over to the posse office, I got a text from Lyndy. Short and sweet: *Any progress? Been up to my elbows with medical claims but good overtime pay.*

I texted back, *Swim tonight or tomorrow?*

She replied, *Working tonight but tomorrow should be good.*

I put a thumbs-up on it and told Augusta I'd be back after the usual lunch hour. "I'll order you a ham sandwich from the deli," she said. "I know you're not going to eat over there. And steer clear of their coffee. It was probably brewed during the Industrial Revolution."

"You got that right. And thanks!"

• • •

The first thing I noticed when I drove into the parking lot in front of the posse office was that none of the cars were evenly spaced out between the white lines. Some were over the line, others were somewhat diagonal and one actually took up two spaces. Yeah, no doubt about it, the three book club ladies had arrived, along with Herb and friends, not to mention a slew of gardeners from the club.

Sure enough, when I stepped into the office and looked around, I noticed an open door to a large conference room with rows of occupied chairs. I slipped in discreetly, hoping to seek out Maybelle, but instead Herb spotted me.

"Hey, cutie, what brings you to our midmorning interrogation?"

Temporary insanity.

Before I could answer, Deputy Bowman walked to the front of the room and spoke.

"Thank you all for coming. We appreciate your time. If you neglected to sign in when you entered the building, do so now. I am circulating a list. It is imperative you give us your phone number and email."

"How many times do we have to do this?" someone asked, but Bowman ignored him and continued to speak. The voice sounded like Gussie's but I wasn't sure. Peering around, I noticed Joyanne with Ona and Aneta while Tunnie and Marlie were a few seats away. As for my mother, she was at the opposite end of the room, and that was just as well.

"I will be as succinct as possible regarding the situation that brought all of you here," Deputy Bowman grumbled. "Now then, as you're aware, the Maricopa County Sheriff's Office, along with consultants from Williams Investigations, is looking into the recent homicide of Sun City West resident Barry McGuire, along with a severed hand that was found in a compost heap a few days prior. Do not misconstrue what I am about to say."

"Oh, brother," someone else sighed, but Bowman kept talking. "We have not been able to ascertain if the severed hand is, in any way, connected to Mr. McGuire's murder. We are still analyzing the situation."

A hand flew up in the air and it was Louise. "Can you analyze it later? I'm supposed to play Mexican Train at the women's club in forty minutes."

"I assure you," Bowman said, "this is extremely important or our office would not have insisted you been here. We called you in because of a recent development. As you know from the news outlets, Mr. McGuire's death was deemed a poisoning. His system contained an extraordinary amount of nicotine and the patch he wore was cut, forcing the toxin into his system rapidly."

"If you know what killed him, let the woman go to her card game," Orvis shouted.

"Dominos," Louise replied. "It's played with dominos."

"I don't care if it's played with tiddlywinks. Listen carefully, everyone, this is important." The irritation in Bowman's voice was gradually reaching a crescendo and I prayed no one else would interrupt him.

"In addition to the compromised nicotine patch, Mr. McGuire had ingested a potato toxin found in the tubers from a nonspecific variety of potato. For those of you who don't know, the nibs or stubs on potatoes are poisonous. Keep that in mind. Obviously, our killer did. And that brings me to the next point."

I spotted Maybelle seated a few rows in front and there was an empty chair behind her. Wasting no time, I made my way toward it and sat as Bowman continued with his explanation.

"Given the fact that we are dealing with two different types of toxins, the probability exists that there are two killers. Then again, maybe one very thorough killer. And here is where it gets complicated. Our office received a tip that Mr. McGuire may have ingested the potato toxin from the nib of a cigar that he had placed in his mouth to chew."

"Ew!" a woman's voice rang out, and other "Ew's" followed.

Bowman went on. "Said cigar nib was found in Mr. McGuire's plot, which leads me to the next point. We may be dealing with three killers or one diabolical, clever, and meticulous killer who's somewhat obsessive-compulsive. Not that I'm an authority on those things, but if it turns out to be one individual, then he or she made sure they got the job done."

For a moment there was absolute silence. And then, there wasn't.

Everyone spoke at once:

"Do you think it's one of us? Is that why we're here?"

"Are you subjecting us to a DNA test? I'm calling my lawyer."

"Three killers? There might be three killers in this room?"

"Three killers, and the sheriff's office can't identify even one of them?"

And finally:

"Can we bring our guns back to the garden?"

Deputy Bowman rubbed the back of his head and then twisted it around. "Deputy Ranston will now explain what we need from you."

Like a skittish rabbit, Ranston jumped up from where he sat and walked to the front of the room. "Anyone in this room who may have knowledge about Mr. McGuire's smoking habits is asked to share that with either Deputy Bowman or me, or one of the two posse officers who are here to assist us. Specifically, did Mr. McGuire partake of his cigars with anyone? Was anyone observed near where Mr. McGuire kept his cigars? Mind you, you are not being asked to 'rat out' someone. You are being asked to assist in a murder investigation. Let that sink in."

"Oh, it sunk, all right," Herb blurted out.

Either Ranston didn't hear Herb or he chose to ignore him. "This will be a confidential conversation and you will be called into one of the conference rooms. Please listen for your name."

As Ranston stood and walked toward one of the small conference rooms, he paused in front of my seat. "Mrs. Kimball. Gregory. Why are you here?"

"I needed to chat with my mother for a few minutes."

He looked around. "She's on the other side of the room. I'll hold off calling her right away."

"Thanks."

He announced Ona's name, along with Aneta, Claudia, and Thira. So far Maybelle was in the clear and I tapped her shoulder. I thought about the direct approach but past experience taught me that guilty parties have no problem lying. Instead of asking her outright about the conversation in the ladies' restroom regarding Barry's cigarette habit, I played my mother's favorite game—the gossip circle!

"I heard they already know who's responsible for Barry's death. Someone taped a conversation they overhead in the restroom right at the agricultural plots. It had to do with Barry's smoking habits. All they're doing is gathering substantiating evidence. Shh! I shouldn't have said anything."

Maybelle spun around in her chair, eyes wide open. "Who? Do you know?"

"Not yet."

"What else do they know?"

"A laundry list of who had it in for him."

"Who didn't?"

"That's why opportunity is going to play a big part in this shindig. Face it, everyone had a motive, and as far as means, it was easy—nicotine patches and potatoes. Not like cyanide or arsenic. Whoever murdered Barry had to have the perfect opportunity."

"That man was as predictable as the sunrise. In his garden while it was still dark, puffing away on nasty cigars, or chewing on them like a Neanderthal. Then he'd mosey around everyone else's gardens and make sarcastic remarks. That is, when he wasn't poisoning people's cucumbers or cutting their water lines. I couldn't prove it in a court of law but my gut and everyone else's told me he did it."

"Um, yeah. I kind of noticed that animosity between the two of you when I first came out to see my mother's plot. Any reason why he was so antagonistic?"

"I think he just wanted me out of the club and out of the agricultural plots."

"Why?"

"Because I saw him monkeying around in Ona and Aneta's garden one afternoon and shooed him away. He said he was just curious as to what they were planting but I think he wanted to poison their cucumbers too. I told Ona and Aneta about it and they said they'd take care of it."

As in murder?

"Take care of it how? Did they say?"

Maybelle shook her head. "None of my business. I wouldn't have been at all surprised if they found a way to get even, but I don't think they'd go as far as killing him. It was over cucumbers, not a gold mine. But their plot wasn't the only one Barry scoped out. He was in Racine's as well. She told me about it one afternoon when his name came up while we were weeding."

"What happened with Racine?"

"Barry accused her of growing marijuana and told her he'd keep his mouth shut if she paid him off."

"Was she? Did she?"

"No. She grows lavender and lots of herbs. She told him to take a long walk off a short pier or she'd file a police report for harassment. I don't think it went any further."

Just then, Bowman called Maybelle, my mother, Louise, and Lucinda. Since I had told Deputy Ranston I came here to see my mother, I had no choice but to remain until her conversation with him ended. I took out my phone to check emails when I noticed Joyanne had moved back to where Tunnie and Marlie were seated. I put my cell phone back in my bag and decided to make it a foursome.

CHAPTER 31

No sooner did I say hello to the women when my mother rushed toward me. "You didn't have to come here, Phee. Unless those deputies wanted someone from your office. Oh, never mind. You can tell me later. I've got to hurry. Thanks to this interrogation, our Murder Mystery Radio Show had to make a switch with 'Sally's Salad-Making Techniques.' It's dreadful. She spends fifteen minutes explaining how to cut lettuce. Anyway, Myrna and I are on the air at two p.m. I want to grab a bite first. Call me later."

My eyes rolled around in their sockets longer than humanly possible.

"I didn't know your mother had a radio show," Marlie said.

"You're kidding?" Tunnie crinkled her nose. "It's a hoot. And their combo murder mystery and fishing show is even better."

"On KSCW?"

I nodded. "Uh-huh." Because no radio station in its right mind would have them on the air. "I probably should get going. I popped in here to check on my mother but it seems as if she didn't need moral support. These sheriff office questionings usually unnerve her." Or the deputies.

"You got that right." Tunnie sat up and perused the room. "I have been so frazzled lately with everything on my plate that I didn't even remember putting in the wash the other day. And this morning's time-consuming session didn't help. There's a rumor circulating that they know who killed Barry but want to eke out a confession from one of us. Good luck with that." Then she turned to Joyanne. "What's with you and the Zlatkova sisters? You've been tighter than Scrooge's purse strings."

Joyanne shrugged. "Gardening stuff, that's all."

Suddenly, Herb appeared out of nowhere with Orvis and waved for me. I excused myself and walked over to them.

"Orvis got it wrong," Herb announced, his voice bellowing across the room. "It wasn't Gussie he saw. It was a woman. Like I said, Orvis had been drinking."

Good grief. What was he drinking?

"Not my fault all those gardeners look alike with the denim coveralls and gardening gloves."

"So who do you think overheard the conversation in the ladies' room?" I looked at the wall clock and knew I had to hurry back to the office.

"Someone who looked like Gussie after I had a few rounds of beer."

"That's not much help, Orvis."

Joyanne, Marlie, and Tunnie were all thin as could be, as were Ona and Racine. Aneta was average build and a far cry from Gussie's frame. Thira

Planted 4 Murder

was slender and shapely so that excluded her, but Claudia and Maybelle were on the zaftig side.

"Orvis felt as if he should say something to the deputies so he told Ranston what he overheard."

"And?" I raised my eyebrows.

"And nothing." Orvis brushed something off his shoulder but I didn't want to know what. "The deputy said it was hearsay."

"Um, it really is."

"Anyway, cutie, I did us all a favor. After Orvis told me what happened, I went over and told Ranston to drag in Claudia and Maybelle and question them."

"Herb, they're questioning everyone now!"

"Yeah, but they don't know what Orvis knows from what the Gussie look-alike said."

"Oh, brother. Look, I've got to get back to the office. If anything happens, let my mother know, okay. Only call Williams Investigations if it's an emergency."

"You got it. And you can thank us later."

I gave them both a half wave and darted out the door before the afternoon got any weirder than it already was. Once back at work, I gave Augusta the blow-by-blow description of my visit to the posse office.

"We only have a few minutes, Phee, before your mother's radio show is on the air. I meant to tell you, I turned on KSCW this morning and thought I had the wrong station. It was the most annoying shrill-sounding woman expounding on the textures of lettuce. I didn't find out until later that the shows were switched. I should have realized it before when you mentioned the impromptu meeting with the deputies."

"I can't afford to miss work time by listening to it."

"No, you can't afford to miss what those two women divulge. How about if we just have our Alexas play the station and we can work at the same time. We can multitask. We were doing that before it became a word."

"Okay. Just keep our fingers crossed they don't compromise the investigation."

"Or start a new one."

• • •

I must have missed the introduction to the "Cozy Mystery Hour" with my mother and Myrna because the first thing I heard when I asked Alexa to play KSCW was, "Today's theme is cozy mysteries featuring gardening and poisons." It was my mother's voice and I wanted to respond with, "How about duct tape and a silencer?"

Multitask my foot! I started to enter some figures onto the Excel spreadsheet but what I heard next made me reconsider.

"You'd be surprised what lies beneath the very ground where so many of our crops are planted. And I'm not talking about rocks or worms, am I, Myrna?"

"Absolutely not, Harriet. In fact, Alice Castle, when she wrote *The Murder Garden*, could very well have been writing about our very own agricultural garden right here in Sun City West."

"And what about *Buried by Buttercups*, that wonderful cozy by the late Joyce and Jim Lavene. They certainly knew their poisons."

"Just like the perpetrator in our own backyard."

And there it was. An invitation for every cozy mystery reader to jump on the rumor train and ride it out.

"I'm sure we're not telling anyone anything they don't already know, but the two separate investigations pertaining to a severed hand and the body of a Sun City West resident who was discovered in one of our agricultural plots has now widened."

"Just like it did when we read *Arsenic in the Azaleas* by Dale Mayer a few years ago. Didn't they discover a finger or something and then they dug up the rest of the body? The finger was just the tip of the iceberg. Or corpse, as it turned out."

"Oh goodness, it's one of our call-in listeners. Let's take the call. Hello, this is Harriet, with whom am I speaking and what would you like to ask?"

"This is Carmen on Aleppo Drive. Are you saying that there's more to that severed hand? Like another body in the ground?"

"Do you hear that?" Augusta called out. "Your mother and Myrna not only opened a can of worms, they're serving it for dinner!"

"Shh! I know."

"Thank you, Carmen. At this juncture in time, we cannot say, but everyone is on edge. Especially since the means for murder appears to be a commonplace one."

"Oh, my! Would I have such a poison in my house and not know it?"

Then Myrna took over. "Do you smoke? Are you trying to quit?"

"No."

"Then you don't have to worry about the first poison."

"The first poison?" The alarm in Carmen's voice was obvious. "You mean there's another one? Or more than two?"

Back to my mother. "Make sure you wash and peel your potatoes."

Then Myrna again, "You don't have to peel them if you're baking them, but you should remove any of those little nibs or stubs. And if I were you, I'd cut deeply into the core of the potato when removing them."

"They're poisonous? You're saying they're poisonous?" Then, Carmen yelled out, "Frank, from now on we are eating rice. Plain white rice. Do you hear me?"

Who didn't.

I stood and walked back to Augusta. "I can't take much more of this. I can only pray Bowman and Ranston aren't tuned in. Or Nate and Marshall for that matter."

Augusta nodded. "Oh no. Did you catch that last part?"

"No, what?"

"Your mother just said, 'Consider this a public service announcement: Be on the lookout for a woman wearing a dark hoodie with the logo of the LA Raiders. And for those of you who don't know what that looks like, it's a Viking with a helmet and swords behind his head.'"

I stood, wordless, as Myrna's voice bellowed, "Not a Viking, Harriet, I think it's a pirate. And now we will take one more phone call before our time slot is up."

"This is Indira. I'm in the expansion district. I hope that's far away from the murder plots. Are you saying the woman with the hoodie is the killer?"

"So sorry, Indira. We are not at liberty to say."

"'Not at liberty to say'? 'Not at liberty to say'? Good heavens! They've said everything else!" My cheeks were warm and my pulse raced.

"Calm down, it's not that bad. They've said worse."

"True, but I think this time they may start a community panic. In retrospect, we would have been better off if Paul's fishing tidbits were on that show!"

Chapter 32

By the time I got home from work, the Sun City West rumor mill had been working overtime and Lyndy was the first to inform me.

"Good thing we're swimming tomorrow night," she said. "It would take me way too long to tell you what my aunt heard. And worse yet, what she passed on to everyone else in her gossip chain."

"Ugh. It gets worse by the minute. At least Nate and Marshall are on the case so maybe, with these new pieces of information about the cigar stubs and the mystery woman, they may get somewhere."

"By the way, I caught a snippet of the radio show. What a hoot! Guess rice sales will be going up."

I laughed and told her I'd be in the pool tomorrow by seven. Then, my aunt Ina phoned. Marshall still hadn't arrived home yet so I had a few minutes to chat before starting dinner.

"Oh, good, Phee, you're home. Do you have any idea what the temperature is like in Vancouver?"

"British Columbia or Washington?"

"Canada. But it's probably the same. They're both up north."

"Are you and Uncle Louis planning a trip?"

"Didn't Marshall tell you? Louis just found out a few minutes ago. The Royal Canadian Mounted Police contacted the FBI regarding the theft of a rare LaPerm cat belonging to a high-ranking official. The FBI referred them to Williams Investigations and—"

"Don't tell me. They're headed to Vancouver. But why is Uncle Louis going? It's not like Las Vegas with all the gambling."

"Your uncle is acquainted with, shall we say, an underground network of entrepreneurs who may be able to lead them in the right direction. But in all honesty, I think he wants to be out of the way for my annual Edgar Allan Poe readings."

"I see. Well, I'm sure Marshall will give me the details." As I spoke, I pulled up the weather app on my phone. "Forties and fifties expected this week in Vancouver with cloudy skies, some rain, some sun."

"Your uncle will just have to pack with no expectation for weather whatsoever. By the way, I left a message for your mother to stay away from that agricultural plot. My neighbor said there's a killer on the loose over there."

"I think the only thing on the loose is my mother's lips. But thanks."

"Anytime. And don't worry, I won't mention Vancouver to her. You can break the news."

Magnificent.

When Marshall and Nate returned from Las Vegas a few days ago, Marshall mentioned that he and Nate may be called upon to investigate similar cases. I pushed it off to the back of my mind, figuring it would be months from now. If ever. But right now? In Canada? And the timing couldn't be worse with our own murder investigation hitting dead ends.

The sound of the garage door opening signaled Marshall's arrival and in seconds, he announced, "I've got to tell you something."

I smiled. "It's in the forties right now in Vancouver. Fifties expected this week. Maybe rain. Maybe not."

"Uh-oh. Did Augusta call you? I know Nate texted her."

"Not Augusta. Aunt Ina."

Marshall slapped his forehead with the palm of his hand and rolled his eyes. "I should have figured as much. I'm sorry, hon. I only found out about it a little while ago and you had already gone home."

Rushing over, I hugged him and planted a kiss on his neck. "I'm not upset. My mother may get somewhat theatrical with the news, but I understand what juggling cases is like. Besides, Bowman and Ranston knew about your prior agreements to work these cases. How did they take the news?"

"Better than expected, which worries me. Bowman said they 'had a plan' to trap the killer but needed to work out the kinks."

"Do they even have the slightest idea who that is?"

Marshall shrugged. "Ranston said they devised a method to assign points to each of the suspects and from there, make a determination according to the amount."

"Points?"

"Yep. The usual for motive, means and opportunity, plus background and character traits. Not to mention nuances."

"Is this something the sheriff's office does as a rule?"

"No. It's a Bowman-Ranston original. Nate's still in shock. We spoke with Rolo and he's moving along with his deep dive. At least there'll be some credibility when the deputies decide to make a move. Hopefully, our case in Vancouver will have been resolved by then and we'll be back in time to pick up this one."

"Come on, you must be hungry. I can nuke anything from our Trader Joe's assortment or make stir-fry."

"What microwaves the fastest? I'll eat that. By the way, how did your mother's radio show go? Or should I avoid the topic? Usually, the deputies tune in for fear of panic being spread in the community, but they didn't realize the time slot had been switched. They assumed the show was replaced for the midmorning. We never got a chance to ask Augusta because we were dealing with the Canadian matter."

"Uh, just as well. You may want to eat your dinner first."

"Tell me over dinner. I'll change and wash up. This iron stomach can handle anything."

And while Marshall's iron stomach handled the BOLO that my mother and Myrna blasted, mine was in knots. Not so much from the radio show, but the reaction awaiting us when my mother learned Nate and Marshall would be out of town for a while. I figured I'd let her know in the morning. No sense ruining a perfectly good night.

* * *

In retrospect, I should have texted my mother last night about the Vancouver case but I decided to wait it out until my Wednesday morning break. Then I pushed it off until lunch. Then, until the afternoon. By then, the guys had located a missing sibling and found evidence of a cheating spouse. I had just stepped out from my office to get some coffee when I heard Nate's voice.

"That clears our docket for a while," he announced when he and Marshall bounded through the door around three. "We paid our dues today, working the Sun City West cases. Now it's Bowman and Ranston's turn."

"And Phee!" Augusta said. "You don't think she's going to sit here twiddling her thumbs and tallying numbers while you're gone."

I couldn't discern the look on Marshall's face but his words were familiar enough. "As long as you don't do anything that will put you in danger. And please remind your mother that Streetman isn't a Rottweiler."

"Right now she's convinced he's a bloodhound."

The remainder of the day moved at a steady pace with no surprises. Unfortunately, that changed the following morning. With their flight to Vancouver scheduled for Friday, Nate and Marshall had a number of odds and ends to shore up. They were out of the office before I even arrived. Augusta rummaged through the file cabinet near the window while I busied myself with the Keurig.

"Oh, no!" she exclaimed. "What in God's green earth did I ever do to deserve this?"

"Deserve what?" I pushed the blue button and turned to her.

"Look out the window and see for yourself."

I took a step forward and froze.

"Cat got you tongue?" She laughed. "And he's with Mini-Moose, no less. In twenty seconds they'll be through this door."

Wonderful. Mini-Moose. Just what we need. Paul's fishing buddy and

Sun City West's billiards manager. Next to him, Paul's as polished as King Charles.

"Paul is off to the side. Please don't tell me they're carrying dead fish with them. Or smelly bait."

"Why do you suppose they're in Glendale? This is the business district, not a lake."

"I don't even want to know, but it can't be good. Honestly, Paul's like one of those newly hatched flies that refuse to leave you alone."

Augusta shuddered. "Yeah, but you can swat those."

Then, the door flew open and we got our answer.

"Morning, all!" Paul's voice was as chipper as ever. "You'll thank us for this. The Moose and I were on our way to Saguaro Lake when we decided our news couldn't wait until the afternoon. We wanted to fish at dawn but we got hungry and wound up having a double breakfast at Over Easy. The Moose ordered the —"

I put a hand on my hip, and with the other hand motioned for Paul to get to the point.

"Okay, okay." He turned to Mini-Moose. "You can tell her what you ate later."

Or not.

"Get to the point, Paul," Augusta said. "I'm not getting any younger."

"Like I said, you'll thank me. I know who Barry's killer is. It's Maybelle. And I think he's not the first one she axed."

Chapter 33

"And how do you know this?" I asked.

"You want to tell her, or should I?" Paul looked at Mini-Moose.

"Just tell us." By now, I had reached the apex of my limit with Paul.

"Fine. Mini-Moose and I had a boatload of fish entrails and some old bait that we no longer wanted to use. We gutted the fish for a Kiwanis cookout and got paid a pretty penny. Anyway, we didn't want the entrails and such to go to waste. That's when I remembered that when you grind them up, you can use them for plant fertilizer. Isn't that right, Moose?"

The big guy nodded. "Yep."

"So, in a spirit of generosity, we drove over to the community gardens to dump the grindings onto the freshly tilled plots. Santi was elated and so were Gussie, Orvis and Racine. Even those emaciated hippy women and Claudia thought it was a good idea. Herb and the guys were okay with it, too. And they said your mother, Lucinda, and Louise wouldn't care."

Until they smelled it.

"Anyhow," Paul went on, "the Zlatkova sisters weren't around so we did them a favor and dumped the entrails in their garden, but we might have overdone it. No worries. The Moose used a shovel to mix them into the soil where it had been tilled."

"What does any of this have to do with Maybelle?" I widened my eyes and waited for a response.

"Oh, yeah, Maybelle. She pitched a fit! And I don't mean one of those little hissy fits women have but a super-duper, arms waving in the air fit! She told us to steer clear of her garden and that everything was tilled and prepared for more planting. Told us if we dared to put anything on the ground in her compound, she'd have us arrested for vandalism, trespassing, and civil rights."

"Civil rights?" I looked at Augusta and she shrugged.

"Yeah," Mini-Moose added, "Maybelle said she had rights as a citizen to do whatever she wanted with her land."

"Um, I believe the term *civil rights* has to do with—oh, never mind. And by the way, I'd avoid saying hissy fit and women in the same breath. But what makes you think she's the killer?"

"The way she guarded her garden, that's what. She's hiding something and I'll wager it's under that recently plowed or tilled swath of land in her plot. She shooed us out of there as if we were about to expose government secrets. If you ask me, she's the culprit. In fact, I wouldn't be surprised if the body belonging to the hand is buried under her precious tomatoes."

Then, Mini-Moose looked around, and even though no one other than us was in the office, he whispered, "We should go there at night and dig it up."

"No! No, we shouldn't. Both of you sound like my mother. There is no concrete evidence of Maybelle harboring skeletal remains. And nothing whatsoever to suggest she murdered Barry McGuire. All you'll wind up doing is getting yourselves in trouble. Look, if it will make you feel any better, I'll let Nate and Marshall know when they get back from Canada."

"Canada? Don't tell me they've gone up there to fish?"

"Yes," I said, "but not for the kind with fins and gills. Listen, next time you guys decide to do a good deed, please run it by someone other than the two of you."

"Come on, Moose." Paul yanked Mini-Moose's arm. "I want to get to Saguaro Lake before the afternoon."

I walked them to the door. "Thanks for letting us know. Have a good day."

Thirty seconds later, Augusta sprayed the room with Lysol and turned on the standing fan. "The AC will only make the fish odor stronger. Maybe the fan will disperse it."

"We can only hope."

Thankfully the morning proved to be productive for Augusta and me. We rewarded ourselves with club sandwiches from the deli that were enough for two meals.

"I still smell fish," she said after we had eaten. "I may have to go full-blown meat eater for a while."

"Yeah, I know what you mean. Can you believe Paul and Mini-Moose? But I did check it out on Google and sure enough, dead fish are used as fertilizer. So I guess it was a good deed after all."

Or so I thought. Shortly before five, when the day wound down, I got a call from Lucinda.

"Sorry to bother you, Phee, but is there any chance you could come over to the agriculture gardens to give us a hand? There's sort of a situation going on."

I cringed. "What situation?"

"Your mother brought the dog and we can't catch him. He's running from garden plot to garden plot rolling in dirt. It must be the ground-up fish entrails that Paul graced upon us. Your mom tried luring him with all sorts of treats but apparently he prefers stinking dead fish. Lots of people are here and they're really pitching a fit. And there's more."

"Lucinda, if she can't catch him, how am I supposed to?"

"You're faster. And more adroit."

I couldn't argue with that and I didn't need my mother to fall and heaven forbid break a bone.

"Fine. We're wrapping up here and I'll drive over. I'd offer Marshall's assistance but he and Nate are out of the office. They fly to Vancouver tomorrow on another case and need to get some things done before."

"I understand. See you soon. And wear a hat if you have one. You'll know why when you get here."

"Trouble in paradise?" Augusta asked when she saw the look on my face as we were about to lock up for the day.

When I told her, she couldn't keep a straight face. "Have fun. At least Streetman is wiggling around in fish entrails and not human remains."

"Yeah, small favors, huh?"

I sent a quick text to Marshall and he responded with a screaming emoji.

A half hour later, I had all I could do to keep my own face from resembling the emoji.

When I parked my car outside of the gate and walked in, I was flabbergasted. The sky was filled with birds and it looked like a scene from Alfred Hitchcock's *The Birds*. No wonder Lucinda told me to wear a hat. Then I recalled something Paul said—"We might have overdone it."

As I hustled to my mother's plot, the frenzy of gardeners all but overtook me. And all I heard was "What do we do? How do we get rid of them?"

Birds were everywhere. In the air. On the ground. And pecking on the soil. To add to the fiasco, Streetman was in his glory. He flew past me and buried his head in the garden plot belonging to Gussie.

"Phee!" my mother shouted. "Grab him. Run over and grab him."

Something wet dripped on my forehead and it wasn't rain. Will this nightmare ever cease?

I charged toward the little stinker but he skirted around me and landed in Joyanne's plot, where he rolled around like a monkey. My voice got louder. "Wait until he tires out!" Like that would ever happen.

From Joyanne's plot, it was on to Tunnie's and then Orvis's. A never-ending chain of chaos on four legs. Finally, he landed on top of Maybelle's precious tomato plants. But that didn't last long. One sniff and he must have realized her plot was fish-entrail-free.

Moving closer to him, I saw he had something in his mouth, but what it was, or where he got it, was anyone's guess. I figured it was a chunkier piece of fish and I felt like strangling Paul and Mini-Moose.

With the prize possession in his mouth, Streetman settled underneath a patch of lavender in Racine's plot. Thankfully, she'd left earlier in the day so she didn't witness him trampling her lavender. I closed her garden gate and snuck up on Prince Valiant. And when I reached to grab him, I got the surprise of my life—he had a small bone in his mouth and it wasn't from a fish.

Chapter 34

My mind raced with horrific thoughts. What if more body parts were underneath the garden plots? And whose were they? Or maybe it belonged to the owner of the severed hand.

And then, I got my answer. When my daughter Kalese, now teaching in St. Cloud, was in high school, she broke a bone in her foot when she played powderpuff football. I still remember the X-ray. The bone Streetman had in his mouth bore an uncanny resemblance.

"You got him!" my mother called out as she and Lucinda walked toward me. "Take whatever garbage is in his mouth and toss it. I'm putting him right back in his stroller."

"It's not garbage."

"Well, toss it anyway. It's been in his mouth."

"Mom, I'm pretty sure it's a human bone." And just then, a flock of larger birds landed a few feet from us. I shooed them away and sneezed from the downy feathers that were in the air.

"Let me see."

Seconds later, Lucinda announced, "We found another bone! *Otro hueso! Ay! Cuerpos muertos!*" Her native Spanish flowed like a river. "*Cuerpos muertos debajo la tierra!* Dead bodies everywhere!"

And then, silence. Silence before chapter two in the torturous saga of "Why Does She Bring That Dog Everywhere?"

I tried to collect my thoughts but it was as if I had a total brain freeze.

"Are you all right, Phee? By the way, your blouse has bird droppings on it."

Sure. What else is new?

Claudia rushed over to us with Joyanne at her heels. They were immediately followed by Gussie, Orvis, and Maybelle.

"What's going on?" Gussie asked.

"Harriet's dog found another human bone. Didn't you hear them shouting?" Claudia gave Gussie a look.

If the situation was anything like the last time, it would take hours to extricate the bone from Streetman's mouth. Still, it had to be done.

I sighed and looked at the crowd of gardeners that now included Tunnie and Marlie. "Does anyone have any food? I can try to lure the bone away from him."

"Don't!" Maybelle shouted.

"Yes, don't," Joyanne added. "That dog is a snapper."

"Snapper or not," Maybelle's voice got louder and faster, "I say we

Planted 4 Murder

leave well enough alone. We don't really know if it's a human bone. For all we know, it could be chicken bones. KFC is down the road and the supermarkets all sell fried chicken."

"We really can't risk not reporting it." By now I was beginning to wonder if Paul's assumption about her had some validity.

Then she added, "Face it, they'll show up again with that plant-stomping forensic crew and my prizewinning tomatoes will become pasta sauce before they're even harvested. I planned to showcase them at the Maricopa County Garden Expo."

"Maybelle's right," someone shouted. That was followed by a few others saying "Leave it alone" and one "Haven't we endured enough agony around here?"

Joyanne walked to where I stood and squeezed my arm. "I know you want to do the right thing, Phee, but face it, we don't really know where that bone came from. Your mother's dog has been running all over the place. It's quite possible he found it over by the railroad yard. That fence is easy for a dog to get through. Especially one his size."

"I say we forget the whole thing. The sheriff's office hasn't even been able to garner information on an entire hand. Not to mention an entire body! Calling them will only result in more interviews, gardens being roped off, and idiotic declarations from the administration." Gussie made a thumbs-down gesture and walked away.

Meanwhile, my mother finished putting her little man in the stroller and returned to where the crowd still stood. "He's gnawing on that bone, Phee. There's not going to be much left of it by the time he's done."

"Let it go." Maybelle was adamant. "We'll all look like fools if they come to find out it was the daily special at Putter's Paradise."

One by one, the gardeners returned to their plots, but the birds still hovered around, occasionally landing in flocks on the ground, where everyone shooed them away. As they moved further away, I heard someone say, "I'm headed to Lowe's to buy netting. I'll be darned if those flying rats eat my seeds and do their business in my garden."

Complaints notwithstanding, I was still uncomfortable about keeping the information from Bowman and Ranston. When my mother and I were no longer in earshot of everyone, I whispered, "Nate and Marshall are still in town. What do you say we snatch that bone from your Roman gladiator and I'll have our guys send it to our lab. If it is human, then it can be compared to one with the ring on it."

"Put on my thick gardening gloves. Lucinda's got some chorizo in a cooler. Maybe the spices from that sausage will distract him."

"We can always pray."

As luck would have it, it wasn't the chorizo that distracted him. It was a fly. An annoying horse fly that flew in front of him and got snatched up in the same second that he dropped the bone.

I never moved so fast in my life and frankly, I was astonished that I did. And although I didn't need the garden gloves to save me from a visit to the ER, I was grateful not to deal with a disgusting, sticky bone with no hand sanitizer in sight.

"Here," my mother said. "It's a napkin that I had in my pocket. So the bone won't get contaminated."

"Uh, I think it's a little late for that, but I'll pass this treasure along to Marshall."

"Let me know what they find out."

"Williams Investigations uses a private lab, but in cases like this, the bone may have to be reported to the authorities."

"Just make sure my Streetman gets the credit."

I grumbled, rolled my eyes and said I'd call her. Then I got into my car and turned on the windshield fluid and wipers. Thanks to Paul and Mini-Moose, there was enough bird poop to warrant a visit to the car wash.

Thank goodness for Salad and Go, because that's exactly what I did on my way home. I figured Marshall wouldn't want a heavy meal before an early flight, and I had lost most of my appetite smelling fish entrails in the community garden.

"Before we sit down to eat," I said to him a little while later, "there's something I need to show you. And a favor I need to ask you."

"Uh-oh."

I retrieved the bone from the refrigerator in the garage and held it in front of him.

Marshall narrowed his eyes and looked. "Please tell me you got this at the butcher shop for Streetman."

"No, he got it for himself from the one of the garden plots. I'm keeping my fingers crossed it's from an animal but I think it's from a human foot."

"I can see where the larger bone separates into a toe. Looks human to me. Which plot? And did someone call the sheriff's office?"

"That's the favor." I let out a long breath of air and explained in great detail the negative sentiment of the gardeners when it came to the deputies, and the fact that no one knew exactly where the dog found the bone. "Streetman ran around that entire area like a lunatic so we have no idea whatsoever as to which plot it came from. When he wasn't pawing and digging, he was rolling and rubbing."

"You do realize that this could be evidence of foul play, especially if it's from the same body as that severed hand."

"I realize. And it really should be examined in the forensic lab. That's why I hoped you'd say something to Bowman and Ranston. I could drop it off at the posse office in the morning."

"They might still cordon off the area, if that's what the gardeners were concerned about."

"I know. But maybe they'll take it at face value and have it examined first. After all, they're not going to glean any new information from interviewing the same people."

"I'll phone Bowman and text Nate after we eat. Keep in mind that if it matches the prior find, then that entire area will be deemed a crime scene and planting may be put off indefinitely."

"Then again, it could be a giant chicken leg."

"Only in your dreams. Come on, I'm starving."

• • •

Nate and Marshall were on the first flight to Seattle by five the next day. From there, a forty-three-minute wait and on to Vancouver. I agreed to drop off the bone at the posse office in Sun City West before work. And while the gardening crew basked in the misguided belief that the discovery was behind them, I knew better. And it was only a matter of time.

CHAPTER 35

"The correct protocol would have been to contact our office upon the discovery of that bone," Bowman said as I handed him the box that contained it.

"You do know that gardening crew, don't you?"

"Aargh. Say no more. We'll have this tested and compared to our other sample. Then we'll take it from there. Do me a favor. Please persuade your mother to leave her ankle nipper at home, will you?"

"I'd like to leave him in Australia. A large ocean separates us."

Bowman actually laughed and I told him to have a good day.

"Good morning, Augusta," I said as I opened the door to the office. "Remember yesterday afternoon when you said it was a good thing the dog was only rolling around in fish guts and not dead bodies? Well, you spoke too soon!"

"What? Who did the little whipper-snapper unearth this time?"

"Not a corpse. A partial. Maybe."

"I'm going to refresh my coffee for this one."

Augusta raised her eyebrows when I relived the saga of Streetman gnawing on what possibly could have been a human bone. Then she topped off her coffee cup and shook her head. "Never thought I'd be saying this in a million years, but maybe Paul and Mini-Moose may be right about Maybelle hiding something, or someone, under those prizewinning tomatoes of hers."

"But who? And what possible motive? Now, if it was Barry, I might be tempted to agree with you. Especially since Maybelle had experience with butcher knives and cleavers. But still, it's a stretch. Anyway, we'll know more once the forensic lab completes its comparative analysis. In the meantime, the only thing I want to compare are the last two months of expenses."

"Knock yourself out." Augusta chuckled as I walked into my office and switched on the light. I didn't emerge until midmorning, when I got a text from Marshall telling me they were about to board a flight into Vancouver. I texted back, *Gave Bowman Streetman's gift. Let me know when you land.*

I prayed that was the last bit of mischief that dog would get into, but unfortunately, it was only the precursor of "worse things yet to come." Only it didn't begin with the dog. It began with a barrage of phone calls to Williams Investigations regarding sightings of women clad in hoodies with questionable insignias.

"Why are they calling our office?" Augusta demanded while we ate our lunch. "That was the fourth call in less than two hours. Why us? Why not the sheriff's office?" I started to respond but she continued. "And not even close! Minnesota Vikings. Tampa Bay Buccaneers. And two that sounded more like Disney characters."

I gulped. "I think my mother or Myrna might have mentioned us on their radio show. And face it, we're less intimidating than the sheriff's office. What did you tell them?"

"What I always do in those cases—'I'll make a note of it for our detectives.' Then I give them our email and tell them to provide details and contact information should we need to reach them."

"Then what?"

"I push Delete when I get the email."

"Let's hope that's all we're dealing with while the guys are gone."

Lamentably, it wasn't. Apparently, Paul and Mini-Moose were unfamiliar with the expression leave well enough alone. I should have known as much when Paul expounded on his theory about Maybelle. That'll teach me to pay more attention to what comes out of his mouth. Especially when it's followed by a plan of action.

The stark blue light emanating from my alarm clock read 3:43 a.m. when the landline rang. I knew it couldn't have been Marshall because he calls my cell number and not the home phone. In addition, we had just spoken a few hours ago when he checked into the hotel.

That left my mother, who viewed cell phones like gadgets and landlines like actual phone systems. I picked up the receiver, expecting to hear her voice, when I heard Mini-Moose's instead.

"Paul lost that card with the name of the bail bondsman you gave him. Do you have the number handy?"

"Moose? Is that you? It's almost four in the morning. What's going on?"

"Paul and I are being detained at the sheriff's office in Sun City."

"Detained as in questioning or detained as in arrested?"

"Uh, maybe a bit of both."

"Oh, brother. Please don't tell me this involves something with the conservation office. I'm not familiar with those licensing laws. And why did you and Paul have to get up so darn early? Were you poaching fish?" If there is such a thing as fish poaching.

"No, more like grave-digging."

"What??" Up until that moment, I thought I was dealing with something that made sense. "What do you mean by grave-digging?"

"Don't get mad at Paul. I thought it was a good idea at the time."

"Um, maybe I should just give you the bail bondsman number and let him deal with it."

"Don't you want to know what happened?"

"I don't mean to sound dismissive, Moose, but whenever I hear the expression 'I thought it was a good idea at the time,' I know for sure that it wasn't." Thoughts of my mother and her friends immediately came to mind and I shuddered.

"I'll tell you anyway. Here goes."

I wanted to hang up but something compelled me to stay on the line. I pulled the covers up to my neck, moved another pillow closer, and settled back to listen. If nothing else, it beat getting up at such an early hour.

"So, anyway, me and Paul thought about how Maybelle was probably the one who had a corpse underneath her tomato plants. And then Paul figured that maybe the nutrients from the dead body were what was giving her plants all that growth and size."

"So you dug up her plants? That's what you meant by grave-digging?"

"Hey, someone had to. And we couldn't wait around for those pokey deputies."

"Fine. And then what?"

"So, here's where it got a little out of hand. Paul turned on the spigot and dampened the ground, although it was pretty soft to begin with. We used our fishing lanterns so we could see but then, out of nowhere a pack of javelina show up and scare the daylights out of us. Had to be at least five of them. Paul was convinced they'd attack us so we made a getaway to the fence over by the railroad yard. Paul thought he could pry the metal apart and get through it but he got stuck. Really stuck!"

"I think I can piece together the rest. You had to call the fire department to cut him out of there, right?"

"We never got the chance. The railroad inspector got a report of vandalism and was already on the premises. He called the fire department."

"And the both of you were placed in custody for digging on private property?"

"That came later. First we were arrested for trespassing. Hey, do you think there's any chance you could stop at Circle K or QuikTrip to pick up something for us to eat? The hot dogs are good and they've got those big sausages, too."

"Are you kidding me? You woke me up from a sound sleep and I either go back and snooze or make myself some strong coffee. Either way, the answer to that is a solid no! Grab something to write with. I'll give you the number of that bail bondsman. Call me later at the office. After nine. Got it?"

"Yeah, I suppose."

I don't know who laughed louder, Marshall or Augusta, when I told them about Paul and Mini-Moose's escapades a few hours later. By then, I had settled into the office and blissfully attacked a small pile of invoices. Around noon, Paul phoned to inform us that "we were released on our own reconnaissance."

"You mean recognizance," I said. "You and Mini-Moose weren't involved in any military operations."

"Whatever. We just have to appear in court and pay a fine."

"Wonderful. Now, will you please keep away from the agricultural plots? I know you mean well but you'll only muck things up."

"We wouldn't be doing this if we weren't convinced Maybelle murdered someone and buried the body under those tomatoes of hers. But maybe we can find another way around it."

"Yeah. It's called keeping a wide berth."

Chapter 36

I was glad it was Saturday and I only had a half day to work. I was groggy from my early morning wake-up even though I had enough espresso in me to start my own java joint. Nate informed Augusta that the Canadian authorities needed to keep this operation under tight wraps so not to expect too much detailed information.

He also mentioned that Rolo was involved as well and to field any calls or communication from him. Marshall texted me that as well, in addition to mentioning that my uncle had some rather nefarious connections in Chinatown and they were about to "get going." I knew it wasn't for moo goo gai pan.

At a little past noon, as I was about to call it a day, Joyanne called.

"Hey, Phee, sorry to bother you, but do you know anything about some of the gardens being tampered with? I figured your office might have been informed."

I felt the heat in my face and was glad we spoke over the phone. "Uh, no. What happened?"

"Maybelle's tomato patch looked as if it had been disturbed and one of her plants was uprooted. She said it looked deliberate to her. Then, the Zlatkova sisters said their pristine soil looked as if an elephant had trampled over it. They bought coiled wire to place around their prize areas, even if it is a violation. To top it off, Aneta announced that it was easier to beg forgiveness than ask the official question."

"Maybe it was an animal. Javelina are everywhere this time of year. Not to mention raccoons and skunks."

"Maybe. But the situation is not sitting pretty with the gardeners. The heat is a stressor enough this time of year. Throw in the external pressure of a murder or two looming over us and well, let's just say tempers are getting thin. By the way, I'm glad you didn't contact the deputies regarding that bone in Streetman's mouth. It would have only made things worse around here."

I rolled my eyes and prayed there wouldn't be a match with the severed hand. "I suppose."

"Sorry to have bothered you. Have a nice weekend. Maybe the sheriff's office will have some answers this coming week."

Don't bet on it.

Then, out of the blue, Cecilia Flanagan phoned me shortly after I arrived home. At first, I imagined something horrific happened to my mother in her latest 'hotspot for murder,' but as soon as Cecilia mentioned

College of the Holy Cross, the tension in my neck diminished.

"I know I shouldn't have butted into the dead hand investigation, and of course Barry's sudden demise, but I knew I could be of help, especially since things are stalling."

"Um, help how?" I clenched my jaw. "You brought over some lovely holy water to the gardens. That was helpful, I'm sure."

"Yes, yes, but I'm talking about earthly help, not spiritual."

Oh no. Now what?

"I'm a graduate of the College of the Holy Cross in Worcester, Massachusetts. Granted, it was years ago, but I still maintain my connections. Were you aware that the college is one of the top learning centers for the study of classical languages?"

"No, I wasn't. But what does that have to do with the investigations?"

"Why, the gimmel ring, of course. Your mother told us that it was a three-band combination and that the forensic jewelers couldn't piece together the names or message on the two rings they found."

"Uh-huh." I wasn't sure where Cecilia was going with this, but I had an uncanny feeling that if I stuck it out, she might actually have something valuable to add to the mystery. "Go on. I'm listening."

"When your mother told the book club ladies to discreetly see if anyone wore such a band, I had an epiphany."

Heaven help us!

"And then what?"

"I contacted the granddaughter of my late ancient Greek professor, Esme Albright, and asked if she knew of anyone at the college who was proficient enough in classical languages to piece together the letters isavet eta dra ov on. And she did! And that's not all. The professor who agreed to study the existing letters on the ring was able to piece it together. At least to the point where it would make sense."

"Was it Medieval English? Greek? Latin?"

"Albanian."

"Albanian?"

"Yes. Albanian. And if the translator is correct, and I have no reason to doubt his expertise, the three rings would spell out 'Friendship, Loyalty, and Fellowship,' in Albanian, of course."

I was stunned. "Of course," I muttered. "That would make sense. Nate and Marshall learned that gimmel rings were used as messages of betrothal or friendship. And this one was a medieval replica. Only with an inscription in Albanian. If that doesn't confuse things further, I don't know what does. Say, do you have this information in writing?"

"I have it in email. I'll forward it to you and you can share it with those deputies. For some reason, they're quite dismissive of my input and observations."

I was about to remind her that her observations included dead bodies that were later found to be lawn decorations and palm fronds, but instead, I thanked her and asked her to forward that email immediately.

When the call ended, I let out a long sigh and smiled. It was the first time in days that actual progress on the severed hand case had been made. And by Cecilia of all people!

I texted Nate and Marshall to let them know but I didn't expect to hear back for a while. Then, I phoned my mother to let her know.

"Now aren't you glad we're investigating those murders as well?" she asked.

"One murder. One questionable finding, but yes, the ladies have been very helpful."

"Your aunt invited me to her upcoming Edgar Allan Poe reading. I told her I might be coming down with a cold. Don't use the same excuse if she calls you."

"No worries. I'll probably be working anyway."

• • •

When Monday rolled around, I started to tell Augusta about Cecilia's call when I walked into the office, but before I could say a word, she blurted out, "Bowman left us a phone message. Here—listen to it. I wish that man would enunciate his words. Tell me if he's saying something about an ostomy bag or did I miss something?"

"Gee, I hope so."

She pushed the speaker button and we both listened to his loud, garbled voice. "Expecting information from the osteolomy office of one Clea Koff. She's the top expert. Let your boss and your husband know."

Augusta and I looked at each other and played it again. Then, a third time.

"Maybe we're better off looking up Clea Koff," I said. "I'll google her."

Seconds later, we got our answer. "It says she's a forensic scientist specializing in osteology, the study of bones. That would make sense. At least Bowman's referring to that bone Streetman found and not some stomach issue of his."

"I wish that man would speak English." Augusta lifted her coffee cup and took a large sip.

"Must be the sheriff's office had some connections and are pushing through on evidence. And speaking of which, I've got some news from Cecilia."

"The former nun?"

"We don't know that. But I did find out she graduated from College of the Holy Cross."

"That would explain things."

I grinned and proceeded to inform her about the translation on those rings.

"Albanian, huh?" Augusta adjusted her tortoiseshell glasses and bit her lip. "That certainly complicates things. If you want my take, those deputies will jump back into the Barry McGuire case. I figured it got stalled somewhere."

"Yeah, the minute our guys boarded the plane for Vancouver."

Augusta rubbed the back of her neck and winked.

"Oh, no. I know what you're thinking. You're getting worse than my mother."

"Our office can't be dilly-dallying with this stuff until Christmas. We've got the same information those deputies do. Plus, we've got Rolo at our fingertips."

"More like on our burner phones, but yeah, I suppose . . . so, what did you have in mind?"

"For starters—"

And then the phone rang. So much for "starters." As soon as Augusta picked up, I knew it was trouble. She placed her hand over the receiver, grimaced, and mouthed "Paul." Then I grimaced as I listened to her end of the conversation.

"Uh-huh . . . Yeah . . . Really? . . . Are you sure? . . . Fine. Did you get your fingerprints on it? . . . Never mind. Why didn't Mini-Moose tell Phee? . . . I see. Sure, bring it in."

"What? What was that all about? And what's Paul bringing in?"

"A small red gem got caught up in the grooves of his boots when he and Mini-Moose started digging around Maybelle's plot. He said when they watered it, the ground loosened up. He didn't realize the stone was stuck in the grooves until this morning when his boots dried out."

"Hmm, maybe Maybelle did bury something there. Only it wasn't a body."

"My thought as well. I suppose we'd better inform Frick and Frack but let's give it our own look first. What do you say?"

I shrugged. "At this point, I'm game for anything."

"Good."

CHAPTER 37

"Shouldn't I get a receipt or something for that?" Paul asked when he handed me the unusually dark red stone.

"Oh, for goodness sake, Paul. If it will make you feel any better." I studied the gem and took note of its shape. It was not an ordinary cut, that was for sure. "This could be a cheap costume piece or it could be the real deal."

"The real deal what?" Paul scratched his ear.

"A ruby."

"Oh."

"Look, there's a reputable jeweler a block away. I'll have them check it out during my lunch hour and get back to you."

Paul ran his hand through his thick, bushy hair and nodded. "Okay."

I handed the gem to Augusta, who furrowed her brow and eyeballed it. "I'm no jewelry expert but this appears to be real. Hold on a sec." She opened her desk drawer and took out a small magnifying glass. "It doesn't look like resin or plastic. Hard to say with that red color."

"I'll take that receipt after all," Paul said.

I scribbled something on a Williams Investigations card and gave it to him. "You do realize that if that stone turns out to be really valuable, or questionable, we'll have to give it to Bowman and Ranston."

Paul gave a nod. "And they'll have to give me ten percent of its value. That's the law, isn't it?"

"I'm not sure but you can deal with it later."

"Okey-dokey. Catch you later. I'm heading over to Bass Pro Shops to check out their new reels. Might want to do a radio segment on the latest fishing rods and reels."

"Sounds very enlightening."

Augusta all but choked and turned away as Paul left the office.

"I'll get the Lysol," I offered.

"Don't bother. I now keep an extra can in my desk."

• • •

I picked up Subway subs for us for lunch after dropping off the gem at Cranemoore Jewelers. One of their jewelers specialized in rare stones and agreed to study it once he finished with an appraisal for a brooch.

"I'll pick it up after work," I told him. "Just let me know the cost."

"No cost unless it's for an appraisal. I'm just giving you an idea of its worth and authenticity."

I thanked him and headed to Subway, anxious to bite into an Italian BMT with extra jalapeños.

A short text came in from Marshall, informing me that they were "engaged." Code for moving at breakneck speed. And although those exotic animal cartels were treacherous in their own right, it wasn't as if they were dealing with drug smugglers or worse.

The rest of the day was as mundane as they get, but when I got a call from Cranemoore Jewelers at a little past four, my jaw dropped.

"Where did you find this item, Mrs. Kimball?" the jeweler asked. "It's a near-perfect ruby and its value is priceless."

"A friend of mine found it and brought it to our investigative agency."

"I would notify the authorities if I were you. It could be a stolen piece. The FBI has a database for that sort of thing."

And a federal prison.

"Absolutely. I'll lock it up in our safe and call the sheriff's office. They can take it from there. And thank you."

"No. Thank you. It's not every day one gets to examine a piece of such magnitude."

Especially since it's been stuck to the bottom of Paul Schmidt's muddy boot.

By seven that night, two things happened. An agent from the Federal Bureau of Investigation in Arizona, along with Deputy Bowman, met Augusta and me at the office to retrieve the ruby. In the interest of saving them time and aggravation, we had Paul join us as well. This time it was the FBI who gave Paul a receipt, as well as our office.

"You mean I stepped into a gold mine?" Paul shouted. "What are you folks waiting for? Call an excavation company. Rent a tiller. Dig up Maybelle's plot! For all we know, she could have King Tut buried in there."

Augusta and I exchanged glances but kept quiet. Then, the inevitable call from my mother. And this time on my cell phone.

"Phee! You are not going to believe this. Mini-Moose has been yammering all over the bowling alley that he and Paul discovered something really valuable under Maybelle's tomatoes. She got wind of it and staked out her plot like one of those lone ranches in Idaho or Montana that resemble fortresses. Of course, we all knew that was coming when Joyanne told everyone what Maybelle said about the place getting trampled. Face it, no one can keep their mouths shut."

"Actually, Mom, I'm aware of it but please don't say a word. Paul did find a red gem but it could have come from anywhere. It was stuck under one of his boots. No telling what fishing hole he came from."

"Mini-Moose said they were digging up Maybelle's garden to look for a body."

Those guys simply do not know when to keep their mouths closed.

"I can't believe he admitted that. They're in enough trouble with the sheriff's office. Don't make it any worse by fueling the fire."

"I'm not Myrna. I can be circumspect."

"Good."

"So, do you think there might be a body under there? And maybe Barry found out and Maybelle murdered him? That would explain everything."

"No, it would not. Not without evidence."

"That's why we have a sheriff's office and those two deputies. They need to pull up their big-boy pants and get to it!"

"I'm sure that's exactly what they're doing. Listen, I'll talk with you tomorrow. Meanwhile, not a word. Okay?"

"Fine. Call me in the morning."

When things quieted down, I approached Augusta and leaned over her desk. "Do you have that detailed description of the gimmel rings?"

"Sure." She tapped her keyboard and an instant later the printer fired up. "Here you go—the complete summary."

Unlike my usual scanning, I perused every word. "I'll be darned. Here, read paragraph two."

Augusta adjusted her glasses and crinkled her nose. "I'm with Paul. Time to dig." She handed me back the paper.

"What are the chances? I mean, it's not definitive."

"It's close enough for my comfort."

I let out a long breath and brushed a wisp of hair from the side of my face. "The analysis of those gimmel rings pointed to idents that were believed to have held gemstones. According to this report, each ring held one gem."

"With that ruby red stone in their possession, the forensic lab won't have any trouble determining if it came from one of those rings. Begs the question—where's the other ruby?"

"We don't know if the second stone was a ruby. Or if the first one is a ruby, for that matter."

"My money is on a ruby."

"I hate to say it, Augusta, but I concur. Now what?"

"I had an original plan but now we can scrap it and move on."

"To what?"

"My favorite game in the world, Wait and See."

"Oh, brother."

CHAPTER 38

Having the FBI breathing down the neck of our local sheriff's office meant a turnaround in record time. Less than twenty-four hours for a solid analysis. The agent left our office before eight, and now, at three the next day, a fax rolled in with the news.

The gem was indeed a ruby, and not just any old ruby, but one that was nearly priceless due to its intense "pigeon blood" red color coupled with its weight and cut. As for origin, that was yet to be determined. That was the first shoe to drop.

But the second came as no surprise. The stone matched the gimmel ring's setting like Cinderella's glass slipper. Still, there was no evidence that connected Paul's find with Maybelle's plot. True, he and Mini-Moose traipsed over there, but they also traipsed everywhere else in the vicinity, including extricating themselves from Santi's vines and stirring up some dirt in Gussie's garden. Even Paul admitted that "one patch of dirt in the dark looks like every other."

A half hour later, Bowman sent our office a fax of his own. *When are your men getting back? Calls are going to voicemail. Texts are going unanswered.*

"Do you want me to answer or do you?" Augusta asked when she showed it to me.

I laughed. "Let me. I'll be more diplomatic."

In short, I explained that their radio silence wasn't deliberate on their part and that they were unable to make contact due to the extreme undercover investigation.

"That should buy us some time," I said. "Must be this new discovery is prompting more questioning from the sheriff's office and Bowman's patience is wearing thin."

"What about Ranston?"

"The man was born without patience. Glad I don't work in that office." I barely spat out those words when who should phone our office but Ranston himself. Thankfully, Augusta took the call because I was already doubled over laughing. So hard in fact that she had to turn away from me.

Other than "Uh-huh," "hmm," and "okay," Augusta was unable to form full sentences. When she put the receiver down, she looked up and rolled her eyes. A skill we had both mastered.

"He wanted to clarify the urgency for Mr. Williams and Mr. Gregory to return to the area ASAP."

"We already know. He and Bowman don't want to get hives interviewing those gardeners again."

"Well, that, too, but there's more. The detectives are convinced there's another valued gem from that other gimmel ring. Not to mention the third ring that has so far managed to elude us."

"Shouldn't they be more focused on Barry's killer than a valuable ruby?"

"Here's where it gets interesting. The deputies think the two situations might be connected."

"That's news to us. Up until now they've dismissed that theory. Did Ranston tell you what changed their minds?"

"He sure did. Hold on for this one. That ruby underwent extreme forensic testing and it was found to have particles of Solanum tuberosum on it."

"Potato poison?"

"Indeed."

I shrugged. "Questioning the same suspects isn't going to get those deputies anywhere. That crew is as tight-lipped as I've ever seen."

"Not if you know where to find the weak link. And as much as I'll kick myself for saying this, there's only one way to do that."

I froze. "You're not suggesting—"

"Get ahold of the book club ladies to get them talking. They certainly don't have any trouble with that."

"Yeah, for the women, maybe. But not Gussie or Orvis. Cecilia will cower, Myrna will scare the daylights of them, and the others will . . . I don't know . . . bore them to death talking about sewing, soap operas, and birds."

"Well, give it some thought. This has been dragging on way too long."

Fortunately for Augusta, another opportunity presented itself and my mother jumped on it like Streetman after a freshly coiffed poodle at the dog park. I found out about it after nine that night. I had just gotten a text from Marshall, putting my mind at ease that they weren't in immediate danger. And while it didn't disclose much, it was enough to ensure that I'd get a decent night's sleep. No sooner did I turn off the lamp by my bedside when the landline rang.

Now what?

The caller ID was my mother's and I snatched the phone from the cradle and said, "What now? Did Streetman ingest something questionable? He always does that after the veterinary offices are closed."

"My little man is fine. I meant to call you sooner but got stuck listening to your aunt pontificating about Louis being in Vancouver and how he always manages to miss her literary soirees."

"Okay. What's up?"

"All of us in the agriculture club got an invitation from Racine. There's going to be a blue moon this Thursday and she thought it would be lovely if we were to gather in the garden to enjoy her homemade dandelion wine and rejuvenate in the moonlight."

"That's a new word for it."

"Racine said she only serves her wine at special occasions and felt as if the gardeners needed a tranquil evening to decompress from the unfortunate incidents."

"Another new word for 'murders.'"

"Never mind, but I thought perhaps you'd care to join us. Marshall is out of town so it's not as if I'm cutting into your social schedule."

"My social schedule consists of chores, swimming, and sleeping. Besides, I don't drink and neither do you. Or any of the book club ladies. In fact, didn't Cecilia tell us that the half thimble of wine at communion made her loopy?"

"It's more about fellowship. Besides, we can bring fruit drinks or iced tea. Knowing the men, they'll forgo the wine and dive into a six-pack. Or go to Curley's Bar altogether."

"Aren't you forbidden to be in the garden after dusk? I thought that was an edict from the rec center."

"Edict schme-dict! No one pays attention. So what do you say?"

The word *no* was at the tip of my lips but then I realized something. This was the opportunity Augusta proposed—eking out information from the gardeners. "Sure, why not?"

"Racine said it will start at seven. You can come here first and say hello to Streetman and Essie."

"Um, I'll meet you at the garden. Most likely I'll be running errands after work and grabbing a quick bite."

"You're welcome to invite Lyndy if she doesn't have plans."

She'll find some.

"Thanks, but she's got a full schedule with Lyman."

"I asked your aunt but she's tied up with that Edgar Allan Poe thing."

When I said good night and put the receiver back in the cradle, something didn't sit well with me. My mother is as devious as they come and it didn't take a genius to figure out she had something planned. Especially if the gardeners were going to indulge in dandelion wine. And if my memory served me well, dandelion wine was more of a spirit than a wine since it didn't come from fermented grapes. And, since it contained a much higher alcohol content. For sure, my mother wasn't about to pass on this opportunity and neither was I.

∙ ∙ ∙

When I told Augusta on Wednesday, she shared the same sentiment and added, "If I didn't have canasta tomorrow night, I'd stop by. I can envision it now. Hippie gardeners reliving Woodstock with dandelion wine, survivalists chugging anything with alcohol, and your mother's book club taking notes like Nancy Drew on a field trip."

"If that's all that happens, I'll consider it a success."

It wasn't. In fact, it was more like the sinking of the *Titanic*, only louder and faster. The last normal thing I remember was leaving work, changing into jeans and a sweatshirt and grabbing a quick meal at Pollo Loco on Happy Valley Road in Peoria. Not wanting to destroy another pair of sneakers, I dug out some old hiking boots and wore them. Fashion was not the first thing on my mind.

Traffic headed into Surprise and Sun City West was on the light side and I arrived at the garden at a quarter to seven. Racine stood at the gate and handed me a plastic tulip-shaped wineglass. "Welcome, and join us under the ramada. I added fairy lights this afternoon when everyone left. Doesn't it look lovely?"

I turned my head and took in the haze that emanated from the ramada's lighting. "Yes, magical and whimsical." *And wacky as all get-up-and-go.*

Marlie, Claudia and Maybelle were already there, and with their bodies leaning toward one another, it appeared as if they were engaged in a serious conversation. Next thing I knew, Gussie walked in and said, "You've got to be kidding me. I'm not drinking out of a tea party glass. I brought a six-pack of Michelob and when we finish that, it's off to Curley's. Blue moon or not." Then he stretched his neck toward the ramada. "Did anyone bring chips or pretzels?"

Racine shook her head. "No, but Thira and I made crudités and cucumber finger sandwiches."

"Crud what? Never mind. I'll grab a burger later." Gussie stomped over to the ramada, where he was met by the ladies and Orvis, who had just emerged from the men's room. I thanked Racine and walked over, hoping my mother's crew would get a move on.

A few minutes later, Tunnie walked in with Joyanne. The two of them wasted no time taking seats next to the other three. I stood off to the side, eyeballing the gate as I tapped my foot on the ground.

"Howdy, folks! Did anyone bring any marshmallows to toast?" It was Herb's voice and it echoed across the garden plots. "I brought beer."

"Me, too." This time it was Kevin.

"Great minds think alike." Kenny waved a six-pack in the air and joined his buddies.

"Hey, cutie," Herb called out when he saw me. "Where's your mother and the other women?"

"On their way, I'm sure. She probably had to walk the dog."

"I don't think so." Kevin pulled the tab off of a beer and laughed. "That's the little ground sniffer now, pulling her across the path."

Sure enough, my mother brought Streetman. This time without his stroller. I was hopeful she banked on a short night, but I was wrong. Dreadfully wrong.

"Phee! Sorry we're late. Lucinda and Louise are on their way. I also invited everyone else and Shirley and Cecilia are on their way. Racine said it would be fine. It's an informal get-together, not a business meeting."

Then, as if on cue, Racine walked to the center of the ramada like she did when I first met her, and welcomed everyone to their "Blue Moon Soiree." With that, she circulated around pouring dandelion wine into the flutes as if it was bug juice at an elementary school campout.

I watched the expressions on the men's faces as they sniffed their glasses and I tried not to laugh. Then I watched them open their beer cans instead. I decided to try a small sip, but no sooner did I put the glass to my mouth when I heard the loud blare of a siren.

"Must be an accident on Grand," Gussie said. "Give it a minute and the rest of the emergency response will come. Wonder if it's north of us or south. Hard to tell from here."

"I can see the lights from the red and blue flashers," I said. "But that's all."

"Funny, there should be emergency vehicles by now." Kevin stood and tried to gaze into the distance. "Must be it's further up the road past the Grand."

"Okay. That settles it," I said. "I have just appointed myself the designated driver. And I'm sure Cecilia will be happy to be the other one. We can pick up everyone's cars in the morning."

"Fantastic!" Orvis announced. "Now we can chug away."

"This isn't a frat party." Racine put her hands on her hips. "It's a respectable evening as we partake of some spirits in moderation as we enjoy the moonlight."

"Or not." It was Herb's voice. "Look who's coming through the gate! And it's not Shirley and Cecilia."

I didn't need to look. The blinking red and blue lights just past the gate told me all I needed to know—the sirens on Grand were none other than Bowman and Ranston coming to pay us a visit. And I was certain it wasn't with the intention to bask in the moonlight.

Chapter 39

"Is Tunilla LaCroix here?" Bowman asked. "We have a search warrant."

Tunnie handed her wineglass to Joyanne and stood with her arms crossed. "At night? You want to search my plot at night? In the dark? What do you think I'm growing? Deadly nightshade?"

"Not your plot. Your garage."

"My garage? What on earth do you expect to find in my garage? And at this late hour, no less. There must be some mistake."

"There's no mistake," Ranston said as he fumbled through a handful of papers. "And as for the late hour, you can blame that on the county judge. We presented the affidavit that established probable cause."

Tunnie wasn't about to go along. "What probable cause?"

"We found a partially filled coffee mug in Barry McGuire's refrigerator and had it tested for toxins. Results were delayed due to some mix-up, but the results were clear—the lip edge contained Solanum tuberosum, or potato poisoning in layman's terms."

"That doesn't mean it came from me. Why would I give Barry a coffee mug?"

"Shh!" Joyanne said. She poked Tunnie and put a finger to her lips. "Don't incriminate yourself. They probably think it's your mug."

"Very astute, miss," Ranston said. "We know for a fact the mug originated from Ms. LaCroix. There's a small sticker on the bottom with one of those cutesy labels. It read, 'From Tunnie's kitchen.' It was evidence enough for the judge."

"Oh my heavens!" Tunnie threw the palm of her hand over her heart. "So that's where it wound up! That scoundrel Barry must have pilfered it from our springtime garden lunch a few months ago. I wondered where it disappeared to. It was part of a set from Red and Howling."

"That's a wonderful company," Shirley said. "Whimsical and delightful. I happen to own three Christmas mugs myself and—"

"Enough with the Christmas mugs," Bowman bellowed. "We're here to escort Ms. LaCroix home while our forensic crew searches her garage."

I looked at my mother but didn't say a word. The entire scene felt more like a setup than sheriff's office business.

"I'll drive myself if you don't mind," Tunnie said. "I haven't been arrested, have I?"

The deputies looked at each other before Bowman replied. "Drive straight home. No monkey business. We know where you live."

In the background I heard a few "oh brothers" from the men as the three of them left.

"What do you make of that?" Claudia asked. "Tunnie of all people. I mean, I know she believed Barry poisoned the soil in her garden and that's why her plants wilted, but I don't think she'd go that far to murder him."

"Unless she didn't." I fixed my gaze on Joyanne's crew as well as on Ona and Aneta, who had passed the sipping stage of wine and had moved on to full gulps thanks to Racine's refills.

"Think they'll find anything?" my mother asked.

If anyone wanted to answer they never got the chance because Thira suddenly shouted, "Harriet! I think your dog peed on my ankle. It's soaking wet!"

And then, a similar remark from Maybelle. "My foot's soaked. What's your dog doing?"

"He got me, too," Marlie said. "I thought maybe it was just some moisture from the air since everything's aerating right now."

"Streetman can't possibly be peeing on all of you at once." My mother handed Louise her wineglass and walked over to where the women were seated. Maneuvering the dog on his long leash and reaching for her phone, she managed to tap the flashlight feature and point it to the ground. "It's not Streetman. Look! Puddles are coming up from the ground."

At that moment, all I could think of were the lyrics from the *Beverly Hillbillies*: "And up through the ground came a-bubblin' crude." Only this wasn't oil. It was water. Something must have sprung a leak somewhere. I tried not to laugh but it was futile. The water may have started out slow but it began to saturate the ground in record time.

"Gussie! Do something!" Racine yelled. "You're the one who has the key to the water shutoff. Turn it off before all of our plants drown."

Without hesitating, Gussie thundered to one of the outbuildings, and within seconds the bubbling from the ground stopped. "Some idiot turned on the main water supply," he announced. "I'm not the only one with a key. And there's a sign right over the faucet that says 'Main shutoff. Do not use without permission.'"

Then he crossed his arms and surveyed the group. "Okay, which one of you thought that would be funny? Because it's not. Wasting water is costly. Not to mention prohibited by the governing laws for this organization."

I looked around but my guess was as good as Gussie's. A few folks were milling around and chatting while they indulged on Racine's wine, but in the scant light it was impossible to discern who was where. The greater question was why? Why would someone turn on the water. Unless . . .

"Mom," I said. "I need you to show me your garden. I haven't seen it in a while."

"What? In the dark? Why all of a sudden do you want to see my garden? Louise, Lucinda and I will be back tomorrow. You can see it before or after work."

"I'm curious about something and it can't wait. It'll plague me."

My mother stood, sighed, and grabbed the dog. "I'll be right back," she told everyone. Then she grabbed my elbow as we walked toward her plot. "What's really going on? What are you up to?"

"More like what someone else is up to. Face it, no one in their right mind turns on the main water line. Especially ecology-conscious gardeners. Whoever did it, they needed a distraction."

"Oh, please don't tell me you think someone else got murdered."

"Murdered? No. But something. Come on, we need to have a look-see."

I kept the flashlight feature from my phone low to the ground so as not to call attention to us as we maneuvered past Santi's thick vines.

"Do you notice anything out of the ordinary, Mom?" I asked.

"Everything looks out of the ordinary in the dark."

We kept walking and then, sure enough, a reason for the distraction. It looked as if someone had started to snip the coiled wire surrounding the Zlatkova sisters' plot and must have gotten scared away with the arrival of Bowman and Ranston.

"Whoever it was must believe Ona and Aneta have something to hide," I said.

"Let's go find out. It's a chance I've been waiting for—to put Streetman's sniffing skills to the test."

"Not now! Not here! Not with everyone yards away from us. You can put his skills to the test on your block."

But it was too late. The little stinker jumped out of my mother's arms, leash and all. He wedged himself underneath the makeshift wire barricade and made a mad dash for the rear section of the Zlatkova plot.

"Grab him, Phee! Before he gets caught up in something."

"Before he gets caught up in anything? I'm the one who'll get caught up in what's left of the coiled wire! Call him!" Who was I kidding? On a good day, Streetman ignored commands.

I bit my lip as I watched the dog start to dig.

"What if that dog unleashes something?" It was the first time I could actually sense fear in my mother's voice. Face it, no one needed to find another corpse.

Suddenly, the word *unleashed* gave me an idea. Streetman was still attached to his leash. If I could find a way to grab it, I could, conceivably, pull him out. I looked around, hoping to find something to pull the loop end toward me. A stick. A long rod. Anything! Unfortunately, the only thing the

Zlatkova sisters had were flower pots.

"Give me a second, Mom. I'll be right back."

"Where are you going?"

"To play Tarzan." Without waiting for a response, I hurried over to Santi's vines and used a small nail file that I had in my bag to snip one of his larger, sturdier ones. Needless to say, I forgot the vines had thorns and tendrils, causing my fingertips to bleed. No matter. I pulled the vine out from its surrounding greenery and charged over to where Streetman was still fixated, tossing soil in the air.

Then I outstretched my arm and moved the vine to the loop of the leash. It took four attempts but I finally snagged it and gave it a pull. When it was less than a yard away, I grabbed it and gave it a yank. "Any second and I'll be able to pull him out of there!"

On what planet?

I tugged the leash, expecting the dog to come toward me. Instead, he refused to move. I leaned forward and tugged harder. Next thing I knew, I lost my footing and landed face down in the murky ground.

The odor from the damp soil was sour and made me recoil, but it was nothing compared to my clothing, which was now saturated from the groundwater that had seeped up when someone turned on the spigot.

"My goodness, Phee. I never knew my little man had so much strength."

I stood, handed her the leash and glared. "Well, now you do!"

"I wonder what he was so fixated on. We've been working on pungent odors like rotten meat and sulfur odors like rotten eggs."

"Maybe the Zlatkovas used eggshells in their garden. Aren't they supposed to keep away snails?"

"Yes, they are. Hmm, could be Paul's fish entrails too. As I recall, he said he and Mini-Moose dumped a ton of them in their garden."

"That has to be it. Another reason to keep that man at arm's length."

"I think you spoke too soon. Look down the path. If I'm not mistaken, isn't that him?"

I squinted and edged forward. "Ugh. If that doesn't complete the evening, I don't know what does."

Chapter 40

"Yoo-hoo! It's Paul. Can you hear me?"

Like a marching band at the foot of my bed.

"We can hear you," I said. "Why are you here and how did you get in? The gate's in the other direction."

"From the railroad yard. One of the workers is an old fishing buddy of mine and he wanted to show me some new lures he got at a bargain."

"At this hour? In the dark?"

"It's not dark over there. They've got quite the lean-to. Besides, he was on duty. They've had a lot of trespassers lately and the railroad inspectors are worried about sabotage to the tracks."

"Okay, that answers why you were there, but why did you come over here?"

"Orvis sent me a text that Tunnie was arrested. Never can be too sure with him. I decided to find out for myself. I like being on top of things."

I rolled my eyes, thankful he couldn't see in the dark.

"She wasn't arrested." My mother walked toward him with Streetman tucked under an arm. "The deputies got a search warrant for her place."

"Then they must think she did it. Murdered Barry or cut up a body. Either way, Orvis wasn't too far off."

"Too far off?" I nearly shouted. "That's how rumors get started. Do everyone a favor and don't say anything."

"Only if you tell me what you're all doing here."

"Drinking wine," my mother answered.

"I'm serious." Paul crossed his arms and looked around. "What's everyone doing here? Orvis wouldn't say."

"My mom's right. Racine made some dandelion wine and wanted the gardeners to drink it under the Blue Moon."

"Harrumph. And people tell me I've got a screw loose. Hey, why is the ground so wet?"

"Someone tampered with the main water supply. And before you say another word, that's why I'm so wet!"

"I wasn't going to say anything. I'm always wet from fishing."

I tried not to shudder. "Listen, if that's all you wanted to know, we need to be getting back. We were just taking the dog for a stroll on his leash."

"Watch out for the wet spots. The ground is so dry that the excess water remains on the surface. It takes a while to saturate, but when it does, it'll bring up anything that's underneath it, including a body."

"Honestly, Paul," my mother said. "Do you really believe there's

Planted 4 Murder

another body buried in here? Wasn't finding the hand enough?"

"I'm not so sure. That ruby came from a ring. And that ring came from a finger. And that finger—"

"We get it. And don't pick up where you left off regarding digging around Maybelle's plot."

"No sirree. I came up with a better idea. Especially since Nate and Marshall are out of town. And especially since I could be looking at a hefty finder's fee."

"What idea?" Streetman squirmed and my mother shifted him to the other arm.

"I get Mini-Moose to cozy up to Maybelle and see if he can romance it out of her."

At that point, every nerve in my body hit high alert. "That's, by far, the worst idea you've ever had. Listen, I don't mean to disparage Mini-Moose's charm, but he's no Casanova. How about if you let things ride for a day or so. I promise I'll reach out to our cyber-investigator and see if he can make headway. If not, then, well, I'll let you know."

"Fine. I wasn't too sure about the Moose anyway and it would have cost me lots of beers."

"Um, are you going out the same way you came in?"

"I suppose. Don't need to get hammered on some weedy concoction when I've got cold beer in the fridge at home."

"Good plan."

"If anyone asks," I told my mother as Paul sauntered back, "let's tell them what we told Paul. About walking the dog."

"No one will ask. They're too busy talking. I can hear them from here."

"Paul was right, you know. About the ground. Good thing Gussie was able to turn off the water. And thank goodness they haven't predicted a monsoon."

"Bite your tongue, Phee. Monsoon season won't be over until the end of October. I don't care what Google says about September. They don't live here."

The evening ended without fanfare, but with enough chattering about Tunnie to reach the gossip grapevine by morning. So much so, that no one gave any more thought to who was responsible for turning on the faucet.

• • •

"I'm glad it's Friday," Augusta said when I walked into the office the next morning. "Got our big canasta tournament tonight. My hands have been itching all night. Means I'm going to come into money."

"I hope you're right!"

"How did last night go? Did everyone get snookered on the dandelion wine?"

"No, but someone turned on the main water supply and saturated the ground. Then Bowman and Ranston showed up with a search warrant for Tunnie's house. If that wasn't bad enough, Paul snuck in from the railroad yard because he heard about Tunnie from Orvis and wanted to find out for himself."

"Whoa. Slow down, Phee. You're making me dizzy."

"You? I had to deal with that entire nightmare. Funny, but I thought the water deal was a distraction and I was right. Someone snipped the coiled wire around the Zlatkova sisters' plot. We didn't say anything for fear of starting a melee. But they'll find out soon enough. Whoever did it must have had a good reason to believe Ona and Aneta had something to hide."

"And you're about to find out?"

"In a roundabout way. With a phone call to Rolo. I already landed on wet ground once, thanks to Streetman. I'm not about to go for round two."

"Tell me whenever you want the burner phone."

"Will do. Meanwhile, I need to get some work done. Got a late-night text from Marshall telling me he was fine and not to worry. Said Nate will reach out to you today."

"Whoever would have thought there'd be so much money in exotic domesticated cats. And all this time, my family raised dairy cows."

I laughed and walked into my office, where I remained for the next two and a half hours. Then, I got a call from Lyndy, who picked up her scuttlebutt from Lyman and her aunt.

"This is a first, Phee. Both rumor mills match up. The long and short of it is that a few sheriff cars were at Tunnie's house last night for the longest time. Oh my gosh! You don't suppose someone planted that obliteration knife in the potato bag and set her up, do you? I mean, why else would the sheriff deputies have been there?"

"Unless they found out something else. But I think you're right. Listen, I've got to get back to work but let's touch base later, okay?"

"You got it."

A strange thought crossed my mind but I struggled for a connection. What if it was Tunnie who turned on the water supply in order to cut the wire in the Zlatkova garden? Come to think of it, I didn't remember seeing her the entire time at the wine tasting. And maybe the Zlatkovas had been suspicious of her all along. After all, Tunnie did have a motive for murdering Barry. But what did that have to do with Ona and Aneta? They despised him as well. Unless one of them was responsible and Tunnie found out so they set her up with that knife in the potatoes. Better to point the finger at someone than be at the other end.

I knew I wasn't getting anywhere and without bona fide evidence, I was as bad as the book club ladies.

"Augusta!" I called out. "Can you get me that burner phone?" I stood and walked to the front office.

"I wondered when you'd make the call. Another half hour and I would have done it myself. Here!"

She handed me a phone, still in its packaging, from the locked file cabinet. "While you're at it, see if he knows anything about the Canadian cat situation. His tentacles reach further than ours."

"He'll double bill us." I laughed. Then I made the call.

"I expected your call, Phee. Your boss and your husband warned me. I can't divulge anything except that the cat is a LaPerm. Not that I'm an expert on cats, but this one is a rare breed of rex cat with tight curly hair."

"Thanks, but that's not why I called." For the next two or three minutes, I theorized about Tunnie, Ona, Aneta and Joyanne. "Can you dig deep and find any connection that would link one or more of them? Other than the fact that Ona and Aneta are sisters."

"If I didn't know any better, I'd swear you had my office bugged. I've been studying that Macedonian dynasty for weeks now."

"Macedonian dynasty? Weren't they wiped out in the eleventh century? Gosh, I remember that from my world history class."

"Not that dynasty, although the lineage is the same. I'm referring to a twenty-first-century one that's still engaged in age-old vendettas within their own tribes, for lack of a better word. Do me a favor and steer clear of those women. Sure, they may come across as sweet little peasant farmers, but my intel says different. Wait until your boss and your husband get back before you decide to play with the sharks."

"Seriously? Ona and Aneta?"

"They were taught by the very best, Phee. And I'm not referring to growing crops. Look, I've got another matter to deal with. If you want something to do, look at the new IKEA catalogue. Consider it a heads-up."

"Rolo, I—"

But it was too late. He ended the call in a nanosecond.

I looked at the phone in my hand and thought about his words—They were taught by the very best. And then, something Cindy Dolton said struck me. Something about three of them walking a wolfhound a few years ago. She thought it was their mother. Heavens! Their mother! She could be the one manipulating everything behind the scenes. Maybe Cindy got it wrong. Maybe the dog passed away but the mother is still alive and well. And pulling all the strings.

I let the phone slip from my hand and bent down to retrieve it. "Augusta! Find that Sun City West phone book! I may be on to something!"

Chapter 41

"I think Sun City West is one of the only communities left with its own phone book," Augusta said as she retrieved it from the bottom of a rarely used file cabinet. "Do you plan on calling her?"

"Huh? No, of course not. This is strictly for my own edification."

I turned the page to the Z's and found Zlatkova. Unlike Smith or Jones, it was a "one-of."

"Rats. It reads 'A. Zlatkova.' Ona isn't listed. Or the mother. Whatever her name is. Must be the landline is in Aneta's name. That's not much help. Worse yet, it comes down to another sojourn into the dog park to find Cindy. If she saw three of them with a wolfhound, other people must have as well. And she'll know who was there. That woman's memory goes back to when Sun City West was Lizard Acres."

Augusta chuckled. "I'd say it's worth the aggravation. Face it, no one's plants are worth all that subterfuge. I'm not saying they've got a body rotting under those vegetables, but I'll venture to say they've got something to hide. And a chitchat with Cindy is better than the alternative."

"Did my mother put you up to this? Never mind. I'll see about a park date with His Excellency."

When midafternoon rolled around, Augusta got an email from Ranston. It must not have been so pressing as to be sent by text, or as formal as a fax. Still, it was a communiqué and it read, "For your information—The Maricopa County Sheriff's Office retrieved a Dalstrong Gladiator Series Meat Cleaver from Tunilla LaCroix's garage. The brand-name cleaver was concealed in a twenty-pound bag of potatoes that appeared to be homegrown. It has been sent to our lab for indications of blood or other human fluid. At this time, Ms. LaCroix was released on her own recognizance." Then, in the following paragraph, "We may have nailed it. Will keep you in the loop."

I shook my head at the last sentence. "Even if that meat cleaver is saturated with blood, they have no way to prove Tunnie was the responsible party. And it was Maybelle who worked in that butcher shop. Maybe she paid Tunnie a visit and put the cleaver in with those spuds and not the Zlatkovas."

"But why Tunnie? Why not Claudia or Thira, for that matter?"

"Good point. Tunnie had motive to murder Barry, but he was poisoned, not, well, you know . . ."

"Unless Tunnie didn't murder Barry but had a reason to do away with someone else."

"Wonderful. Now I have no choice but to take Streetman to the park. And the sooner the better."

• • •

"Hold on, Phee," Cindy said the next morning. "Charles Delavan, who's over by the awning, used to have a retriever and I'd always see him chatting with the Zlatkovas. Now he's got that cute Maltese mix. Come on, let's ask him. Streetman's just sniffing the ground. So far, so good."

For how long?

We stepped away from the fence and approached the elderly man with one of those three-prong canes. Cindy introduced me and then got to the point.

"Sure, I remember Elisaveta. Classy lady. Never left the house without her jewelry. Long gold earrings. Brooches. And rings. Even if it was just to walk Igor."

"Remember? Is she—"

"No longer with us. It was quite a while ago. Can't give you an exact year. It was as if she suddenly vanished, but the daughters said she succumbed to a sudden illness."

Or poisoning. Still, someone had to get the body.

"What about a funeral or calling hours?"

Charles shook his head. "I would have thought so, but no. Very private. I was told they had her cremated and the ashes shipped back to the homeland."

"Was there ever an obituary in the paper?"

"Like I said, nothing. That family kept to itself. My late wife always thought the Zlatkova's were involved in international espionage or something equally dangerous. It didn't surprise her that Elisaveta disappeared as if she'd been abducted in the middle of the night. But the daughters didn't give any indication of foul play. They both held to their story—that their mother died following a sudden illness. It was a few months before they sold their small patio home and purchased that large one on Echo Mesa Golf Course. I imagine the mother left all the money in her will to them. That's how it is with parents. They live modestly and then leave everything to their kids, who spend it like drunken sailors. Between you gals and me, I intend to spend every last penny!"

Cindy mumbled something and I think I said something inane like, "Life is meant to be enjoyed." Oh, brother.

We thanked Charles and returned to Cindy's spot by the fence.

"What did you make of that?" I gauged her expression.

"If nothing else, Charles was certainly forthcoming. Maybe a tad too much, but I trust his credibility as far as the Zlatkovas are concerned."

"True. I doubt he has anything to hide." Then I looked for the dog and shuddered.

Streetman had discovered a disgusting clump of dried who-knows-what and I yelled for him to drop it. He didn't.

"Here." Cindy handed me a treat. "Dog trainers would be aghast but hey, they're not dealing with your mother's chiweenie."

I took the bacon-flavored roll-up and swapped it with the "prize" he had in his mouth. No fuss this time.

"What's your take, Cindy? Do you think Elisaveta's death wasn't natural?"

"Sounds rather suspicious, doesn't it?"

"Uh-huh. I hate to say this but Paul Schmidt might have had the right idea about digging up one of the plots. Only he had the wrong one in mind."

"And you're going to convince him otherwise?"

"Heck no! I'm going to figure another way around it. One that doesn't involve Paul. And one that certainly doesn't involve getting my nails dirty or my reputation sullied."

"Too bad this isn't California. We could always pray for an earthquake."

"Or a sinkhole."

"Um, speaking of which, you'd better take a look behind you."

I turned and sure enough, there was Streetman, head down in a freshly dug hole. That dog never stopped. Dirt flew behind him as he and another dog pawed the ground like the forty-niners after gold. I rushed over, snatched him up and kicked most of the dirt back in the hole while the other dog's owner joined me.

"I can't turn my back on this guy for longer than ten seconds," she said.

I dusted the dirt off my clothes with my spare hand. "I think it's five for me."

Cindy shook her head and tried not to laugh. "Sorry Phee, but your mom's dog is a regular sideshow."

"I may need to charge admission."

I thanked her and told her I'd keep her posted.

"Any time. And be careful. Please. If there's one thing I've learned around here, it's that people can be deceiving."

Or dangerous.

Given Rolo's warning, coupled with what Charles told us, the Zlatkova sisters were now at the top of my suspect list. I simply needed a way to flush them out.

Since it was one of my Saturday half days, I called Lyndy when I dropped the dog off and convinced her to spend a "fun-filled afternoon" at my house eating pizza and doing what we did best—internet searches.

"Double pepperoni and you're on," she said. "Lyman's picking me up at seven for a round of miniature golf and fish fry. By then, it will have cooled down. This sticky heat is getting to me but the KPHO weather forecast was hopeful monsoons would move into the valley."

"Did they say when?"

"Before the season ends."

"Talk about playing it safe. Okay, see you at two."

When I told Augusta what I had in mind, she thought it was the first sensible idea I'd had. And one that wouldn't result in running the washer. "Unless you get pizza sauce on your clothes."

• • •

"Where do you want to start?" Lyndy asked from her comfy spot on the couch. "I brought my laptop so we can do double time."

"Public records. I'll look into Elisaveta and you can check the social media on Ona and Aneta. Pizza won't be here for another hour."

By the time we inhaled the aroma of the pepperoni and tomato sauce, we had discovered that Elisaveta Jovanovska Zlatkova was a wealthy widow who emigrated to the United States in the late seventies. Public records showed her birth and citizenship papers, but no death certificate.

"That's odd." Lyndy took a bite from her first slice. "Didn't you tell me she died?"

"Yep. That's what I was told. I wish Rolo wasn't so tight-lipped. It's not as if I'm a government employee. Anyway, this changes everything. Think about it. What if Elisaveta is still alive but suffering from dementia or something. That's a possibility. Some people still think there's a stigma associated with that."

"Charles said the daughters bought a huge house. That could be the reason. Oh my gosh. This is just like *Wuthering Heights* but without the romance."

"Only one way to find out. If that's the case, then caregivers would be going in and out."

"Oh, no. Not a stakeout."

"I don't see any other way."

"Wait a sec. The house is on Echo Mesa Golf Course. Can you find out where?"

"Sure. Aneta is listed in the directory. Hold on." I scrambled for the information I had written down on the Notes app on my phone. "It's on Yukon Drive."

"I'm Zillowing it!" Seconds later Lyndy exclaimed, "Holy cow! It sold for over eight hundred thousand dollars."

"Hmm, that does not smack of someone caring for an ill parent at home. That money had to have come from someone. I'm going to take a Grand Canyon leap and propose that Elisaveta is with her maker."

"And the money is with the girls?"

"Uh-huh."

"Then how come there's no death certificate?"

"It may be under the maiden name. Let's try again."

Lyndy and I held our collective breaths as I tried another search.

"Jovanovska. It's listed all right."

"I don't know about you, Phee, but I'm not sure whether we should leap for joy or cower in fear. This is worse than *Wuthering Heights*. The daughters could have murdered her for the family fortune."

I gulped. "That might explain the severed hand. It was arthritic according to the coroner's report."

"And that gimmel ring. The third band might have simply become dislodged."

"I don't think we should get ahead of ourselves. Darn. Of all the times for Nate and Marshall to be out of the country."

"I'm sure you'll think of something."

"Don't say anything to Lyman. Okay? Not yet. If word gets out to his softball team, I can't imagine what would happen. Heck, Herb alone can spread a rumor faster than a ten-year-old smearing peanut butter on bread."

"No worries. Let's call each other if we come up with a plan."

"Or bail. Whichever comes first."

Chapter 42

At a little before eleven, when I checked the doors and windows before trudging off to bed, a text came in from Marshall: *Rolo texted. Concerned about your sleuthing. Said the players have "spreading roots." Stay safe, hon. We are getting close. XOXO*

Something about Rolo's message didn't sit right. No one says "spreading roots." The expression is "deep roots." And I knew Marshall didn't get it wrong. I also knew Rolo's penchant for cryptic messages. In my mind, it meant one thing: the Zlatkovas didn't act alone. But who did they cozy up to?

My mind twisted and turned for the next forty minutes as I replayed all of the relationships I could think of from that garden crew. A real detective would have gone straight to the murder board, but I was too tired and too lazy. Not exactly the attributes Dashiell Hammett would admire. Sadly, the more I pushed myself to find connections, the more tangled everything got.

Then I recalled something Nate told me a while back. We were all stymied over an international diamond smuggling case with a myriad of suspects when he said, "If you can't single out the relationships, or there's just too darn many of them, look for the inconsistencies in behavior."

He went on to elaborate by explaining that guilty parties are so concerned about concealing their real motives that they play off of the moment at hand. Professing one thing and doing another, hoping no one will realize it.

That made me think. Joyanne was adamant that Tunnie poisoned Barry. Insistent and credible enough to have me scope out the woman's laundry in search of gardening gloves. But we discovered a meat cleaver in Tunnie's bag of potatoes, not a mug. It was the sheriff's office that was credited with that find.

Joyanne had no qualms siccing me on that investigation, and yet, when Ranston questioned Tunnie about the mug, it was Joyanne who told her not to incriminate herself. No one flip-flops like that. Not without good acting skills.

My mind didn't shut off for another forty or so minutes as I rationalized why Joyanne would shove Tunnie into the limelight for a murder or murders she most likely didn't commit. That left Joyanne herself, but for the life of me, I couldn't come up with a motive.

I finally fell asleep but it wasn't restful. When I got up the next day, I thought I had a hangover without going near alcohol. It was only after two cups of coffee that I began to feel somewhat normal. And that's when I decided to pay a visit to the community gardens to see if I could dig up the kind of dirt that wouldn't get under my nails.

It was a little past eight and Gussie was chatting with Santi at the edge of Santi's plot. I overheard a bit of their conversation and cringed.

Gussie's voice was crisp and clear. "Are you sure? The vines look fine to me."

"I meant to trim a big one that served no purpose but it's gone."

"It probably got too brittle and is on the ground somewhere."

"I know my vines like the veins in my hand. It's not on the ground."

"Probably javelina."

"They don't carry off an entire vine."

No, that's something new in my skill set.

"Hi, guys!" I announced. "Have either of you seen my mother? I figured I might find her here."

They shook their heads.

"Hmm, I must have gotten my signals crossed. It doesn't look like there are too many people here this morning."

"It's Sunday. Church and restaurants. Unless there's a football game," Gussie said. "By the way, any news on Tunnie? I haven't run into any of the yakkers."

I did a mental eye roll. "Nothing that isn't public knowledge. The sheriff's office got a tip and the long and short of it is that Tunnie was found to be the owner of the mug with potato poisoning on it. That prompted another search and that turned up a suspicious meat cleaver in her garage."

"Is she in lock-up? Santi asked.

"Not that I'm aware of. But doesn't it appear odd to both of you that she would be behind two murders? And I'm presuming the severed hand was evidence of the first."

"Not as odd as Maybelle going ballistic that no one approach her garden. Or Joyanne for that matter."

"What about Joyanne?" I was suddenly on high alert.

Gussie took a step back from the vines that overcrowded the wire fencing. "Most of us can stand a little dirt. Or soil, if you prefer. Hey, it goes with the territory. Especially when it comes to the tillers. They're meant to mulch the ground. Not shine and gleam in a parade."

I furrowed my brow. "What are you saying?"

"For some incomprehensible reason, Joyanne has taken it upon herself to spit polish the tillers."

"What?"

"You heard me. Normally we hose them off and call it a day. And up until recently, so did she. Then, *kazoom*! It was as though the woman got hit with a disinfecting germ. None of us can get to the tillers until she finishes cleaning them. If you ask me, I think its menopause, but Claudia told me to keep my mouth shut."

"Um, uh, yeah. I would agree with Claudia."

"I ain't saying another word. Joyanne's pretty well acquainted with tilling. Not like the rest of the 'gentleman and lady' gardeners who wouldn't know a rototiller from a wheelbarrow."

I thought back to when I first met everyone at these agricultural plots. At that time, Ona told me Joyanne helped her and Aneta till the back of their plot. Not an easy task. It would take muscle, dexterity, and skill to break up the soil, aerate it, remove debris and rocks, and prep it for planting. Not to mention making sure the ground layers were mixed. I only knew this thanks to Augusta, who happily shared her "life on the dairy farm" with me whenever she got the chance.

"Would you know the last time the rototiller was used?"

The men shook their heads and Santi told me that they didn't keep track. Then he added, "People are supposed to sign the sheet in the shed but good luck with that! Doesn't matter. It's a small area and no one's about to run off with a heavy rototiller."

Not run off. Just get the ground soft and malleable for a body.

I looked around to see if anyone else had ventured into the gardens but it was only Gussie and Santi.

"Do Joyanne or Maybelle usually show up on Sunday mornings?" I asked.

"Not Maybelle. She's probably singing off-key in church somewhere." Gussie bent down and pulled a weed from the ground. "As for Joyanne, I've never seen her on a Sunday morning, but I doubt she's a churchgoer. More likely she sleeps in late from the night before. Why? Do you think they may know more than they've shared?"

"More like a social thing. I can catch them another time. I also wanted to touch base with Ona and Aneta. Since I work most of time, Sundays are easier for me."

Santi swatted something from the nape of his neck and glanced at the Zlatkova plot. "They were here when I arrived at six but took off around seven thirty. They always go to the nine o'clock mass on Sundays and their church is in Surprise. Ona chewed my ears off one day about how wonderful their choir is."

"Santi, did you ever meet their mother? The reason I ask is because a friend of mine used to see her with a wolfhound at the dog park."

"Hmm, that was years ago. Before the sisters bought that double plot in the back of the acreage. Tall woman. Carried herself well. Always telling Ona and Aneta what they did wrong when it came to planting." Then a harrumph, followed by, "Of course, she never offered to get her hands dirty and—"

"That's because she didn't want any dirt to get into the settings on her rings," Gussie butted in. "That happened once when Ona got stung by a wasp and needed Aneta to drive her to urgent care."

"The mother didn't drive?"

"Nope," Santi said. "Told us she had a chauffeur in the old country. Ha! I'm from the old country, too, and the only chauffeur we had was a mule."

"Must be nice to have that kind of money." I looked at Santi, hoping he'd expound on my statement but he didn't. Instead, he looked past me. "Spoke too soon. Looks like Joyanne's coming out of the shed."

Then Gussie added, "If she wants something else to polish, I'm going to offer up my car."

"Has she ever done that before?"

"Nope. Her wacky cleaning frenzy started around the time your dog turned up that hand. Could be traumatic stress maybe."

Or covering her tracks.

My brief conversation with Santi and Gussie boosted my hunch about the Zlatkovas and added substance to my burgeoning theory about Joyanne. All I needed was the courage to go through with a plan that probably should have been tossed in a wastepaper basket. Then again, it wasn't as if anyone else was chomping at the bit to get this done.

Chapter 43

"I'm keeping my end of the bargain," I said to Lyndy when I phoned her from the car. I hadn't even put the key in the ignition.

"Huh? What bargain?"

"We said we'd call each other if either of us came up with a plan. Well, I did. I'm headed out of the agricultural plots. Had a conversation with Gussie and Santi. Joyanne's acting like Lady Macbeth and I think I know why. I think she was in cahoots with the Zlatkova sisters to murder the mother so they could cash in her jewelry fortune. I can't prove it, but I can push Joyanne over the brink with your help."

"Oh, no! It finally happened. You and your mother switched places. Just like that old movie, *Freaky Friday*, with Jamie Lee Curtis."

"Very funny. I'm serious. And I'm not talking about anything wacko." Then I paused. "Okay, fine. Maybe a tad extreme but nothing we can't handle."

"Tell me."

"First, I approach Joyanne and tell her that I know Elisaveta Zlatkova is buried under the Zlatkova sisters' garden plot. I tell her that I have a friend who works in cyber-intelligence in Phoenix and that she remembered me speaking about Ona and Aneta. That should raise Joyanne's eyebrows."

"And then what?"

"I tell her that my friend mentioned a cyber-intelligence investigation regarding stolen gems that the Zlatkovas amassed. That's where you come in."

"Me? I don't know anything about cyber-intelligence."

"She doesn't know that. And you won't have to say a word. You just have to be seen with me."

"Seen where?"

"I'm still working out the kinks. First, I need to ask Joyanne outright if she was the one who ratted out the coffee mug that was found at Tunnie's house. I'll tell her I would have done the same thing. Once I gain her confidence, I'll tell her about my friend in cyber-intelligence. Then, we find a way to be seen by her. Then I introduce you and you play the part. Like I said, I'm still working out the details."

"I thought you said I won't have to say anything."

"You won't. Just tap into a tablet and look serious."

"What do you expect her to do?"

"Dig up that rototiller and find a way to remove the body."

"You're sure it's there?"

"Yes."

"I hate to sound cliché but the devil's in the details."

"No, the devil's from Iowa and handy with farm implements, not fire."

As much as I was ready for a strong cup of coffee, I knew I had to do some legwork regarding Joyanne and the time was now. I locked the car and trekked over to her plot, anxious to initiate the conversation I had rehearsed in my mind. The only trouble was that I had no idea how she would respond. I couldn't very well hand her a script.

With a wide wave, I shouted, "Good morning!" Then I sauntered over. "I came here to see if my mother was here but I struck out. Chatted with Gussie and Santi and was about to leave when I saw you."

"Um, yeah. Hi! Good morning."

"Listen, Joyanne, there's something I wanted to share but haven't had the chance. You can't share this with anyone. Understood?"

Joyanne nodded.

"I'm telling you this because you were so up front about Tunnie and the potato poisoning. But again, not a word."

"I understand."

I moved closer to where she stood and lowered my voice. "Elisaveta Zlatkova, Ona and Aneta's mother, is buried under the rear of their plot. That's why they fortified the area with coiled fence. It wasn't meant for rabbits or javelina."

"Elisaveta? She died years ago and her ashes were sent to the homeland. So I was told."

"You were told wrong."

"How do you know this?"

"I have a close friend who works in cyber-intelligence in Phoenix. While her team was working on another case, Ona and Aneta's name came up regarding decades-old stolen gems from Macedonia."

I waited for a reaction but Joyanne remained stoic. At least for a few seconds. Then, she glanced at the Zlatkova plot. "Did you friend say anything about a search warrant?"

I shook my head. "No, intelligence gathering is quite complicated and things like this take a long time. Not like what you see on TV."

"Do they think the sisters buried their mother?"

"That's too specific a conclusion. All they believe is that Elisaveta's body is under that soil. Look, this has to remain between the two of us. If it gets out, I'll know where it came from."

"You don't have to worry. I won't say a word to anyone."

"I knew I could trust you."

Joyanne kept staring at the Zlatkova plot. "Um, I've got to do a few things here before I head out. Let me know if you learn anything else, will you?"

"For sure."

As I returned to my car, I couldn't believe how comfortable I was with lying. Too comfortable. I told myself it was a necessary skill for eking out information and ultimately rounding up the bad players, but still, it didn't sit easy with me. That's why I became a bookkeeper and accountant. Not a detective.

Now it was time for part B—popping over to my mother's house since I fibbed to Gussie and Santi about looking for her. Not to mention Joyanne. If there was one thing I learned from working at Williams Investigations, it was to cover your tracks.

Streetman's yelping bark could be heard all the way down the driveway. It was followed by my mother's voice, "It's only the Amazon delivery!"

I called out, "It's me! Phee!"

My mother, still clad in her floral summer robe, opened the door. "Phee! Is everything all right? It's so early."

"It's almost nine thirty."

"Don't tell me there's a brunch at Bagels 'n More. We were just there yesterday."

"No brunch. Just me, shoring up a cover story."

"A what? Don't stand there. Come on in. Streetman wants you to pet him."

I didn't have to look down. I could feel the little chiweenie pawing at the bottom of my slacks. I petted his head and that seemed to satisfy the little bugger.

"I made a fresh pot of coffee. Grab a mug and tell me what's going on."

I couldn't remember the last time my mother made a fresh pot of coffee. She was notorious for reheating it days on end. I counted my blessings and took a mug from the cabinet.

"Listen, if Gussie, Santi or Joyanne mention the fact that I was looking for you at the gardens today, play along. I used that as a pretext when I went over there."

"What did I miss?"

"Nothing yet."

"Yet?"

"Promise me you won't pick up the phone the second I leave."

"Honestly, Phee."

"Fine."

With the first sip of coffee going down my throat, I told her about my hunch regarding the Zlatkovas and how it crystallized to include Joyanne once I listened to what Gussie and Santi had to say. My mother, now with Essie in her lap, thought about it for a minute or two and then stood with the cat still in her arms. "Good work. You got her attention. Now we reel her in."

"We?"

"I'll invite the gardening ladies to join our book club at Bagels 'n More for a get-together on Saturday. We'll get her to take the bait and blurt out the truth."

"Saturday is a week away. That's too long. It has to be tomorrow or Tuesday the latest. I can take a few hours off of work. I won't fall behind."

"Okay. I'll let the ladies know. Let's make it Tuesday. Some of the women can't do things at a day's notice. I'm not going to say anything to Herb. He and his cronies will only muddy the waters. And thank goodness your aunt is tied up with that Edgar Allan Poe thing of hers. From what she told me, it involves lots of preplanning with her literary group."

"Better her than you."

"On the bright side, if Joyanne is as involved as you think, she wouldn't miss a get-together where people could be talking about her. Even at the last minute."

"In a world of sophomoric thinking, that actually makes sense. Yeesh. One more thing, make sure no one rats out Lyndy. She'll be posing as a cyber-intelligence expert."

"Don't worry, Phee. The plan I have worked out in my head is practically foolproof."

Practically. Not a word that instills confidence.

Strangely enough, my mother actually made sense. I would be seated with Lyndy, near where the ladies are but not at the same table. I would motion Joyanne over for a quick chat. Quick enough to get her stomach acids roiling, and her feet moving in the direction of the Zlatkova plot.

I was certain Joyanne would signal Ona and Aneta and then duck out of the restaurant and hightail it to where she had helped hide Ona and Aneta's foul deed. And no doubt those Zlatkova sisters would be right behind her. Now it was just a matter of executing the plan. And not messing anything up.

Good grief. I'm involving my mother. If that isn't an open invitation to disaster, I don't know what is.

The expression "when push comes to shove" lingered in my head more than I liked.

Chapter 44

"Tuesday morning? Around ten? . . . Yeah, I suppose I could take a long lunch and work late if I need to. Boy, Phee, you are going to owe me plenty," Lyndy said and laughed when I called her that evening.

"Face it, you want to see this played out as much as I do."

"Have you shared any of it with Marshall?"

"No. They have to remain a hundred percent focused on every bit of info that wafts their way. From what I was able to glean, it shouldn't be too much longer."

"Tell me again, how does your uncle Louis fit into this?"

"Ever hear of 'Six degrees of Kevin Bacon'? Well, in my uncle's case, it's more like two degrees. He made more connections on those cruise ships than most people make in a decade. Rolo Barnes may navigate the dark web, but Uncle Louis navigates the seas like a Navy commander."

"Yeah, I got that impression. Any chance your aunt will show up?"

"None whatsoever. My mother said Aunt Ina is way too occupied with her upcoming literary soiree. And this one will last the entire weekend."

"Yeesh."

"And don't worry about Herb's pinochle crew. My mom isn't saying a word to him. And that means Paul won't know either. I'm counting that as a blessing."

"Me too. Text me the details or call. I can't wait to continue Sleuthing 101."

"I can't wait to trap Joyanne and the Zlatkovas."

"What if you're wrong?"

"Then I'll eat an extra churro bagel and call it a day."

• • •

Augusta was all ears Monday morning when I told her what we had planned for the next day. "Got to admit, you did your homework, but you're going to have to be as convincing as a stage actress to pull it off."

I gulped and let her continue.

"Did you figure out what you're going to do if Joyanne bolts out of there? And what about the Zlatkovas? Who's going to tail them?"

"My mother was going to take care of that detail until I wait a reasonable amount of time and show up."

"Hmm, you may want to shore up things on that end."

I gulped again. "I suppose you're right."

• • •

When I woke up the next morning, I didn't need coffee. Every part of my body pulsated in anticipation of what I nicknamed, the Sting. Only, unlike Paul Newman and Robert Redford, I had good reason to believe I'd be the one to get stung.

By seven thirty, I had completed a pile of invoices at the office and moved on to the monthly spreadsheets. Knowing that Augusta wouldn't have time to duck out for lunch, I got her a croissant sandwich and two frosted donuts from BoSa.

"I nearly had a heart attack, Phee!" she shouted. "I saw the light from your office but didn't realize it was you until I saw the donuts. Thanks!"

"Wouldn't want you to go hungry. I got in super early because I wasn't sure how long the action plan at Bagels 'n More was going to take."

"With any luck, Bowman and Ranston will be able to make an arrest by day's end."

"Yeah, and take credit for it."

"Tell me something I don't know."

• • •

It was a little before ten when I spied my mother and Shirley off to the left on the top tier of Bagels 'n More's new pergola. If Shirley hadn't extended her arm and waved me over, I wouldn't have seen them behind the palms and Ficus trees that gave patrons an added bit of privacy on their enormous multilevel deck.

As I made my way up one of the ramps, Myrna called out, "Good morning, Phee. Glad we came before the heat got to be too much. Cecilia and Louise are right behind me. Not sure about Lucinda or Gloria."

"Look up! That's Gloria on the second tier. A few feet from that elderly couple dressed in plaid. They look dazed."

"At our age, we all look dazed." Then Myrna realized my mom and Shirley were one tier above and announced it.

Next thing I knew, Lucinda blew in like a dust storm. "We've got to talk fast," she said when we were all seated. "Tunnie, Marlie, Claudia and Thira are in the parking lot. They'll be here any second."

"What about Joyanne? Did you see her?"

Lucinda shook her head. "Not yet. But Maybelle's on her way up and the Zlatkova sisters are right behind her."

Planted 4 Murder

My mother leaned over the table and spoke in a low voice, but loud enough for everyone to hear, including Lyndy and me. "Phee's at the table across from us. Behind that bushy Ficus. Her friend Lyndy's there too. Remember what I said when I phoned all of you on Sunday. As far as we know, Lyndy works in cyber-intelligence. But don't say anything whatsoever. Talk about food or gardening, or anything else. Just play along with whatever Phee and Lyndy do. Shh! Here comes Maybelle with Ona and Aneta."

I couldn't hear what else my mother might have said because the other ladies showed up and everyone spoke at once. I kept looking around for Joyanne and began to think all of this was for nothing.

"Is that her?" Lyndy asked. "I see a thin woman with shoulder-length hair on the lower level looking around."

I peered over the Ficus. "It's her! Thank goodness."

Seconds later, Joyanne bounded up the ramp and greeted everyone at the table.

"She hasn't noticed us. When she does, my mother will acknowledge that I was meeting a friend of mine who works for an undisclosed government agency."

"Too bad Streetman can't be undisclosed. He just snatched one of those mini-bagels from the table."

"Rats! He must have been in her lap all this time. So help me, if that dog messes this up, I don't know what I'll do!"

"Relax. See? He's back in your mother's lap and everyone is talking."

I narrowed my eyes and took a good look. Ona and Aneta were seated across from Joyanne with Maybelle on her left and Thira to her right. So far, so good. "The idea is to have the ladies get settled and their orders placed before my mother makes her move."

Tunnie pulled a large canvas bag from a tote that matched the one my mother used for Streetman. Thank you, Vera Bradley. She handed the sack to Maybelle and said, "Here's the potato sack you asked for. I have another one if you need it. The material allows for storage without decay. Although, for some reason it smells a tad like urine. Must be from my musty garage."

"Thanks. I don't think my tomatoes will mind."

The waitress took our orders right away and scurried over to my mother's table. Then, out of nowhere, Lyndy and I heard something we wished we hadn't. It was a loud male voice that announced, "They were biting like piranhas all morning! Fish dinner tonight!"

"Is that—" Lyndy started to ask.

"Oh, it's Paul all right. Of all people. And why here? He usually goes to Putters Paradise. Where did his voice come from?"

Lyndy stretched her neck and pointed to the tier below us on the left.

185

"I can't see who he's with. Those palms are blocking my view."

"Not mine. It's Mini-Moose."

"He better not see us or he'll blow the whole deal. He knows who you are."

"That's putting it mildly. He's been itching to take me fishing. Thank goodness I have a boyfriend."

"We'll keep a low profile and outwait them. Paul eats fast and I'm sure his buddy does too."

"Um, you may wait those two out, but look who arrived on the first tier."

"Oh good grief *no*! I can't believe this. It's Tuesday! Why is everyone in creation at Bagels 'n More. It's not as if they're running a special."

It was Wayne and Kenny. I figured maybe they were coming from the auto restoration garage or one of their clubs.

Lyndy pulled out her cell phone and grimaced. "Power outage in Sun City West. That means the restaurants are closed. No wonder everyone is on this side of Grand, in Surprise."

"At least it's just Wayne and Kenny. And they're not anywhere near Paul."

"How long before your mother points us out and unnerves Joyanne?"

"Not long enough. I wish she'd hurry."

"Enjoy your breakfast," the waitress said as she placed my avocado and tomato bagel in front of me. Then she did the same with Lyndy's bacon and cheese one.

"Relax, your mother's table is getting served now. They have two servers doling out the food."

And then, in a voice that could break the sound barrier, "Hey, cutie! Is that you? And with—"

"Yes. I'm having a work meeting. It's highly confidential, Herb. Say, isn't that Paul over there with Mini-Moose? And Wayne and Kenny are here, too."

"I know. I'm the one who called them. Power's out in Sun City West. A transformer blew on RH Johnson and Grand."

Now, Mom, now! Say whatever you have to say to get Joyanne out of her chair and the Zlatkovas dialing the nearest bail bondsman.

"Great. I'm sure they're anxious to see you."

Unfortunately, Herb didn't get the hint. Instead, he moved closer to Lyndy's side of the table. "Are you going to watch our game tomorrow night? Lyman says we're up against some heavy hitters."

Before Lyndy could utter a word, I stepped in. "I would love to watch your softball game but like I said, I have pressing business since Nate and Marshall are out of town." Then, I raised my voice. "So pressing that I had to involve cyber-intelligence."

"Okay, cutie. You don't have to yell."

By now, my nerves were on edge but relief came when I least expected it.

"Yo! Herb! Get on over here and join the Moose and me. Bring the whole darn pinochle crew. Boy, wait till you see the beauties I reeled in this morning. They're in the back of my truck."

"Sorry, girls. Catch you later."

Herb raced down to the next tier and I let out a sigh of relief that I thought would never end. "Let's pray that was the last of it."

Lamentably, it wasn't.

Chapter 45

I don't remember eating my bagel but I must have because all that was left on my plate was a small sliver of tomato and some crumbs.

"I wish my mother would hurry it up. Normally she'd be done eating and readying herself for chitchatting."

"I think she's readying now. She pointed you out."

"Shh! Let's hear what she says."

"It is impossible to say how first the idea entered my brain."

"I can't hear your mother. Some woman down there is talking."

"Once conceived, it haunted me day and night."

"Sounds like a real looney if you ask me. I'd like to move closer but Paul's bound to rat us out. For once, I wish my mother would speak louder."

"I made up my mind to take the life of the old man."

"What's that woman saying?"

"Darned if I know." *Come on, Mom. Speak up. That wacky woman is drowning you out.*

"I think that woman's talking about killing someone. I don't think she's from here. Her voice sounds very put-on. You know, like in those old thirties' movies. Not British, but sort of."

"Death, in approaching him, had stalked with his black shadow before him, and enveloped the victim."

"Lyndy, we need to wait for an 'all clear' from my mother. Forget about whoever that nutcase is."

"Um, that woman might have murdered someone. Seriously. She's confessing to someone."

And then, another voice.

"It's my turn, Florella. *'Deep into that darkness peering, long I stood there, wondering, fearing, doubting, dreaming dreams no mortal ever dared to dream before.'"*

I could feel my throat closing but not before I heard, *"Quoth the Raven, 'Nevermore.'"*

"Pinch me, Lyndy. I better be dreaming. That's my aunt Ina's voice. This couldn't get any worse."

"Your aunt Ina! No way!"

"Oh, it's her all right. I'd recognize that voice in a coma."

"She knows me. She'll announce it like a sports commentator."

"Can you see where the two of them are?"

"Two of them? Phee, your aunt is with a bunch of ladies. All veiled and dressed in black. Most of them have three roses on their hats. Do you think they're on their way to a funeral?"

"Yeah. Mine."

"They're on the bottom tier directly below us. Lean over the Ficus and see for yourself."

"I'd rather not. This must be part of her literary soiree. They're doing Edgar Allan Poe. All weekend! Or longer! That's why my uncle Louis wanted to get the heck out of town. All the way to Canada to find a cat!"

"Now's probably not the best time to ask, but how's that investigation going?"

"Probably better than this."

Just then, I heard the bellow I expected from my mother. "It looks serious over there or Phee would have stopped by our table. Those government agency people can be so intimidating. Can any of you see what they're doing?"

"Quick, Lyndy! Show me your cell phone!"

Lyndy and I nearly bumped heads as we peered over her messages from Facebook.

"Now what?"

I tried not to look at my mother's table, but it didn't matter. Paul noticed ours and stood. He waved his arms as if he was flagging down an emergency vehicle.

"Keep looking at your phone! I've got to get over there before Paul blows your cover. Pretend you're making a call!"

I bolted from my seat and all but tackled the other customers as I charged over to where the men were seated. Paul extended his arms and I stopped dead in my tracks.

"Whoa! That's quite the welcome! I suppose you're anxious to see what the Moose and I caught this morning."

"Nothing would please me more, but I'm on the verge of pinning down the perpetrators of those murders. That's why my mother's here with the women from the agriculture club and the book club ladies."

"You set a trap? You planned a sting? You should have included me. Okay, it's not too late. What do I do? And before you say a word, the Moose can really run fast if you need him to."

I looked over at Mini-Moose, whose mouth was full with what I presumed to be a whole bagel.

"No running. No changes to the plan. You need to stay right where—Uh, actually, I do need your help. There's a klatch of women dressed in black on the second tier. They have roses on their hats. And veils over their faces."

"A secret murderess society?" Paul turned to Herb and the guys.

I gave Herb a pleading stare and he nodded as I continued to speak. "In a manner of speaking, yes. Yes. A secret murderess society and I just found out."

"What do you want me to do?"

"I need you and the men to keep an eye on them. They have something planned." *Even if it is a nonstop poetry reading.* "The sheriff's office is aware but they're waiting for conclusive evidence. It should be forthcoming. Wouldn't want any of them to vanish before an arrest can be made."

"Got it. We can handle it." Paul elbowed Mini-Moose and I tried not to roll my eyes. Then I rushed back to our table. Having rehearsed the scenario at least once, Lyndy improvised her role like a seasoned actor. "Leave whatever cash you have on the table, the team is on its way. I have to move on it."

I gazed toward my mother who, thankfully, took it from there. "Oh, dear, something must be up. Phee and her acquaintance are leaving in a rush."

Praying her words would be enough to get Joyanne out of her seat, I clenched my fists and turned my head upward to the third tier as Lyndy and I ducked behind a faux Ficus wall. The pounding in my chest increased and for a split second I thought we were in the clear.

But it wasn't Joyanne who stood. It was the Zlatkova sisters and Maybelle.

"Ona remembered she left a pork roast in the oven," Aneta said to no one in particular, but loud enough to reach all three tiers. "So sorry."

As they skedaddled out of there, I heard Cecilia say, "That's a feeble excuse if I ever heard one. Who turns on an oven in this heat? Aneta fell for it. Good job, Harriet. You're a pro at this."

I waited for Joyanne to make her move, but nothing. And why Maybelle? Had I gotten this wrong? By now she and the Zlatkovas were on the ground level and hightailing it to the parking lot.

Then, the worst! It was Florella's voice sans the affected accent. "We've got the dialogue in order, ladies, I think we need to discuss the motivation."

A loud, gruff voice answered, "Indeed. Who killed him?"

Then, "Not who! Why?"

The loud voice rocked the outdoor tables. "Cataracts. The man had cataracts! He was murdered because of his filmy eyes."

Suddenly Paul forgot he was under cover and shouted, "Someone killed Barry because he had cataracts? Geez! A good eye surgeon could have taken care of that!"

Then Kenny and Kevin chimed in. Loud enough to be heard in Boise.

"Those women murdered Barry? Who the heck are they? Someone call the sheriff's office. We all heard the confession."

On no! This can't be happening. Those nincompoops are calling the sheriff's deputies.

"Rats! I've got to clean this up before everything goes up in smoke! Lyndy, follow Ona and Aneta in your car. I'll catch up. Put your phone on Bluetooth and call me!"

"Got it."

I envisioned myself looking like one of those cartoon characters with its ears blowing out smoke. I charged over to Kevin and Kenny with a large white napkin dangling in front of me, for fear of being spotted by Aunt Ina.

"Don't make that call! Do *not* call the sheriff's office under any circumstances."

"Paul heard a confession," Kevin replied. "Something about cataracts."

"He didn't hear a confession. He heard a— Oh, never mind. Just don't call. You'll mess everything up. Trust me. We're on it."

"So we're just supposed to sit here? It's not as if we're at Curley's. There's only so much coffee I can drink." Kenny picked up his mug and took a gulp.

Then, out of the corner of my eye, I watched Joyanne run down the stairs at the far edge of the decking. But she never made it to the bottom. Somewhere between the first and second tiers, she disappeared.

"Not a word to the deputies!" I shouted. "Just stay put and take notes!"

Chapter 46

Lyndy's voice was loud and clear over the Bluetooth. "They're not headed to the community gardens. They're on the frontage road for the Burlington Northern Santa Fe Railroad."

"The BNSF one? Behind the community plots?"

"Yeah, but on the other side. Way on the other side. What should I do?"

"Stay close but not on top of them. Try to see what they're doing."

"Did Joyanne make her move? Are you tailing her?"

"Not exactly. I lost her over the staircase railing at Bagels 'n More."

"Well, I'm looking at her right now. She's climbing into an empty railcar container. Oh my gosh. Do you think they stashed the mother's corpse in there?"

"They wouldn't have had time. Keep watching. What are Ona and Aneta doing?"

"I can't tell. Oh, wow!"

"'Oh, wow' what? What do you see?"

"It's what I don't see—the Zlatkovas. I see Maybelle behind the wheel. I pulled up closer."

"Maybe they're in the backseat."

"I don't think so but it's hard to tell."

"That can only mean one thing if you're right. Ona and Aneta drove separately and are at their plot exhuming the body right now. I thought they would have done that sooner. I've got to hurry over there. And this time I'll call the sheriff's office."

"Like I said, I don't see them but Maybelle just got out of the car and is heading to the railcar where Joyanne went. She's got an empty potato sack on her. It's blowing all over. Geez, maybe they did dig the body up earlier and put it in that railcar. Now they're going to stuff what's left of it in that bag. It's pretty big."

"Then where are the Zlatkovas? I still think they're back in their own plot. I've got to take off before they get away with murder."

"I think they already did. I think I'm watching a payoff. Not a body. It's money and lots of it. I can actually see stacks of bills."

"Are they being put into the potato sack? That many bills?"

"No, Joyanne handed them to Maybelle and took the sack. Good thing Lyman left his binoculars in my car. Talk about luck."

"Drat! I can't be in two places at once. Okay, you call the sheriff's office instead of me. Tell them what you're witnessing and I'll loop over to the garden. Get me on the phone once you call."

"Okay."

Just then I heard an army of sirens on Grand Avenue, aka Route 60. Not the sound that the fire truck sirens make, but definitely police or sheriff sirens. Attributing it to a highway accident somewhere, I spun around and headed to the garden entrance off of 137th Drive.

In the split second since Lyndy got off the phone, Augusta called.

"Phee! Are you still at Bagels 'n More? What's going on? One of the Phoenix radio stations was playing on Alexa and they just announced a possible terrorist situation at that restaurant. SWAT is on the way along with a plethora of state and local authorities."

"I'm driving but can you pull it up on your cell phone while you're on the landline?"

"Yep. Give me a second."

It was the longest second of my life and my imagination paled compared to what was really happening.

Augusta spoke a mile a minute. "The footage shows a line of SWAT team officers surrounding a table of women dressed in black. At least I think it's women. Could be those terrorists. I can't get a good look. Whoever is filming this has to be a good distance away."

"Holy cannoli! It's not terrorists, it's my aunt and her literary group."

"Did you just say literary group?"

"Uh-huh. Look closely. Do you see Paul or Mini-Moose in the crowd?"

"I can't tell. Where are you?"

"Headed to the Zlatkova garden plot. Those two are the murderesses." *If I haven't made a horrible mistake.* "I've got to get off my cell. Lyndy is also in pursuit but at the railroad yard adjacent to the gardens."

"My head is spinning listening to you. What should I do?"

"Call the sheriff's office and tell them that they've made a huge mistake. Tell them the goth-clad women are a literary society. Convince them there is no terrorist plot. Toss in Paul's name a few times. I'm sure he's the one that blew this situation into the next galaxy."

"Got it. Call me back. And Phee, be careful."

Seconds later, Lyndy was back on Bluetooth. "I was on hold for the longest time. They kept transferring my 911 call. When I finally reported what I saw, they said they'd send a deputy over but that there was a drastic emergency off of Grand that involved Homeland Security. What do you suppose that's all about? At least it explains those sirens."

"One big, catastrophic mess. I'll explain later. What do you see? Where are Maybelle and Joyanne?"

"Maybelle's walking back to the car with the money. No sign of Ona or Aneta. Hang on—Joyanne is running toward the fence into the community gardens. She's not carrying anything. There's a silver SUV parked on the road. It has to be hers but she's on foot. Do you think they're going to hurry and dig up Elisaveta's remains?"

"I think Elisaveta is loosely sitting under a top layer of dirt waiting to be transported out of there. Now they're just going to cover their tracks. Darn it. I wish I knew where they're taking that body." Or what's left of it.

"I'll drive to the garden gate and go on foot to the rear of the area where that fence is. Joyanne should be in plain sight."

"What about you? You'll be in plain sight, too."

"I'll stay one garden row over and keep low to the ground."

"I don't have a plan. It's going to be three of them and two of us. I'm keeping my fingers crossed Maybelle drove home." Or to the nearest ATM to make a deposit.

"I'm keeping my fingers crossed you come up with something."

Lamentably, I didn't. But as circumstances presented themselves, I didn't have to. Paul took care of that for me.

When I pulled up to the gate and exited the car, Paul stumbled out of his truck and raced toward me.

"What on earth are you doing here?" I shrieked. "You're supposed to be watching that group of women."

"I put the Moose in charge. I had to take a whiz. You know what it's like when Mother Nature calls."

"Do you hear those sirens? Were you the one who called the sheriff's office about those women?"

"No. You said not to so I didn't."

"What about the other guys?"

"They didn't call either, but a really old guy with a plaid sports jacket did. The woman who was with him kept yelling, 'Make the call, Loomis. Make the call. I recognize that group from an Instagram post. They're home-grown terrorists.'"

"And that's when the man called?"

"No. It was right after one of the women said, 'I must scream or die! Louder! Louder!' She said some other stuff too."

"What other stuff?"

"'Get the terrorist back.' Or maybe it was, 'Get three terrorists back.' I'm not sure, but the guy who heard them must have gotten it right. So don't look at me. I wasn't the one who told the sheriff's office those women were terrorists. I just figured they were domestic murderesses. Like with kitchen utensils or poison."

I bit my bottom lip and tried to piece together what Paul said. "Scream or die! Louder!" Where have I heard that? It sounded awfully familiar. But "getting three terrorists back" didn't.

"Okay. Fine." I forced myself to take long breaths and stay calm. "Tell me why you drove here."

"You're not the only one with detective skills, you know. I figured you drove here because it's the logical place for that body to turn up. Besides, I didn't need to be trapped at Bagels 'n More while that SWAT team took over. Lucky for me, I had to take a leak."

Yes. Let fortune shine upon thee.

And with that fleeting thought, I was back in my eleventh-grade English Lit class. It wasn't *terrorist*. It was *tempest* and the full quote from *The Raven* was "Get thee back into the tempest and the Night's Plutonian shore!" Heck, I had to memorize the darn thing. Too bad thirty years shoved it to the recesses of my brain.

"Shh! Keep your voice low. I don't have time to explain but we've got to catch the Zlatkovas and Joyanne in their unspeakable act."

But before I could utter another word, my phone vibrated and I looked at the caller ID—my mother. I motioned for Paul to stay still.

"Can you hear me, Phee? This is a nightmare. An entire SWAT team surrounded your aunt's table and the turmoil has wreaked havoc on poor Streetman's nerves."

"Streetman's nerves? That's what you're worried about? Mom, they've mistaken Aunt Ina and her friends for terrorists. I don't have time to explain. Try to get their attention before this whole thing escalates."

"I think it already did. A second layer of men-in-black arrived."

"Myrna's the loudest one in your group. Have her stand up and yell that it's all a mistake. Improvise! I'm inches away from catching the killers." I ended the call before she could respond, but the next call came in a flash.

"It's me. Lyndy. Joyanne jumped the fence a few yards down from the gate. Believe it or not, I'm in someone's driveway and I can see everything from their backyard. No one's home and papers are piled up. Must be snowbirds."

"Forget the snowbirds. What do you see?"

"Maybelle. With Joyanne. They're walking down one of those garden lanes."

"Probably to the Zlatkova garden. We have no choice. We've got to follow them and then confront them once they exhume the remains. I'll wait here behind those bushes at the gate."

Paul, who managed to keep quiet for a full three minutes, came to life. "I have an idea. It's one of my best!" Without waiting for a response, he lumbered toward his truck and I peered past the gate to spot Lyndy.

With Paul out of sight, Lyndy and I crept down the path to the Zlatkova garden, making sure we kept a good distance between us and everyone else. We held back, lest the sisters turn around and spot us. Paul, however, did not. I'm not sure if he had that bucket of fish with him when we spoke at the gate, but it didn't matter. He had it now.

The next thing I knew, Ona shrieked, "There's a pile of dead fish on our plot! Lots of them! Big, dead fish!"

Then Aneta, "They're not going anywhere, Ona. Stay focused. Where the heck are Maybelle and Joyanne?"

"I'm over here!" It was Joyanne. "I had to grab a shovel from the shed. Where's Maybelle?"

"Two guesses." It was Aneta's voice. "Waiting for us. Hurry up."

I whispered to Lyndy, "I hope the deputy you asked for shows up soon!"

She whispered back, "I hope he or she shows up, period!"

Chapter 47

Lyndy and I crouched behind a row of pepper plants and watched as Joyanne and Aneta strolled toward Maybelle's plot, pulling a gardening cart as if they were about to enjoy a midmorning lemonade.

"Do you see what I do?" she asked.

"Yep. And I doubt it's Santa's toys."

Meanwhile, Paul must have divided his prize between the two gardens because the next thing I heard was Maybelle's voice. "That stench is going to attract all sorts of vermin. Last thing we need to do is call attention to my tomato patch."

I poked Lyndy. "Best thing we can do is stay still and record what we see on our phones."

She nodded and I aimed my cell phone in the direction of Maybelle's garden. Then I froze. "Oh, no. It's Orvis. Looks like he's by himself, but still . . ."

My knees ached as I steadied myself in a half squat, and when I glanced at Lyndy, she grimaced. Meanwhile, Orvis ambled past us, oblivious as all heck. Then again, we were only inches from the ground and he was otherwise occupied drinking something that most likely wasn't water.

"Ona's making a mad dash toward Orvis. Lucky she's not the one wielding a shovel." Lyndy spit out her observation in a whisper but it was clear as day. "She's motioning to him."

"Yeah," I mumbled. "She's got to get him out of there." *What's taking that deputy so long?*

I expected the cover-up for the dastardly deed to roll out in a slow, methodical fashion, allowing me to capture the evidence on my iPhone. Regrettably, the only thing I captured was what I prayed wouldn't happen.

"Yo! Orvis! It's Paul! Caught some beauties today but had enough in my freezer so I tossed them on a few gardens for fertilizer."

Orvis spun around and replied. His voice was somewhat slurred, but still understandable. "Maybelle must be tickled pink. Not like the last time. Look! She and Joyanne are hand-tilling the soil to get those suckers deeper into the ground. And Aneta is helping. Harrumph. Looks like Aneta brought her own fertilizer."

That's a new name for it.

"Think we should give them a hand?" Orvis continued.

I widened my eyes, unsure of what to do next. Then, before I knew it,

Ona looped her arm around Orvis and shouted, "I think someone tampered with your plants. Come on, I'll show you. Paul should look, too."

"Nah," Paul said. "I don't need to see trampled plants, or any plants for that matter. I'd better give those women a hand. Those are whole fish. You gotta smash 'em real good. Dead center if you want to maximize the nutrients."

"I may retch," Lyndy said in a low voice.

"Join the club."

Appearing to have no choice, Ona escorted Orvis away from Maybelle's lane and the vicinity where her own plot stood.

"Do you think she'll kill Orvis to prevent him from discovering what they've done?" Lyndy's voice cracked.

"I hate to think it, but it's possible. Look, you follow them and I'll keep my phone on Record. Aneta, Joyanne and Maybelle are reburying a corpse so one more probably won't make a difference to them."

"What about Paul? He's headed to Maybelle's garden."

"I'll call him right now. It won't interfere with the other app."

Seconds later, I fabricated a distress call and sent Paul to help Lyndy with her car. Meanwhile, Joyanne, Aneta, and Maybelle continued to dig around in the soil. Anxious to catch them uncovering what, or who, was in that gardening cart, I was irritated when my phone rang.

"Phee! It's your mother. Television news vans just showed up. They're all over the place."

"Didn't Myrna explain?"

"They used one of the bullhorns to tell her she'd be arrested for interfering. Are you sure you can't postpone what you're doing and get back over here?"

"Absolutely not! Look, no one is in any danger. Aunt Ina and her lady friends just have to do what the deputies and police tell them until it gets sorted out."

By now, my eyes literally spun in my head. "Sit tight. I'll get back to you. And whatever you do, do not let that dog out of your sight. Or your lap, for that matter."

I narrowed my eyes to get a better look at the gardening cart but it was hidden behind them. It really didn't matter. I knew what it held. Then, a text from Augusta: *Impossible to get on your phone. Quit yakking. No luck with the sheriff's office. I texted Bowman's private number.*

For the first time in my life, I knew what the word *impasse* meant. And Webster was right—It was "a situation in which no progress was possible." In the past, I always had a few minutes to consider my options, but this time there were too many tentacles. Just a wing and a prayer. I started toward Maybelle's garden hoping I'd be able to convince them the deputies were on their way, but instead, two unlikely players changed everything.

"Are you sure it was birds?" Gussie's voice startled me and I turned to see him and Santi in the lane behind Maybelle's.

"I'm sure all right. Look, I already started the framework for the netting last spring but never got around to finishing it. It shouldn't take us that long. If I didn't have to deal with my garage door opener, I would have been here earlier this morning when it wasn't so hot."

"Yeah. Who in their right mind works on projects midday this time of year?" Then a pause. "I take that back. Look over there. It's a regular women's convention."

That was my opening and I grabbed it. I honestly don't remember shoving the phone in my pocket, where I had already stashed my wallet and keys, but I must have, because it was at my fingertips when I reached Gussie and Santi.

"Not a convention!" I screamed. "A cover-up for murder! Hurry!"

The two men looked at me as if I had been Orvis's drinking buddy but they raced behind me. When we reached Maybelle's garden plot, Joyanne and Aneta took a small canvas tarp out of the garden cart and were about to place it in the freshly tilled soil.

"I know that's Elisaveta's remains in that canvas," I announced.

"What on earth on you saying? We're adding fertilizer."

"You're not fertilizing an acre. I know what you've got there."

With a sudden burst of energy, I charged over to the plot and snatched the canvas from Joyanne's hands. And when I did, a mound of pungent red dust filled the air and made its way to the ground.

"Will someone tell me what's going on?" Gussie asked.

"These women conspired to murder Elisaveta and cover it up. I may have the garden plot wrong, but not the deed."

"Feel free to dig up our plot," Aneta said, her eyes fixed on me. "Ona and I have nothing to hide. And neither does Joyanne. Go ahead. Check out our plots. I don't mind replanting if it will put a stop to your accusations."

I stared at the fertilizer-covered plot and nodded to Gussie and Santi. "As a matter of fact, we'll take you up on your offer, starting with Joyanne's garden."

Gussie shot me a look but I responded with a narrow half eye roll and he got the message. "Yeah, sure. Nothing to lose. What do you say, Santi?"

"As long as I can get my netting done, I'll take a look."

When we were halfway down the lane toward Joyanne's plot, I whispered, "We're wasting our time. There's nothing buried in either of those locations. But I'm certain Elisaveta is further under Maybelle's lovely tomato garden."

"You just saw them adding fertilizer. There was no body or remains."

Gussie crossed his arms and shook his head.

"That's because she was already there. Deeper in the dirt. Remember when you told me how fastidious Joyanne was about cleaning the tillers? She did a heck of a lot of work before this moment."

"I don't understand."

I shrugged. "Joyanne's pretty astute. It would make sense for her and her cohorts to devise a complex plan. Look, we have two choices. We can race back there and get into a melee with them by digging further down in Maybelle's plot, or let them think they've gotten away with something."

"I like the second plan. But who's going to catch them?"

"Not who. What."

"Huh?" Gussie looked at me and then at Santi.

I shot off a quick text to Lyndy and waited for a response. A few seconds later, her thumbs-up emoji told me that our plan was still in play. Unfortunately, so was the one that involved my aunt's literary group.

My phone vibrated and with a quick swipe I heard my mother's voice. "Those obnoxious deputies are here and believe it or not, your aunt is trying to flag down a waitress."

Thank you, Augusta.

"Hold tight, Mom. I think all of this will get cleared up."

"Where are those murderers? The book club ladies and I can drive over once they let us go. I have to end this call. A TV crew is headed toward us. I have to make sure my hair isn't flying all over the place like Lucinda's."

Of course. Her hair. Never mind about the SWAT team and the murderers. Heaven forbid her hair looks bad on TV.

"Stay there or go back home, but do not drive here. You'll only make it worse. I'll call."

"Fine."

When I thought that was it for interruptions, a text came in from Marshall: *The cat's in the cradle.*

I texted back, *Did Uncle Louis have to gamble for its safe return?*

Marshall: *No, but he deserves an Academy Award for acting. Will call tomorrow night. XOXO*

I returned the kiss and hug emojis but didn't say a word about my current dilemma. There was nothing he or Nate could do about it. Lyndy and I were on our own. Then again, we did have Gussie and Santi.

I looked at both men and kept my voice low. "We're not going to exhume a body, Epcor Water is going to do that for us."

"What?" Gussie's eyes couldn't have gotten any wider.

"Turn the main water system on and we'll wait it out."

"Then what?"

"The force of the water from under the ground will bring Elisaveta to the surface in no time. All we need to do is wait it out. Those women won't be able to stop it once it starts."

"Do it," Santi said. "Before those birds mess up all my crops."

Chapter 48

Gussie and Santi headed to the building that housed the main shutoff when Orvis's voice boomed from a few lanes over. He and Ona spied me and made their way over.

"I can't believe you thought my plants were trampled. That's how they always look. If I wanted manicured, I'd join the garden club, not the agriculture club!"

"I heard you yelling back there, Phee," Ona said. "What happened?'

"Sorry. It was a mistake on my part. I misinterpreted some information and thought you and your sister were responsible for your mother's death. Anyway, my apologies. Please let the others know. I'd better be on my way."

Without wasting a second, I hustled back to my car, where Lyndy and Paul waited.

"So we have to sit it out?" Paul asked me. "Can you call Door Dash? I could really go for a meatball sub."

"Door Dash? Are you nuts?"

I unlocked the door and motioned for them to get inside. "We'll have stay in the car with the AC on and off so I don't waste gas."

"How long do you think it will be until the, um . . . until Elisaveta surfaces?" Lyndy asked.

"Doesn't take a dead fish long," Paul said.

To which she replied, "Elisaveta is not a dead fish. And I think she's only bones at this point."

Waiting in the car as Paul droned on and on about anything and everything fish-related was a torture I never imagined. But when it ended abruptly, the torture that followed was worse.

I spied Shirley's Buick out of the corner of my eye and prayed she drove here solo.

She didn't! Out popped my mother, Streetman, and Aunt Ina.

"It was a disaster, Phee! The deputy who resembles a Sonoran desert toad argued with the commander of the SWAT team. The other one barked orders at all of us to leave. Your poor aunt's literary circle was traumatized."

"Well, maybe they shouldn't have dressed like nineteenth-century killers." Then I smiled at my aunt. "Sorry, Aunt Ina."

"I'm glad everything got straightened out," Lyndy said.

Shirley pointed a finger at Paul. "This is all your fault. Going on and on about Barry's murder and cataracts in the same breath."

Planted 4 Murder

I raised my hands. "It doesn't matter. What matters now is what's about to happen."

Against my better judgment, I explained the situation, including our next step—to return to Maybelle's plot while Ona, Aneta, Joyanne and Maybelle contended with an uprooted corpse.

"I expect Bowman and Ranston to get here ASAP, along with that deputy the sheriff's office was supposed to send," I said. "Meanwhile, I'll move in closer with Lyndy and we'll both use our phones to capture video."

I was clear and articulate, but I hadn't factored in Paul. I assumed he'd stay with my mother, Shirley and my aunt, but once Lyndy and I crept nearer to Maybelle's plot, we heard him thunder over there from another direction. But that wasn't all we heard.

A loud shriek cut through the air, followed by another one.

"Something stung me! Darn bees! Its stinger is still on my neck! Help!"

Then, "Hold still, Ona, and let me see."

Aneta's voice was unmistakable. "You're caught on a long piece of wire. Probably from the fence."

"It's pulling me! Get it off! I think I'm bleeding."

"Quit fussing, the both of you. Don't you see what's happening? All that water created a pond in my tomato patch. I can see bones surfacing."

"I see something worse, Maybelle. It's Paul and he's headed this way!"

Joyanne took off in Paul's direction but it was too late. The next voices were Bowman's and Ranston's.

"What idiot got a fishing line tangled up in all these plants? It's crisscrossing the lanes! Watch it, Ranston!"

I kept my head low for fear of getting caught in Paul's fishing line. "The plot! The garden plot! Bones are surfacing from all the water! It's Elisaveta Zlatkova! And this isn't a cemetery. It's a murder cover-up!" The words rushed out of my mouth in one breath.

Bowman continued to shout, but not at Ranston. "Hands in the air! All of you! Hands in the air."

Lyndy, who was now inches from me, tried not to laugh. "They don't have any weapons."

Fortunately, the deputies didn't hear her. "Keep those hands in the air." Then, "Ranston! Get names!"

A third deputy appeared out of nowhere and approached the other two. I stood there, wordless, as I watched the scenario unfold. Including Paul's contribution.

"I snared them! You can thank me. You can thank my new Lixada Fishing Rod Reel from Amazon. Pocket version. In case you find yourself someplace without a full-size rod and reel."

"So much for a bee sting," I heard Aneta say.

The next few minutes were chaotic at best as Bowman, Ranston, and the "body snatchers" exchanged words. Next thing I knew, the deputy made a call and announced that a forensic team was on its way.

"Guess this is over," Lyndy said, but before the final word escaped her lips, Streetman escaped my mother's arms and charged down the lane and right into the muck and mire that housed Elisaveta's remains. He was pursued by her as well as Shirley and my aunt.

"Lordy, Harriet, that dog is not getting into my car all filthy like that."

Five minutes later and the community gardens resembled an outdoor circus. Word, or in this case cell phones, traveled fast and the entire crew flooded the place. No pun intended. I took in the entire fiasco—Herb and his crew, my aunt's gothic-clad literary ladies, the Booked 4 Murder book club and all of the women in the agriculture club. Not to mention Gussie, Santi, and Orvis. It was a regular sideshow.

The only one missing was Augusta and that's because she had the good sense to stay at the office and run interference by telecommunications.

The television crews that swarmed Bagels 'n More were now swarming the community gardens and I wondered if we'd ever get out of there. My prayers were answered an hour and a half later when Aneta, Ona, Joyanne and Maybelle were carted off to the sheriff's office, and most likely, the Fourth Avenue Jail.

• • •

It wouldn't be until late the following day when the puzzle pieces came together, linking Barry McGuire's demise to Elisaveta's. And once that happened, I had Cindy Dolton and Charles Delavan from the dog park to thank for their prior intel.

Poor Marshall got a forty-five-minute explanation when he phoned that night as promised.

"Sorry, hon, but everything was under wraps. That high-ranking official who owned the cat turned out to be none other than the Canadian Prime Minister, which explains all that subterfuge. Remind me never to acquire a LaPerm or any other cat for that matter."

"No problem. When are you coming home?"

"First flight out tomorrow. Nate and I will head to the office for a bit to catch up. Besides, I don't want to wait until you get out of work to give you a hug."

"Make it ten!"

"By the way, your uncle wants to know if that literary soiree of your aunt's is over. He doesn't want to go home until he's sure."

"Tell him the coast is clear. I don't think they'll be doing Edgar Allan Poe any time soon."

Marshall laughed and for the first time in over a week, so did I.

Chapter 49

News of the four arrests was all over social media as well as the regular outlets. Racine called to let me know that they were holding a special information meeting at the ramada to "re-instill the faith in our idyllic garden." I thanked her and passed on the opportunity. My mother, however, told me she intended to go with Lucinda and Louise. All of that in the first hour at the office.

"Okay," Augusta said as she bit into a maple long john donut. "I need to piece this together so it'll make sense when Mr. Williams and Mr. Gregory show up."

"It has more pieces than a quilt, but I put together what Bowman explained to Lyndy and me yesterday and substantiated it with what Rolo found out."

"I may need another donut." Augusta reached behind her desk to the counter and grabbed a plain old-fashioned one.

I leaned against the file cabinet, coffee cup in hand, and took a breath. "We know Elisaveta was a widow when she and her daughters came here in the seventies. What we didn't know was that she had strong connections to a Macedonian oligarchy and more importantly, to their money. Rolo was keeping tabs due to their black-market dealings but Elisaveta herself wasn't directly involved."

"Get to the good parts. We can come back to the history lesson later."

"Elisaveta drew up a will that left everything to Ona and Aneta. House, jewels, investments . . . you get the idea. Anyway, something made her change her mind in the past year and she was in the process of changing her last will and testament to exclude the daughters. That's when they schemed to keep the inheritance."

"You mean murder their mother."

I nodded. "They did it the Agatha Christie way—poisoning her with potato tubers. But they had to find a way to unobtrusively bury the body. That's where Joyanne came in. She was skilled enough to till the soil in the Zlatkova garden and put Elisaveta to rest. But something went wrong."

"Don't tell me they buried her alive!"

"No, of course not. But Joyanne had the rototiller at the garden plot at the same time as they were tossing in the body. It was late at night and they thought they were alone. Joyanne started up the tiller to make the ground look even but she accidently cut off one of Elisaveta's hands with the machine. The hand went flying and the women didn't have time to look for it because they thought they heard someone approaching. When they were done, one of them tossed in in the compost pile."

"Yuck! Did they ever say why they buried her with the gimmel ring on?"

"Ona told the deputies that they were able to remove one gold band but dropped it. When they found it, they did not find the ruby that was set into it. And they couldn't seem to extricate the other two rings."

"Who says you can't take it with you?"

"Very funny. What the sisters and Joyanne didn't know was that Barry was in the garden at that late hour and he saw them toss Elisaveta's body into the freshly tilled plot. That was probably the noise they heard."

"Okay. I can figure out the rest. They used their original poisoning formula to knock him off. Am I right?"

"A hundred percent. They weren't too worried about being caught for Barry's murder because everyone in the agriculture club had a motive to kill him. Maybelle in particular. He poisoned her plants."

"Yeah, about Maybelle. How'd she figure into all of this?"

"The sisters and Joyanne needed a scapegoat, and since Tunnie grew potatoes, she was an easy target. But in order to set her up, they needed something for the deputies to latch on to. That's where that Obliterator knife came in. Maybelle used to work for a butcher shop and was pretty handy with cleavers. So—"

"One of those skinny little snakes put one in a sack of potatoes in her garage."

"Yep. And Joyanne stashed the payoff money in a railcar where no one could get at it. Everyone fell for her plot to frame Tunnie. Myself included. Some detective I'd make. I'm sticking to spreadsheets and account balances."

"I'd say you did pretty well. Two murders solved and no insurance claims for damages from your mother's dog."

"Shh! Don't even think it."

"Do you think Mr. Williams and Mr. Gregory will be disappointed they didn't get to solve those deaths?"

"I doubt it. By the time they file the paperwork on that cat case, I imagine something equally heinous will crop up. And I'm not referring to what's planted in any of those other plots."

"Hey, if anyone asks me, I'm just going to say tomatoes."

Epilogue

As expected, the Zlatkova sisters, along with Joyanne and Maybelle, were arraigned in court and awaiting their trials. Gussie and Santi took over their plots until new club members could purchase them from the women.

Aunt Ina and her literary society decided to focus on the Browning sisters for their next literary soiree in the winter, but that wasn't the only news from the Melinsky household. While tracking down the cat-nappers in Vancouver, my uncle impersonated a Hungarian government official and did such a good job that the Royal Canadian Mounted Police wanted to use him for covert operations as needed. As of late, Uncle Louis was considering it, especially if it coincided with my aunt's literary functions.

Paul became the man of the hour thanks to his skill with a rod and reel, resulting in reeling in the murderesses—literally. In fact, the *Sun City West Independent* did a cover story entitled "Reeled in 4 Murder."

Much to everyone's surprise, my mother's vegetables did really well and she, along with Lucinda and Louise, decided to continue with their gardening. But no one was more pleased than Herb. The recent science news pointed to increased solar activity and he purchased a second plot to "prevent going hungry." Not only that, but he got a few more guys to come on board.

At the behest of Bowman and Ranston, Nate and Marshall made an executive decision to hold off on international cases for the next few months or longer. I couldn't have been more elated.

My mother continued with Streetman's scent identification training but so far, he only excelled when it came to food or stinky garbage. I didn't expect to see him working with law enforcement or any business in the near future, but shh! Don't tell my mother that!

Special Endnote

With sadness, I want to let you know that Jim passed away in January 2025. We were married for forty-two years and coauthored for twelve of them. I miss him every day. But there is a bright side—We always stockpiled our writing and the next two books in this series were written by both of us. In addition, Jim left a detailed Murder Notebook, with plotlines, notes, ideas, and his must-haves. So, essentially, he is still writing with me! Keep laughing and guessing whodunit! Ann.

About the Author

Ann I. Goldfarb

New York native Ann I. Goldfarb spent most of her life in education, first as a classroom teacher and later as a middle school principal and professional staff developer. Writing as J. C. Eaton, along with her husband, James Clapp, she has authored the Sophie Kimball Mysteries, the Wine Trail Mysteries, the Charcuterie Shop Mysteries, and the Marcie Rayner Mysteries. In addition, Ann has nine published YA time travel mysteries under her own name. Visit the websites at: www.jceatonmysteries.com and www.timetravelmysteries.com

James E. Clapp

When James E. Clapp retired as the tasting room manager for a large upstate New York winery, he never imagined he'd be coauthoring cozy mysteries with his wife, Ann I. Goldfarb. His first novel, *Booked 4 Murder*, was released in June 2017, followed by ten other books in the series and three other series. Nonfiction in the form of informational brochures and workshop materials treating the winery industry were his forte, along with an extensive background and experience in construction that started with his service in the U.S. Navy and included vocational school classroom teaching. Visit the website at www.jceatonmysteries.com.

Made in the USA
Las Vegas, NV
18 October 2025

32498454R10132